MACHRIHANISH

A Novel

Dan Miller

Wee Egg Mon Publishing

Wee Egg Mon

*For the Greenock Teetotalers,
the real-life Scots
who inspired
this fictional tale*

The Gowfers

Doon amang the benty knowes
O' far-famed Machrihanish shore,
Oft wi' eager steps we ran
At shinty play in days o' yore.

I's strange the changes tahm brings round',
The shinty play we seldom see,
A gowfin' club comes frae the toon
Tae play alang the benty lea.

Wi' club an' putter, cleek an' ba',
Wi' scarlet flags set in a raw,
Tae show the way the ba' must run,
Twa miles before the gemme is done.

Captain Stewart begins the gemme
Wi' sturdy stroke an' steady aim;
Oot ower the heights his ba' does bang
Hard followed up by Mr. Strang.

Then Mr. Douglas strikes wi' care,

The ba' goes whizzin' through the air;

But if the flag he keeps in view

Tae play wi' him theer is but few.

The Major strikes wi a' his skill

Till once on Balaclava hill,

Alang the sward his ba' does roll

An' pops intae a rabbit hole.

Wi' nibblick he must drive it oot

Or lose the gemme wi'oot a doubt;

Wi' weel-aimed stroke, he strikes it fair

An' drives it frae the hole once moor.

So thus they play wi' pleasure keen

Alang the grassy sward sae green;

They view sweet Machrihanish tide

Where health an' happiness abide.

By James McMurchy, 1888

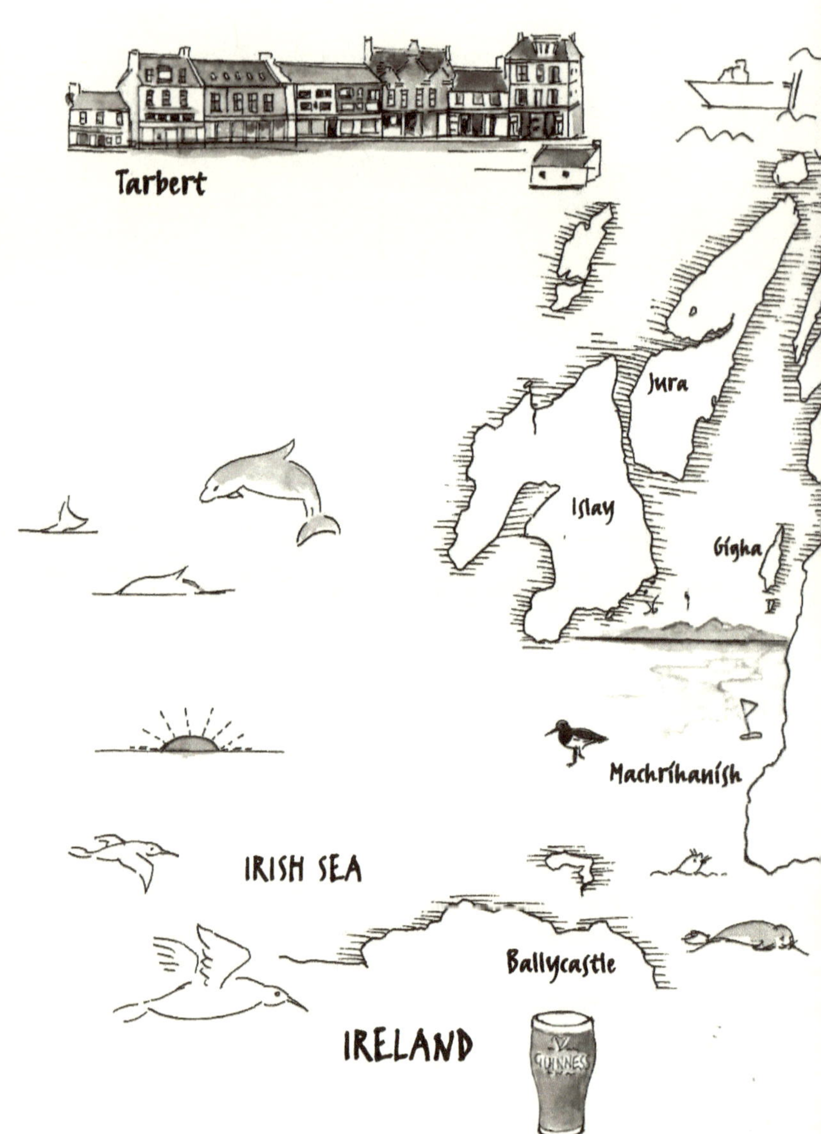

Tarbert
Jura
Islay
Gigha
Machrihanish
IRISH SEA
Ballycastle
IRELAND
GUINNESS

Lochgilphead
rary
Dunoon
Bute
Glasgow
Arran
SCOTLAND
eltown
ty
Turnberry
Machrihanish

Table of Contents

Windblown and Free

Harry Chapin belted out "Cat's in the Cradle" through Kate's cellphone mid backswing, but she wasn't the least bit unnerved. Her 7-iron from the center of the fairway caught the dimpled white Titleist flush, launching the ball with a soft draw to within six feet of the pin.

"Impressive concentration," exclaimed her cart mate Joe, who had been searching for his ball in the adjacent rough.

"Huh?" muttered Kate, already mentally penciling in a birdie three on her scorecard.

"That's some ring tone you've got there, by the way," he said.

"Oh yeah, that," she said. "Big time retro. Works for my dad though. Long story."

"And you're not going to answer it?" said Joe.

"Nope. Playing golf. He'd totally understand. He's basically addicted to the game."

Simultaneously, on the other end of the cellular connection 5,000 miles east, John McAlonan tossed his phone into the empty front passenger seat of his rental car and pulled back onto the A83, the final stretch of a three-hour drive from the Glasgow Airport to Machrihanish Golf Club. Though an American of Irish descent, southwest Scotland—rugged and remote—was the closest he'd ever come to finding a place on the planet that truly felt like home.

Kate's father first stumbled upon this ancient linksland, shaped by God over the millenniums and tweaked by Old Tom Morris in the 1870s, more than 20 years ago during his first pilgrimage to the old country. The sole purpose of that month-long trip? To create a buffer between him and his imploded marriage. A journalist by trade, he arranged for back-up on his beat with the *San Francisco Chronicle*, converted some stock into British sterling, shook off the jet lag of the circumpolar flight and set out with the modest expectation of finding a game or two.

His first stops had been predictable: St. Andrews, of course, followed by Muirfield, Gullane and North Berwick in East Lothian. Then he'd headed north to the Highlands to play a few rounds at Dornoch, Donald Ross' old stomping grounds, making the obligatory detour to Cruden Bay en route. From there he'd worked his way south to Ayrshire and the famed trio of Turnberry, Troon and Prestwick. But it wasn't until three weeks into the journey that he'd crossed the Firth of Clyde on a ferry westbound for Campbeltown and explored the Mull of Kintyre, the inspiration for Paul McCartney's schmaltzy ballad "The Long and Winding Road." That's where he'd found Machrihanish, as well as the seven Scottish members who welcomed him to their club. By the time he'd completed his first loop around those roughhewn links, the locals had embraced him as if he were one of their own.

Every year since, the second week of May became nonnegotiable on John's schedule. His employer knew it. Kate knew it. His ex-wife most definitely knew it. Even the Almighty got the memo, one year clearing—just in time—the airspace over a suddenly active Icelandic volcano whose convulsions threatened to ground all commercial jets in and out of the United Kingdom. No matter how pressing the workload, no matter how tight the finances, no matter how convoluted the routing, John always found a way to reunite with his adoptive clan. Then, without fail, they simply picked up where they'd left off as if 51 seconds, not 51 weeks, had elapsed in between.

Truth be told, time didn't simply stand still at Machrihanish. It shifted into reverse, rolling all the way back to when these eight middle-aged men were boys again, mixing it up on a playground of marram-covered dunes and sandy-soil turf, drenched in an alternating mix of spring showers and brilliant sunshine, windblown and free.

The Argyll coast was in particularly fine form as John made his way that night, the slowly setting sun painting dramatic cloud formations in pinks and purples offset with a dollop or two of green. Wide eyed like a child on Christmas Eve, John was fully in the moment. Deep contentment, so often elusive, held still here. A voice inside his head compelled him to pull over and share the scene with his only flesh and blood, international data roaming charges be damned.

But, predictably, Kate didn't pick up. So John left a voicemail, knocking him out of his reverie and into an all-too-familiar state of muddled distraction. That's a dangerous frame of mind when hurtling around a blind curve in a right-hand drive car on the opposite side of a two-lane country road—into the gloaming.

It's Not a Date

O ne more for the road?" said Joe as he watched Kate consume the last of her Cosmo in the muni's *Brady Bunch* vintage clubhouse bar. "I just checked my phone. The Sepulveda Pass is a freakin' parking lot. Might as well wait it out here."

"Tempting, but gotta scoot," she said, her green eyes scanning her mobile device. "Steven and I are meeting up at the Hollywood Bowl tonight."

"Steven, huh?" muttered Joe as he studied his beer. "Who's on the bill?"

"Don't know and don't really care. He sprung for a box."

"Whoa! A private box?" said Joe, looking up. "Sounds like

a date to me."

"It's *not* a date," she shot back, brushing aside her long dark chocolate hair. "We just enjoy each other's company. Trust me, last thing I need right now is a boyfriend."

"Helpful to know," he said. "Guess I'll have to find someone else to take this Lakers' playoff ticket off my hands."

"Lakers!? You're joking, right?"

"Strangely, no. It's the real deal. My client hooked me up. Every once in a while, all those late nights and weekends servicing a multi-million dollar account produces some perks."

"And I don't have a shot?"

"Not this time, Katie. The game's Tuesday night."

"Damn! I'll be in New York."

"Precisely."

"Maybe there's a way out of it. I've got this app on my iPad. I could videoconference it in."

"GoToMeeting ain't going to cut it, Katie. Not if you're still hellbent on making partner by the time you're 35. This is our anchor client we're talking about."

"Clients! Amazing how they're always getting in the way of a wonderful life."

"Actually, I could make a pretty compelling case that your life is rather wonderful *because* of those clients," said Joe. "In fact, Exhibit A is waiting patiently for you out in the parking lot."

"The Porsche? Well, OK, you've got me there. I must admit, I do love that car."

"Lucky car," mumbled Joe.

"Huh?"

"I said you're one lucky girl!" exclaimed Joe.

"If that were true, I'd be at Staples Center on Tuesday, not babysitting a senior VP who—how can I put this nicely?—is completely clueless."

"Well, if he had a clue, he wouldn't need you or our firm. We're talking job security."

"Oh crap!" exclaimed Kate, her eyes once more transfixed on her phone. "I really gotta get out of here. Thanks for the game, Joe. Same time, same place next week?"

"I'll text you the details. Will give me an excuse to feed you a full report on the Lakers, not to mention the celebs in the stands."

"Don't rub it in," said Kate, reaching for her wallet to pay the bill.

"Save it. I've got this one," said Joe. "I might not be much of a player. But I always settle my gambling debts."

"You're a good man, Charlie Brown. See you in the IMs."

Exactly What She Wanted

Kate eased into her Boxster's leather seat, heated just shy of scalding by a Friday afternoon of Los Angeles sun trapped within the metal-and-glass bubble. No debating the greenhouse effect here. She started the engine, cranked up the AC and plugged in her phone, taking the opportunity to recharge the battery while also, alas, confirming Joe's dire traffic warning. What should have been a 20-minute cruise to her condo in Santa Monica was now looking like a 60-minute slog. Steven had offered to pick her up on his way to the Bowl. Clearly, that wasn't going to be logistically feasible now.

"Time for Plan B," she thought. "I'd better text him."

Kate made her way to the 405 on-ramp and wedged the

Porsche into the barely moving train of cars, rendering her roadster's 265 horsepower and race-tuned suspension moot—and its manual transmission a workout for her left leg's hamstring. But at least she still had her phone, a USB cable, and the latest version of Pandora to calm her nerves. She deftly scrolled through her list of custom stations, settling on Eric Clapton. The app cued up a mellow acoustic version of "Layla," just as her phone vibrated, alerting her to Steven's reply.

"Got it. CU @ will call. Try for 7:30," she read.

She looked up just in time to slam on the brakes, the cars ahead having screeched to a halt.

"Damn!" she blurted, before averting her eyes once more.

"Will do my best," she texted back.

There was a time, not so long ago, when freeway claustrophobia would have sent Kate careening into an emotional tailspin. But that was before she recognized and was willing to acknowledge, with pride actually, that she is—and always has been—a control freak. If you ask her, she will tell you: She has a vision for her life. She knows how it will play out and what it will be. Not just believes, *knows*. This knowing is her rock, her comfort. As long as the big picture continues to come steadily into sharper focus, she can let the small distractions—like an LA traffic jam—roll by like just so many harmless clouds in the sky. Or at least that was the strategy recommended by that video series on meditation techniques she downloaded last week.

Then, just as she was about to congratulate herself on her newfound emotional maturity, the music changed. Van

Morrison was now serenading "Tupelo Honey" through all 10 of the Boxster's speakers. And just as suddenly, those benign wisps of white turned dark and threatening.

"Not funny, Pandora," she said to no one as she peered over the crest of the car-choked Sepulveda Pass.

Music and memories forge an amazingly powerful bond. Certain songs, no matter how hard we resist, snap us back to the time and place where we first heard them. Kate, so at peace a moment ago, was now caught in this vortex, hurtling into reverse, back to her childhood home, back when her parents hovered together nearby, back when the boundaries were clear, back when her family was a solid, single and indestructible unit. Van Morrison, one of her father's favorites, was definitely on the sound track of that movie.

Somewhere during the second verse, Kate found herself sinking into a melancholy mist. More than 20 years had passed since her parents, over Saturday morning breakfast, tried to explain how their feelings for each other had changed but that their feelings for her never would. As an adult, she understood the nuance—at least on an intellectual level. But emotionally? The distinction was far too subtle then and, if she were completely honest with herself, still disturbingly fuzzy now. She loved her parents. She knew her parents loved her. But that didn't change the simple fact that something very fundamental was lost that day at that kitchen table—the same table where her father served her chocolate-chip waffles, just the way she liked them, and where her mother and she decorated Christmas cookies together, their personal holiday tradition. Try as she might, she'd yet to fully forgive them for taking those moments—and the untold more that had yet to arrive—away from her.

It didn't help that her father never seemed to be fully present in California—the center of her life—after that first tour of Scotland. Every year since, he escaped to Machrihanish for a week physically and pretty much the balance of the year on every other level. That disconnect dovetailed nicely with his job, the lead beat writer for the San Francisco Giants, that ensured he'd be on the road for at least half of Major League Baseball's six-month regular season, not counting spring training on one end and—in the good years—the postseason on the other.

And then, before Kate knew what hit her, her mother met Frank who made it clear, though he never actually came right out and said it, that he had no intentions of playing the role of stand-in parent, virtual or otherwise. A fierce tug-o-war ensued, with Kate and Frank on opposite sides of her mother, who played the role of the rope. At some point—was it late middle school or early high school?—Kate simply lost the will to fight and, reluctantly, released her grasp. And her mother, distressingly, seemed to let go, too.

So Kate made a pact with herself: If she couldn't rely on her parents to create a secure and predictable world, she'd just have to do it for herself. It wasn't something she ever voiced, let alone committed to paper. It was more as if a switch, deep within, had been flipped—not as a conscious choice but as an unconscious response to events beyond her control. Bottom line: The arc of her life had been altered, irrevocably.

Looking back, perhaps it was all for the best. Thanks largely to that inner drive, Kate's life had since been defined by a run of exceptional achievement. In elementary school, she never hesitated to go toe-to-toe with the boys, both in the classroom and on the playground, clearly emerging as a leader among her peers. That led directly to the teacher recommendation letters she needed to secure a spot in the most prestigious private school in town where, throughout her middle and high school years, she was a big barracuda in a small but impeccably groomed pond. Academically, anything less than an A was unthinkable. Politically, class president was inevitable. Athletically, stardom was assured.

In this latter category, team sports held a particularly strong allure. She was the shortstop on the softball team, the point guard on the basketball team and the captain of the water polo team. She also managed to squeeze in a couple of seasons on the golf team, recruited by her best friend, Allison, whose father served as the coach while he wasn't making a living as the head pro at the local country club. Combining his grip, stance and swing fundamentals with her natural athletic ability quickly made her competitive, sufficient to be included on the short list of players chosen to play in matches.

Her father, for the first time in years, suddenly took notice and nearly mustered the will to reengage with his daughter. But much to his dismay, Kate didn't fall in love with the game the way he did when he was her age. For her, it was merely a means to an end, yet another outlet for her voracious appetite for competition. So when, after graduating from high school, she made her great escape 3,000 miles east to a liberal arts college's ivy-covered cocoon, she left her clubs behind in her father's garage to gather dust—and to remind him, each time he saw them, of what might have been.

Her need to succeed, however, survived that crucial transition fully intact. If anything, the bigger stage only intensified it. Kate always played to win, whether that meant making the dean's list each semester or leading her sorority to intramural championships on various fields and courts. In between, she set her sights on a career in advertising, pursuing through unpaid internships the practical experience that would pad her resume and establish her professional connections.

That groundwork paid off when she landed an entry-level job with a leading New York City-based agency upon graduation. Two years later, she pounced on an account supervisor position at the firm's Los Angeles office. Five years after that, she knocked—not so gently—on the door to management and it opened. Now, after just three more years, she was on the fast track to the top.

Outwardly, she surrounded herself with the trappings of her personal crusade. There was the Boxster, of course, as well as the two-bedroom high-rise condo overlooking Ocean Boulevard and the crashing Pacific surf below, not to mention the makings of a lucrative high-growth stock portfolio. But inwardly? That was a more complex question. The first level down was crystal clear: financial security and relationship simplicity. Attempt to venture deeper, though, and the way forward became decidedly murkier. Kate had simply conditioned herself not to go there.

And the people who floated through her life—no one was ever fully ensconced in it—followed her lead.

Take Joe, for example. At 36, he was four years older than Kate, just far enough removed to have begun to sense the emptiness at the heart of a life dedicated solely to the pursuit of legal tender. Marriage, or at least a deeply committed relationship with the right woman, had begun to have some appeal. And the romantic in Joe entertained fantasies that Kate could be the one. But the pragmatist knew better. He'd never openly admit he had a crush on her because he realized, just as assuredly, that he had no chance. More than that, she knew it, too. And she knew that he knew. That made Joe a safe haven for Kate, someone she could commiserate with about work, battle it out with on the golf course (assuming Joe's male ego could accept the gift of a stroke or two) and, if pressed, share a small personal revelation. He was the quintessential boy next door: good-looking but not handsome, fit but not buffed, clever but not brilliant. When an opportunity presented itself, like the round of golf they'd just played, their lives could almost intersect in a meaningful way. Almost.

Joe was on point about one thing, though: Kate really did have a wonderful life. She certainly worked hard for it and, by all rights, had genuinely earned it. That little girl, whose illusions of security were shattered on a seemingly benign Saturday morning so many years ago, got exactly what she wanted. And yet, no amount of self-satisfaction could whisk away the unanswered, let alone unasked, question that nipped incessantly at her heels like a lost puppy: Did she get what she needed?

Commence the Hostilities

The subtle lines radiating from Margaret's blue eyes deepened slightly as she checked her watch, then relaxed again as she cast her gaze from behind the bar and across Machrihanish's timeworn clubhouse dining room. There, in a darkened far corner, Angus was holding court. Three of his countrymen, in various states of inebriation, sat to his left around an oak table laden with pints of Guinness and snifters of single malt. Three more sat to his right. Though not another soul graced the premises, Margaret knew there'd be no retreat to the solitude of her private flat on the structure's upper floor any time soon. Not while the big man was on a roll.

"Grab yer glasses, boys, grab yer glasses," said Angus, the

fireplace's peat flame giving his ample cheeks a ruddy glow. Big-framed, barrel-chested and bear-like, it was no longer obvious that the group's self-appointed leader was once a standout on the Scottish national football team with aspirations of making a living at it. Ask now, newly retired after a 30-year stint with the UK Border Agency, and Angus would readily admit he's lost a step or two of speed and gained a stone or two of girth. But that doesn't mean time and toil have diminished his fertile mind or fearless manner. Angus doesn't simply find comfort on this stage. He owns it.

"I's tahm tae make a toast an' commence the hostilities, uh Ah mean the festivities, in an official manner an' all," he blustered in a tortured Glaswegian brogue that even his friends at times struggled to decipher. Strangely enough, they'd discovered over the years that the more Guinness they consumed the clearer Angus' diction became, as if the malty brown liquid functioned like some sort of super decoder ring.

"Noo? But John's na' heer yet. Shooldn't we wait?" said Gavin, ever the stickler for gentlemanly protocol.

"We've *been* waitin', Fauntluhroo," said Angus, using the term of endearment he'd personally assigned to the group's most affluent member. Gavin, though, was no blueblood. For that matter, none of those assembled could stake a claim to a royal line, dotted or otherwise. Rather, Gavin was more new money than old, having climbed his way up to the rung of vice president on the Royal Bank of Scotland's executive ladder, the crowning achievement of his 57 years. As such, while he moves with ease among the upper crust, he's never lost sight of his more humble upbringing. It's this collection of misfits, he'd tell you, as well as golf's egalitarian nature that help keep him grounded—Angus' penchant for infuriating caricatures notwithstanding.

"Fauntleroy?" replied Gavin, intentionally adopting a proper British pronunciation. "Aye, an' so it begins. If ye insist on goin' theer, Angus, the least ye coold dae is make use o' ma proper title."

"Ah beg yer pardon, ma Lord," said Angus.

"Tha's Little Lord Fauntleroy tae ye, if ye please" said Gavin, straightening his back and tilting his head a tick. Gavin had learned long ago it was far wiser to go with the flow of Angus' ribbing than attempt to resist.

"Aye, Ah stand corrected," said Angus. "Ba ma calculations, Johnny Mac should ha'e been heer three hoors ago. Methinks he missed his connection a' Heathrow."

"Nae surprise theer," said Gavin, whose chosen profession forced him to consume a steady diet of business travel. "Personally, Ah'd rather take ma chances tiptoein' through a mine field than try tae clear the security checks a' tha' Rube Goldberg o' an airport."

"Ah'm sure he'll toorn up on the first tee in the moornin'," said Angus while Machrihanish's more than 100 year's worth of past club captains, immortalized in high school yearbook-like portraits hung on the clubhouse walls, looked on with benign bemusement. "He's ne'er failed us, nigh on 20 yeers runnin' noo."

"Aye, 'tis true," said Bernard, absent-mindedly repositioning his glass on its cardboard coaster. "John wooldn't miss this week for the woorld. Ah dare say he loves this place e'en more tha' we dae, an' we were practically born an' raised heer."

"Speak for yersel', Monkey Boy," said Angus, pushing yet another of his mates' hot buttons. Translation: Bernard made his living as a writer, but of the corporate communications variety—not the finely crafted prose of one Bernard Darwin, considered by many to be the United Kingdom's finest golf writer and, by actual fact, the grandson of Charles Darwin. Thus, in the alcohol-soaked recesses of Angus' tortured brain, the balding and bespectacled Bernard begat Darwin which begat Monkey Boy. "But Ah dae know this: Johnny-come-lately woold be gravely disappoonted in us if we dinna uphold oor traditions—especially on his account. Besides, the clock is tickin'. We dinna want tae wear oot oor welcome wi' Margaret on oor first night, noo dae we? We ha'e a loong week ahea' o' us."

"But an hour shy o' midnight? Wha' a shockin' state o' affeers!" said Alister. The group's resident physician, one of the few remaining true country doctors, had been dividing his attention between the conversation inside and the parade of threatening storm clouds outside, clearly visible through the clubhouse's panoramic bank of windows that peer out on an often turbulent North Atlantic sea. Ever the tactician, Alister was visualizing how he would attack each hole if the evening's wind continued to blow in the same direction and with the same intensity during the morning's opening round. "Why Ah remember, na' so long ago whe' ye, Angus, woold just be rampin' up tae full speed a' this hour, na' lookin' tae power doon. Coold it be tha' Father Tahm has finally caught up wit' us?"

"Finally? Wake up an' smell the Metamucil, Doc," said Malcolm, his gnarled right hand setting down his pint with surprising gentleness. If Gavin staked out one extreme on the group's socio-economic spectrum, Malcolm held down the other. Like Angus, he was a formidable athlete in his youth, though blessed more with brute force than graceful agility. As such, Malcolm excelled as a boxer and also made a bit of name for himself on the local rugby pitch. But all that remains of those hard-knock days now are an off-kilter nose that, like a restless housewife's furniture, has been rearranged one too many times, and a pair of matching tattooed forearms that pound sand with the same ferocity they once pummeled an opponent's midsection. Unlike Gavin and Alister who were spoon-fed golf by their forebears, Malcolm took up the game much later in life when he felt the need to hide his rough-and-tumble exterior under a more gentrified veneer. Then, much to his surprise, golf set its hook into him. Now, in his late 40s, Malcolm doesn't simply play the game. He is a student of it and its lore. "Ah dinna know aboot ye fine chaps, but Ah must admit tha' Ah strooggle just tae git oot o' bed in the mornin'. An' tha's *after* Ah've popped an anti-inflammatory or two."

"I's na' the years, Malcolm, 'tis the miles," countered Gavin, placing a hand on Malcolm's shoulder. "An' ye, ma dear friend, have racked up soom serious miles on tha' body o' yours. I poosh paper for a livin'. Ye poosh loads. Serious loads. Bricks, loomber, cinder blocks an' the like. Ah canne imagine a week o' gowf woold be much o' a boorden for ye."

"I's na' the gowf, 'tis the drinkin'," chimed in Ewan. At 42, the long and lean redhead was the youngster of the group. He was also its most accomplished player, with a textbook swing that generated seemingly effortless power and an intuitive short game that rarely dropped a shot. He owed his prowess in part to a favorable gene pool, but perhaps even more so to a father who put a club in Ewan's hands when he was still a wee lad. A true natural, Ewan was the dominant player among his peers through prep school and held his own against Scotland's best at university. But soon thereafter, unexpectedly and inexplicably, he hit an imaginary wall. One failed attempt after another on the United Kingdom's mini tours eventually forced Ewan to admit that, for all his physical gifts, he lacked that intangible something that's needed to cross the thin green line between top Scottish Golf Union amateur and viable European Tour pro. Yet, it's a reality that—further burdened by 60-hour weeks as a software engineer, 15 years of marriage and two daughters under the age of 10—he's yet to fully accept.

"At the start o' the week, Ah'm a scratch player," he said. "Ba the end, if Ah foolishly try tac keep pace wi' Angus on his throne, Ah'm a 15-handicapper. Tha's why, in case ye hadn't noticed, Ah've been sippin' water a' night—well, at least since ma inaugural pint o' course. Ah'm boond an' determined tae keep ma wits aboot me this tahm."

"Oh, spare us, Roy!" said Angus, making the tenuous link between Ewan and Roy Hobbs, the ill-fated baseball prodigy at the center of the movie *The Natural.* "If wit translated intae gowfin' proficiency, Ah dare say Ah'd be knockin' it aroond wi' the likes o' Colin Montgomerie rather than this soorry lot. Instead, Ah stumble along wi' a meager government pension an' a gemme tha' leaves me ne'er moor tha' one or two wayward swings away from total an' ootter oblivion."

"Ah'll second tha' motion," blurted Donald, who, true to form, was having a hard time getting a word in edgewise. It's not that the group's elder statesman passed the evening in silence, content to simply sip his Scotch, sit back and take it all in. Quite the opposite. Donald's need to express every thought that passes through his brain is akin to breathing: it's utterly involuntary. Even more astonishing, the well never goes dry, no matter how trivial or random the flow.

As such, his friends—who really do care deeply for this strange little man—have mastered the art of being in the same room with Donald without fully engaging with him. Make eye or, more to the point, ear contact and—experience has taught them—they will be caught helplessly in his verbal spell. Give him an audience and there is simply no stopping him. Perhaps the isolation of retirement after 40 years teaching physics to boarding school boys is to blame for this quirk. Or perhaps it's just the way he's always been wired. Once or twice a night, though, the 70-something Donald could still be counted on to rise above the surface of his stream of unconsciousness, catch a breath and merge with the communal craic. This was one of those rare moments.

"Ma gemme is absolute rubbish thi' year," said Donald.

"Nae, make tha' for the past 10 yeers."

"Ye, on the other hand Ewan," continued Angus, not pausing to acknowledge Donald's lament or the monologue that was certain to follow, "make yer way aroond the links as if 'tis a guid walk *un*spoiled, nae matter how much single malt we inject intae yer system."

"Well, Ah appreciate the kind woords, Angus, at least Ah thin' tha's wha' they were," said the freckle-faced and still boyish Ewan. "But, fact is, Ah'm a feel player. An' if ma head feels like 'tis aboot tae explode, which is inevitable if the drams are somewha' less than wee, Ah canne play worth a lick. Tae quote the great Dirty Haahry, a man's git tae know his limitations."

"Limitations!? How dare ye ootter such a woord in oor midst?" burst Bernard, slamming his pint flush against the hardwood. "Lest we forget, we all make oor way tae this seaside oasis specifically tae shed the daily constraints o' oor various lives. Nae significant others, nae progeny, nae daily grind, nae obligations—save tae share in oor life's love: the swingin' o' the club, the strikin' o' the ba' and the gazin' at oor handiwork as it soars majestically toward the target."

"All well an' guid, Bernard, but ye left oot the best part: the drinkin' o' the Scotch," added Malcolm.

"Ah did indeed, ma guid man!" affirmed Bernard. "In this place an' wi' these friends, theer is nae such thing as limitation. Nae hesitation. Nae guilt. Nae explanation. Just pure indulgence. Aye, indulgence. Noo tha's the operative woord o' the week."

"Ah Monkey Boy, ye dae ha'e a way wi' the Queen's English,"

said Angus. "But, truth be toold, 'tis gettin' harder an' harder tae keep this week as 'tis, e'en for me. Reality weighs heavy on us all, ma friends. Take, for starters, oor economy which, if ye'll excuse me Little Loord, is thoroughly buggered."

"Nae apology required," said Gavin. "Ye dinna know the haulf o' it."

"Spare us the gory details," said Angus. "Meanwhile, none of us is gettin' any younger. An' oor children dinna seem tae be gettin' any aulder. Ah mean, they haven't moved oot. Or maybe they did an' they moved back. Or some such nonsense. All Ah know is, theer was a tahm when ma life progressed along a straight line. Noo, it feels moor like 'tis spinnin' aroond in circles."

"Soonds like gowf," interjected Alister. "Try as we might wi' this gemme, we always end up right back wheer we started—physically, emotionally, psychologically. Maybe life is simply imitatin' art, uh, Ah mean the gemme."

"Maybe, in the end, it all merges intae one," offered Gavin. "Noo theer's a soberin' thought. All these years, we've held tae the belief tha' theer was our tahm at Machrihanish an' then theer was everythin' else—an' nary the two should intersect. Perhaps we simply need tae soorrender tae the notion tha' there is nae distinction. Perhaps life really is one big adventure an' all o' it—the guid, the bad an' the ineffable—is tae be embraced, wi'out joodgment."

"Wha' in heaven's nemme is this gibberish, ye two muppets?" said Angus in mock disgust. "Ewan might na' be gettin' mad wi' it. But ye, Gavin an' Alister, most certainly ha'e been, an' most certainly are! I' only confirms ma original premise, so easy tae forgit amid this tedious digression: tha' 'tis indeed tahm tae call it a night. Drink up, mates, afore one oor moor o' us makes a complete arse o' hi'sel'. An' afore Margaret gives us all the heave ho. Wi'oot further adae, heer's tae a week o' guid friends, guid gowf an'—if the fates allow—guid weather. Cheers!"

"Cheers," echoed the choir.

"An' let's also raise a glass tae oor intrepid Yankee, in hopes tha' he's managed tae extricate hi'sel' from Heathrow's nasty clutches."

"Aye, tae Mac. Cheers!" was the reply.

"Sleep well, laddies. First group is off a' 9 bells sharp."

Pathetic and Predictable

"Really!?," said Kate to no one in particular as she bent down to retrieve the keys she'd fumbled while trying to unlock the door to her condo. A hazy dawn partially illuminated the lock. But her disconnect was more about a lack of focus than a lack of vision. The night had not gone according to plan.

If it had, she would have been here hours ago. Instead, she found herself stumbling across the threshold of her safe haven decidedly behind schedule. And for what? A bottle (or was it two?) of Cabernet? A few bites of grilled salmon? A shared slice of tiramisu? A handful of twinkling stars bright enough to break through the glare of the city's lights? A friend who happens to be a guy with an apartment that just happens to be on the way home? And a libido that, it seems, grows stronger the more she tries to contain it? In retrospect, the sequence of events was all so pathetic and predictable. That was the worst of it. How, in heaven's name, could a woman with her skills have slipped up like some naive college co-ed?

Kate closed the door behind her and scanned her living room. Everything was in its place, just where she'd left it in a rush for Steven and the Bowl. The eclectic mix of furniture, discovered methodically piece by piece, from garage sale to Craigslist post to trendy retail store and back again. The burgeoning art collection, some original and some limited edition prints, each displayed in pricey custom frames. The freshly vacuumed oriental rugs set off by a deep-grained hardwood floor. Like a shot of Red Bull after too little sleep or too much alcohol, even that small dose of her personally crafted reality was enough to help her, slowly, begin to regain her footing. By the time she'd slipped off her shoes and traversed the 30 feet from the entryway to the nearest bathroom, recovery mode was in full swing.

The voice in her head, emboldened, set the record straight: "What happened, happened. It's done. In the past. It wasn't real. It wasn't me. This condo is real. These things are my things. In this space, I am me. Time to move on. Get back on plan."

A normal human being would have processed the moment by falling face first into bed—lights off, shades drawn, silence comforting. But Kate went the other direction. She suited herself up for a morning run. A little pain would produce a measure of gain. At least that's how she calculated it.

Nikes doubled tied? Check. GPS watch engaged? Check. iPod charged? Check. Earbuds in place? Check. Adorned for battle, nothing external could get in—not even the shudder of Kate's cellphone, buried in the purse she'd cast aside on her kitchen table, as it beamed in a call from an unidentified number.

A Perfect Day for Golf

Gavin slipped his mobile back in his pocket and allowed his gaze to drift through the clubhouse windows and out to the first tee—just a mere flip wedge in the distance. A powder blue sky, dotted with puffs of cotton, merged seamlessly with a softly rolling turquoise sea. A Scottish flag, hung half-mast from a pole near the pro shop's front door, furled and unfurled lazily in a warm spring breeze. On the beach, an elderly couple worked their way unhurriedly amid the rocks and seaweed, their golden retriever scampering to and fro a few yards ahead. Further out, a flock of oyster catchers—black-and-white sea birds that had become Machrihanish's de facto mascot— circled the waves effortlessly, then, one by one, dove head first into the water in search of their daily sustenance.

It was a beautiful day for golf. Check that: it was a *perfect* day for golf. Yet, eerily, Gavin didn't spot a single club-wielding soul making his or her way down the green swath that demarcates the first hole. It was as if the view through the window had been transformed into a living, breathing Edward Hopper painting: stunningly beautiful at first glance, then cold and emotionally detached upon closer inspection.

Eventually, the hubbub in the far corner of the dining room diverted Gavin's attention, which was just fine by him. This was no time to be alone, especially with one's thoughts.

"Were ye able tae reach her?" half-whispered Angus as Gavin rejoined the group.

"Voicemail, assumin' Ah ha'e the right number," responded Gavin. "Lucky tha' Ah still ha'e it saved in ma phone."

"So ye got tae play Shinnecock taegither?" inquired Bernard.

"Well, Mac an' Ah did," said Gavin. "His daughter set it up wi' a member an' was goin' tae join us. But at the last second, she got called away on business. She was in New York a' the tahm. Noo she's in LA."

"So tha's eight hoors then, 5 a.m.," interjected Ewan. "Probably still sleepin'. We can only hope she's na' alone when she awakes an' listens tae yer message."

"Well, actually, Ah didn't tell her. Na' the kind o' thin' ye put in a voicemail, seems tae me," said Gavin. "But Ah made it clear tha' she needed tae call as soon as possible. A bit o' a reprieve."

"For her or for ye?" asked Bernard.

"Both," said Gavin. "A part o' me is still holdin' oot hope tha' the facts, as we know 'em, will somehow miraculously dissolve intae fiction."

"Aye, 'tis a nightmare from which all o' us, in one fell swoop, woold happily awake," said Angus.

"Wha' did Alister say, *exactly*?" implored Malcolm.

"Tha' he got a call in the middle o' the night from the country doctor based oot o' Tarbert. Goes ba the nemme o' Dixon. Apparently the two went tae medical school taegither, back in the day," said Gavin. "Dr. Dixon told oor doc tha' theer'd been a car accident. Tha' the driver did not survive but tha' his car's GPS system, strangely, did, an' tha' it was pointed directly at Machrihanish. Apparently, Alister always makes a stop in Tarbert on his way heer each year tae catch up wi' his old friend. So the local doctor put two an' two taegither an' thought, 'Hey, maybe Alister knows this poor soul.'"

"OK, but how dae we know, for certain, tha' 'tis Mac?" asked Malcolm. "We're na' the only people who go oot o' theer way tae play gowf heer, ye know. Thanks tae the Internet, oor little playground is no longer oor little secret."

"True enough. But Dr. Dixon foond a driver's license," said Angus. "If oor friend's nemme was John Smith, we might have reason tae hope. But John McAlonan?"

A pall fell over the room, interrupted by a random mix of barely audible gasps, guttural sounds and labored sighs. Words simply did not apply. Six pairs of eyes diverted their attention about the room, deftly avoiding direct contact lest they burst into tears. After all, men don't cry—least of all Scottish men.

Then, Gavin's phone rang, breaking the tension—but only for a moment. As he registered the incoming number, his friends attempted to read his face for clues.

"Kathleen?" Angus managed to ask.

"Nae. Alister," replied Gavin, raising the phone to his ear. "Hello, Doc? Aye, we're all heer…in the clubhoose…nae, Ah think Ah'd rather stand…so i's confirmed…Gawd help us… wheer are ye noo?…wha' happens next?…is theer anythin' we can dae?…Ah see…tha' could take awhile…aye, Ah left a voicemail for her…i's still very early in LA…so ye'll be headed back soon?…we'll be heer…wheer else woold we go?"

Gavin girded himself to replay the other half of the conversation for his friends, but Angus cut him short.

"Nae need, ma old friend. Nae need."

Sorry to Bother You

Technically, Joe wasn't asleep when the phone rang. But that's not to say he was fully awake either. The fact is, he'd spent the last hour drifting in and out of a vague state of consciousness, taking in the random thoughts—from the mundane to the momentous—that tend to bubble up to the surface in the quiet of a Saturday morning with no place to go and no one to go there with, even if he did.

"Sorry to bother you so early, especially on a Saturday," said Kate calmly. "But I had to call someone."

"Yeah, well, what's up?" replied Joe, still in a haze.

"I don't quite know how to say this, but…I won't be able to go to New York on Monday."

"Huh? What? Katie, please don't tell me this is about that Lakers game?"

"I wish it were that simple, Joe. Really, I do," she said. "I just got off the phone with a guy in Scotland. I'm not going to New York. I'm definitely not going to the game. But I could be going to Scotland. I don't know. I barely remember this guy. Maybe he's making it all up?"

"Whoa! Slow down," said Joe, gradually getting his wits about him. "What's this about some guy in Scotland?"

"He's a friend of my dad's. I set him up at Shinnecock when I was working out of our New York office. My dad's over there now. Or, I guess I should say, he was."

"Huh? I just woke up. I'm not following you."

"It's my dad!" she finally blurted out, forcefully. "He…was killed…in a car accident!"

"Oh my God," said Joe, softly. Then, a beat or two later and a decibel or two louder, "Oh my God, Katie."

"It's OK. I mean, uh, I'm dealing with it," she said, her composure nearly betrayed by an almost imperceptible hesitation.

"Katie?" said Joe, quickly gaining focus.

"No, really," said Kate, back at full strength. "I'm OK. I just thought someone should know. Sorry to bother you with this. But I'm going to need some backup. For New York."

"Kate, there's no need to apologize. New York? That's the least of your worries. And if you're thinking you have to go through this alone, think again. I'm coming over."

"That's really kind of you. But not necessary."

"Well, I'm coming anyway."

"Really? No, I couldn't ask that of you."

"Really, yes. And it's not about you asking. It's about me telling. I know you're accustomed to getting your way. But I'm going to pull rank. I insist."

"Well, if it'll make *you* feel better."

"Yeah, it will. I'm on my way."

New York? Fuggedaboutit

Joe needed less than an hour to jump out of bed, pull on some clothes, stuff his hair under a faded Dodgers hat and race across town along the city's still quiet streets. By some fluke, he managed to find just enough vacant curb right in front of Kate's condo complex to accommodate his battle-tested Toyota.

"Wow, that was fast!" said Kate as she opened the door. "Sure hope you didn't break any laws getting here."

"Uh, don't think so," said Joe, caught off guard by her playful tone. "But if I did, I'm sure I could have talked my way out of the ticket. I mean, under the circumstances. Didn't want you to be alone."

"You're so sweet," she said, motioning to him to take a seat on the sofa. "But, like I said on the phone, I'm fine. Really. I mean, yeah, I'll admit, it's a shocker. Preposterous really. It doesn't seem real."

"But it *is* real, right?" said Joe, noting how Kate had pulled herself together: the still slightly damp hair of a shower, the fresh change of clothes neatly pressed, the hint of blush on her cheeks and mascara on her eyelashes—when he was expecting mascara on her cheeks and blush on her eyelashes.

"According to Gavin. That's my dad's friend. In Scotland. But it sounded like he was getting it second hand. I'm not sure. This thing came completely out of nowhere."

Joe hesitated to respond, still taking it all in. He tried to imagine how he'd react if someone had just told him that his father had died. He tried to crawl inside Kate's head and view reality—this suddenly altered version of it—as she was seeing it. He tried to imagine a middle-aged Scot thousands of miles away, dialing his phone and struggling to find the words to convey this awful news to a young American woman he barely knew. His head swirled. And for a moment there, he sensed that Kate's very orderly living room had begun to swirl, too. Then he looked up, connected with Kate, and it all came screeching to a halt. If it's true that a person's eyes are the windows to their soul, then Kate—her green eyes devoid not only of tears but even a hint of redness—was, at this crucial juncture, jarringly soulless.

"So," said Joe, moving past the vision, "are you saying there's a chance your father is still alive?"

"Maybe," Kate responded. "Gavin said I'd need to go there. To, uh, identify the body. The local police are in charge. He said…here, wait, I took some notes."

"You never miss a beat," said Joe.

"Yeah, well, you know me. Anyway, the police have the body now but they need to hand it off it to what they call a procurator fiscal. Gavin said that's the Scottish equivalent of a lawyer who takes charge of the situation, including making arrangements for a coroner."

"Really? Is that necessary?" said Joe.

"Apparently, yes," she said. "It was an accident, so they have to do an autopsy. When that's done, they can issue a death certificate. But they won't do that without the approval of the next of kin. Which would be me."

"So you need to book a flight to Scotland. Like, now," said Joe.

"I don't know," she said. "Seems like there's got to be another way. I mean, maybe I could just have Gavin do it. He's there. He knows how this works. There's got to be someone I can call or email. Even find a fax machine if that's what they use. Ask them to text me some photos. Delegate my power of attorney or some such thing. I mean, this is crazy! I'm supposed to be flying to New York on Monday. That's the plan, right?"

"That *was* the plan," said Joe, gathering himself. "Katie, neither of us really knows what's happened. It sounds like the people on the scene aren't entirely certain either. But

I do know this: you need to go to Scotland. The sooner the better."

"I guess," said Kate unconvincingly.

"Look, you've never been through anything remotely like this before. Neither have I. We're both floundering in uncharted water here. But Katie, whenever I've found myself in over my head, I've always trusted my gut. It's never let me down. Never."

Joe paused, just long enough to see Kate look away and stare blankly through her living room's bay window.

"Listen, Katie! My insides are telling me to tell you, in no uncertain terms, that you need to face this head on. And furthermore, if you try to dance around it, you'll regret it for the rest of your life. Do you get what I'm saying?"

"What about New York?" she said.

"New York!? Fuggedaboutit," said Joe in a poor excuse for a New York accent. "I'll go to New York. You go to Scotland."

"But you've got Lakers tickets," she said, finally reestablishing eye contact.

"Really?" he replied. "*Really*!?"

"I know, I know," said Kate, her shell flexing slightly but resolutely refusing to break. "I'm just talking. Babbling. Trying to take it all in. I'm out of my element here. And I don't like it. I don't like it one bit."

"I get that," said Joe. "But you know what Katie? It's OK. I know you pride yourself on being prepared for everything. But there's just no way to anticipate something like this. So you know what? It's OK to fall apart. You have my permission, not that you need it. To be perfectly honest, you're kind of freaking me out that you're not."

"Yeah…well…I probably should," said Kate. "I'm sure, eventually, I will. But I'm just not there yet. I'm sorry."

"What do I know? I'm probably the one who's completely off base here," said Joe, pulling back. "Perhaps we should focus on the facts. You have a passport, right?"

"Yes. Still valid," said Kate. "Thanks to that girls trip to Cancun last summer."

"What about flights?"

"Already checked. Nothing direct from here to Glasgow, but I can connect through London. If I leave tomorrow I can be there first thing Monday. Do what I have to do and be back by midweek. Get this over with. Get back to my life."

"If that's what you want," said Joe.

"I don't want any of it," said Kate with an ambiguous mix of defiance and exasperation. "But if this is what I need to do, then I'll do it. You should know by now: That's my M.O. Take care of business. Put it behind me. Move on."

"You're right. I of all people," said Joe. "Let's get busy then."

Her Most Precious Possession

Kate spent an ungodly proportion of her young professional career on airplanes. She'd earned gold status on American in her first six months on the job, then rose steadily to executive platinum by her fourth year, where she's resided ever since. Yet not once amid all the hours and all the miles did she ever fall asleep while aloft. The Type A in her simply couldn't bear to pass the time and not be productive. So she fires up her laptop as soon as possible after takeoff and keeps it going until right before landing, plugging in a back-up battery—or two—if needed. Occasionally, she might indulge in a book on her iPad. Even rarer, she'll watch an in-flight movie. Mostly she works. At least it makes the time go faster.

But this flight, an 11-hour non-stop from LAX to LHR, was different. She could feel it in her bones. Sleep deprivation was partly to blame. She hadn't fully closed her eyes for more than a minute or two since she spoke with Gavin. Actually, for that matter, the night before—spent partly with Steven—was hardly restful. Even someone of Kate's hard-driven makeup can keep fatigue at bay for only so long. And unlike her laptop, she didn't have the benefit a back-up battery to prop her up.

So, once nestled into her seat and numbed by the drone of the 777's engines, she opted to plug in her earbuds and, deliberately, search for tracks that would quiet her brain and relax her body. She scrolled up. She scrolled down. She searched by artist and by album. Nothing resonated.

Frustrated, Kate wandered over to her phone's voicemail app where the last message from her father remained safely stored yet, surprisingly, still-to-be played. Perhaps now, amid the pseudo solitude of a red eye, was the right time to push the little green triangle that, tantalizingly, stared back at her from her phone. Kate's right index finger, seemingly of its own accord, moved into position and hovered there for a second or two, precariously near the point of no return. But before it could do the deed, her conscious mind kicked back in and aborted the mission.

It wasn't that Kate feared what she would hear. Quite the opposite. In the less than two days since it was created, her father's voicemail had become her most precious possession—and she had become a sommelier who knew that a bottle of Chateau Lafite Rothschild would lose most of its value the moment she popped its cork.

Truth be told, Kate's decision to preserve the voicemail in a state of suspended animation was more coping strategy than inspired genius. It allowed her to remain in the moment, rather than come to terms with an unexamined past or face an unanticipated future thrust upon her by forces beyond her control. And it helped keep *those* questions at bay, questions that, as a young girl, she had trained herself to repress. Questions that, as soon as she touched the play button, would return with a vengeance and demand an accounting.

Not now, though. Not in this place. Instead, Kate pulled her earbuds loose, shut off her phone, reclined her seatback slightly and took refuge in the view through the plane's window. At first, all she saw was darkness. But slowly, as her eyes adjusted, a shimmering array of stars broke through. Light at the end of the tunnel, perhaps?

Then moments later, Kate did something she'd never done before in more than a million miles of flight: she drifted off to sleep—deeply, peacefully, unashamedly.

Ah, the Bluebells!

Gavin, by all appearances, is a patient man. He observes first and acts second. In part, this is due to a genetic predisposition to introversion. But even more so, it's a learned response that has served him well. As in golf, when he finds something that works, he sticks with it.

Ask him to explain and he'll tell you that every situation, like the sea, is highly fluid. The trick, he says, is to read the waves, jumping on only when the right one comes along. Then, after you ride it out, you paddle back into position and wait, patiently, until the next set crests. Observe, act, reset, repeat—in that order. That's not to say Gavin ascended the corporate org chart by always going with the flow. Far from it. Yet, by the same token, he knows that those who insist on swimming against the current will, invariably, exhaust themselves without actually getting anywhere. Instead, Gavin navigates a middle course, balancing a preference for premeditation with—when circumstances call out for it—a burst of spontaneity.

This was clearly time for the latter.

"Oh for fuck sake!" exploded Gavin, as he leaned on his Jaguar's horn for a full five count. "What in heaven's nemme are those guys daein'?"

Inside the Machrihanish clubhouse, Angus and Malcolm shot a glance to the car park and then to one another as the blare shattered the morning's tranquility.

"Much obliged tae ye, Margaret, for the provisions," said Angus, loading the last of the filled rolls, crisps and assorted candy bars into a plastic bag. "But me thinks Gavin has a burr under his high-priced saddle. We'd best be away."

"I's the least Ah coold dae, Angus," said Margaret. "It shakes me tae ma core tae think wha' tha' poor gurl must be goin' through. Please let her know tha' she's moor than welcome tae stay wi' me if she be needin' a shoulder tae cry on. Ma guest room might nae be up tae her usual five-star standards. But 'tis hers for the askin'."

"You're a guid wumman, Margaret," replied Angus. "Consider it done, though Ah canne say exactly when we'll be back. Alister is already on his way tae Tarbert tae consult wi' the authorities. We'll rendezvous wi' him theer, wi' Mac's daughter, assumin' everythin' goes accordin' tae plan."

"Just breaks yer heart," said Margaret.

Angus and Malcolm stepped into the sunshine, hands full, just as Gavin let loose with another blast. The big man, who rarely misses a beat, called shotgun. Malcolm, not in a mood to make a fuss, settled into the spacious back seat.

"Wha' took ye so long?" said a flummoxed Gavin as he fired up the XJ's supercharged V-8. "If we're na' theer tae greet Kate when she walks through the Glasgow Airport arrivals door, Ah'll ne'er forgive masel'. Or the two o' ye."

"Oor apologies Gavin, truly," said Angus. "But 'tis at least a six-hoor journey theer an' back. As lovely as Scotland is this tahm o' year, ye canne eat the scenery."

"How can ye think o' food a' a tahm like this?" Gavin retorted.

"Ah hear ye, Fauntluhroo. Really, Ah dae," said Angus. "But we've got tae keep oor strength up. This is a marathon, ma friend, na' a sprint."

"Besides, think o' the tahm we'll save," interjected Malcolm. "As far as we're concerned, this is a non-stop flight an' ye're cleared for takeoff, Pilot Gavin. Ye'll be happy tae know tha', in addition tae the nibbles, Angus an' Ah paid oor respects tae the gents. We are guid tae go!"

"Yep, in one end an' oot the other," said Angus.

As Gavin pulled onto the main road, he noticed Bernard just outside the pro shop, sitting on a bench that overlooks the first tee and the expanse of sea and sand that must be cleared to reach the fairway—the reason why most experts agree that Machrihanish's is the most intimidating opening shot in golf. But instead of driver and ball, Bernard was facing his fears this morning with journal and pen.

A bit further on, all three of the motorists spotted Donald on the beach, alone, wandering aimlessly. True to the alias Angus had long ago chosen for him, Don-Don appeared to be carrying on a heated conversation with no one but himself.

And then, just as the Jaguar's eight-speed transmission settled into overdrive and the angular sedan hit its stride, there was Ewan making his way solo across a footbridge that spans the burn fronting the second green, his sticks strapped to his back.

All seven of John's friends were soldiering on, each in his own way.

Roughly 500 miles to the south, Kate awoke with a start as the 777 touched down at Heathrow. At first, she didn't know where she was. "In my condo, it's Monday morning after a wild weekend and I slept through my alarm," was the first thought that surfaced. Then came, "No wait: I'm on a plane and I've just arrived in New York." That was followed half-a-second later by "Scratch that. I'm in England, on my way to Scotland, to…" From the outside looking in, the disorientation passed quickly and harmlessly. But for Kate, the momentary loss of context nearly induced a panic attack.

As she regained her wits she also began to gather her things. That included double-checking—no make that triple-checking—the pocket in the seatback in front of her to ensure nothing of value was hiding between the in-flight magazine and the Sky Mall catalogue. Once, pressed to make a connecting flight, Kate had left an expensive set of noise-cancelling headphones in her wake. Every flight since, she vowed to never let that happen again.

That's when she discovered the UK landing card that a flight attendant must have slipped in the pocket while she slept. For most people, this would have been a non-event. They'd simply take a minute or two after deplaning and before approaching customs to find a seat in the gate, pull out pen and passport and fill in the simple form. But for Kate, who is most definitely not like most people, it was as if she were seven years old again, had just arrived at the second grade classroom of Mrs. Plakas, her all-time favorite teacher, and realized, in utter horror, that she'd forgotten to do her homework.

"Great! On the ground five minutes and I'm already behind," she scolded herself.

Kate followed the signs that led, labyrinth-like, to the UK Border Control. The queue for the locals was short and churning. But the line for everyone else? Serpentine, sluggish and, thanks to the REM-wrecking impact of an overnight flight, populated by what appeared to be the extras from a low-budget zombie movie. Kate, alas, was at the end of it. Good thing she still had a full two hours until her connection to Glasgow. With a bit of luck, she just might make it.

It was slow going for the Jag as well, which meant Gavin was doing a slow burn. There are only two roads in and out of Kintyre, the two-lane A83 along the west coast and the at-times-single-track B842 paralleling it to the east. Both bend and meet up at either end, in Campbeltown to the south and near Kennacraig to the north, forming an elongated oval approximately 25 miles lengthwise. Gavin went with the A83, undoubtedly the prudent choice. Unfortunately, on this particular morning, he wasn't the only one who opted for the same tactical maneuver.

"Why 'tis tha' when Ah have all day tae make this drive, the path ahead is free an' cleer. Yet, when tahm is o' the essence, seemin'ly every able-bodied Scot wi' a motorized vehicle is boond an' determined tae impede ma progress?" lamented Gavin.

"Well, *'tis* Monday," offered Malcolm. "Workin' day for workin' stiffs. Prime tahm for lorries. In fact, if Ah weren't on my hols, such as it is, Ah'd be behind the wheel o' a lorry masel' this very moment, nae doubt raisin' the ire o' some rich bloke like yersel' hyperventilatin' in his luxury car much like this one. Gavin, they're just tryin' tae make a shillin' or two an' put a little food on the table. I's nothin' personal."

"Ah know, Ah know," said Gavin, straying slightly into the right lane to assess the passing potential on a slightly less curvy stretch of pavement. But, as if choreographed, an oncoming car flashed into view around the upcoming bend. Gavin had no choice but to retreat to his lane and back off on the accelerator. "I's just tha', a' this pace, we'll ne'er git theer."

Angus, meanwhile, had already begun to make a dent in Margaret's care package, though the travelers were no more than an hour out of Machrihanish.

"Care for a roll, Gavin?" he said, attempting to soothe the normally staid banker. "We've got tuna, ham an' a savory lamb cutlet tae choose from."

"Appreciate the offer, Angus, but nae, thank ye," said Gavin. "Ma stomach's basically in ma throat, which tends tae put a damper on one's appetite. Maybe on the way back, after we pick up oor passenger."

"So Fauntluhroo, I ha'e a question for ye: When ye made yer gran' tour o' America an' spent tahm in New York, did ye actually git tae meet Mac's daughter?" Angus queried.

"Soorry tae say, nae," replied Gavin. "John arranged a couple o' possible meetin's. The round at Shinnecock, o' course. Then theer was the ferry oot tae the Statue o' Liberty. John's ancestors, an' Kathleen's for tha' matter, arrived from Ireland ba way o' Ellis Island. He also arranged a quick bite at Katz's, the New York deli made famous ba Meg Ryan in tha' movie wi' Billy Crystal, if ye know wha' Ah mean."

"Aye, Ah dae," interjected Angus. "Bloody brilliant, tha' scene was."

"Well yeah, anyway, as Ah was sayin', each tahm we were tae get taegither, Kathleen begged out. Her job is rather demandin', it would seem. But Malcolm, ye'll be happy tae know tha', unlike the lorries, Ah dinna take it personally. Ah have a rather demandin' job masel'. Thin's happen. Ah understand. But Ah coould tell John was disappoonted, maybe even a wee bit embarrassed. Ah got the sense it was a recurrin' theme between the two o' 'em."

"Aye, 'tis a shame," said Malcolm. "Ah must confess tha' Ah dinna exactly go oot o' ma way tae spend tahm wi' my da' when Ah was Kate's age. Makes me want tae look him up after this storm passes."

An uneasy silence filled the cabin. Angus refocused his attention on the faintly greening countryside as it rushed by. By mid-May, the collage of ash, birch and alder trees should have been fully leafed. Instead, the landscape's renewal was unspooling in super slow motion—the byproduct of a particularly brutal winter followed by a persistently cool spring.

Then, out of the corner a slightly moistened eye, Angus spotted something that triggered a wry smile. Time to lighten the mood, he thought.

"Ah, the bluebells!" he exclaimed with as much syrupy sweetness as he could muster. "Dae ye see 'em, Fauntluhroo? Dae ye see 'em?"

"Ah see 'em, Angus," said Malcolm joining in the game. "I's na' grand, Gavin? I's na' grand?"

Gavin fumed.

"Ah woondered how loong ye'd wait tae play tha' card," he said.

Years ago, as Angus and Gavin were making the drive to Machrihanish for the golfers' annual reunion, that now infamous bluebells phrase—much to Gavin's horror—had escaped from his mouth before he could take it back. Angus, instinctively, gobbled it up. Then, each succeeding year without fail, he regurgitated it at Gavin's expense—and always to maximum effect.

In his defense, Gavin's namby-pamby adoration for the delicate Scottish wild flower, also known as harebells, put him in fine company among some of his more celebrated UK countrymen. For example, Sir Walter Scott, in his epic poem *Lady of the Lake* penned: "A foot more light, a step more true, Ne'er from the heath-flower dashed the dew; E'en the slight harebell raised its head…" And Emily Bronte, in her classic novel *Wuthering Heights*, waxed equally poetic with: "I lingered round them, under the benign sky; watched the moths fluttering among the heath and harebells; listened to the soft wind breathing through the grass; and wondered how anyone could ever imagine unquiet slumbers, for the sleepers in that quiet earth."

Gavin, however, like Pavlov's pooches, was instantly annoyed. But this time, after absorbing the blow, he had to admit that he was also genuinely relieved. For a fleeting moment, the gloom that hung over the three old friends lifted and they remembered what, originally, had brought them here. If only that moment could last.

"Why aye, Angus, noo Ah see the bluebells, too," said Gavin, playing along. "An' they are, indeed, quite lovely. How thoughtful o' ye tae point them oot for us."

Simultaneously, Kate—anything but a fragile bluebell— wandered amid the man-made wilds of London's Heathrow Airport. Her departure gate for Glasgow was, of course, in a different terminal than that of her arrival. So she boarded a shuttle bus and, the instant its wheels were set in motion, was transported beyond the airport's safe zone. As such, when she disembarked on the other side, yet another security queue greeted her. This one came equipped with retina scanners, a further assault on jet-lagged eyes.

That hurdle cleared, Kate calculated she still had at least

20 minutes to forage for food and compensate for the in-flight breakfast she'd slept through. First up in the terminal's central hub was a faux pub, replete with grizzled Londoners bellying up to the bar, though it was still shy of 9 a.m. Under the circumstances, the tragic scene had a certain allure. But Kate, who still clung to some vestige of self-control, pressed on in hopes of finding a more life-affirming option. That's when she spotted a self-service café, something called Pret a Manger.

"That's more like it," she thought to herself.

After assessing her options, she grabbed a falafel and halloumi hot wrap, a pomegranate and orange yoghurt pot and a cup of hot vanilla chai tea and made her way to the cashier. Then it dawned on her that she'd yet to procure any local currency.

"Credit card OK?" she asked the female attendant.

"Yes, of course love, no problem," was the response.

Thoroughly peckish, as the locals would say, Kate inhaled her frou-frou food then checked the airport monitor for the latest flight information: Her gate still hadn't been assigned.

"Strange system," she thought as she retrained her sights on an ATM, intent on loading up on pounds. But no matter how many buttons she pushed, the machine refused to cough up any cash.

"What's the deal?" she said out load, albeit softly. "I just got paid last week. What a country!"

Rebuffed, Kate rechecked the monitor. This time it told her not only that her flight was departing from gate 13 (of course!) but that the plane was already boarding.

"What the fu…," she said more forcefully, catching herself before voicing the closing consonants. A second later, she downshifted into a slow trot, her wheeled carry-on scurrying along behind her.

The Jaguar was also picking up speed. Once north of the bottleneck at Tarbert, the big cat widened its gait into a full canter along the coastline of the appropriately named Loch Fyne. Soon, the trio would clear the royal berg of Inverary—a tidy town known for its a stately 18th century castle—and approach the route's northern apogee, where they would sweep hard to the right before tacking south toward Loch Lomond and their final destination.

Gavin, mellowing to the purr of his highfalutin feline, loosened his grip on the steering wheel. That's when it occurred to him that, in their haste, they must have zipped past the turn in the road that had been John's last without uttering so much as a word. No point in bringing it up now.

Instead, Malcolm, who was starting to feel a bit peckish himself, let loose an anguished sigh.

"Ah canne believe we're goin' all this way an' wullny be makin' a stop for oysters," he said, motioning to the Loch Fyne Oyster House, a landmark establishment that, for more than half a century, had beckoned to motorists as they rounded the A83's big bend.

"Ah feel yer pain, X-man," said Angus, opting for the nickname he'd bestowed upon Malcolm long ago. The source? Could have been the civil rights firebrand Malcolm X. Or perhaps it was a nod to the Marvel Comics serial of the same name and Malcolm's mutant-like strength. Then again, Malcolm, like John, was divorced. So to his former wife he was "the Ex." And then there was the fact that when Angus first met Malcolm, he was a golf neophyte who had a penchant for playing X-out Titleists, sold at a discount due to their minor cosmetic blemishes. Knowing Angus, it was probably some combination of all the above. "Give me half a chance an' Ah'd happily doon a bucket or two o' those slippery beauties in one sittin', all ba ma lonesome."

"Well, if ye did, ye wouldn't be lonesome for long," said Malcolm.

"How dae ye figure?" asked Angus.

"Raw oysters are an aphrodisiac," said Malcolm. "Casanova used tae eat 50 for breakfast e'ery mornin'. An' he had ower a hundred lovers, at least tha' he was willin' tae own up tae."

"Oh, Malcolm. Tha' old tale," chimed in Gavin. "Ye're far too street-wise tae fall for tha'."

"Nae, 'tis true," protested Malcolm. "A team o' American an' Italian scientists proved it. Has tae dae wi' supercharged amino acids an' zinc, or some such. Apparently the little mollusks practically ooze this stuff from theer pores, assumin' they have pores. Especially durin' breedin' season. And this just happens tae be breedin' season! Ah shudder tae think, Angus, wha' would happen if ye really did suck two buckets' worth o' nature's little Viagra into yer system."

"Well, for starters, Mrs. Angus would be in serious danger," said Gavin.

"Mrs. Angus, Ah mean Rosemary, woold be seriously

shocked," replied Angus. "This is all very amusin', Malclom. But how, pray tell, dae ye happen tae know all this?"

"I's called readin'," said Malcolm. "Ye should try it sometahm."

"Touche!" said Gavin. "Well played, sir."

Angus, who wasn't nearly as skilled at taking jibes as he was at delivering them, looked away.

Outside, he noticed that the roundabouts now appeared with increasing frequency and the traffic was thickening. Inside, he was less aware that his shoulders had begun to tense and his heart to race. Somewhere around Dumbarton, pastoral splendor had begun to lose the battle with suburban sprawl. And, quite frankly, it wasn't putting up much of a fight.

"Just two miles tae the Erskine Bridge," he said with a harrumph. "Then the airport."

Goin' All Sherlock on Me

Gavin practiced his pirouettes in the arrivals area, trying to keep one eye on the passengers who trickled through the auto-opening doors in front of him and another on the bustle of activity behind. The latter is where he'd last seen Angus, who begged out—he claimed—to tend to his bodily functions. But 15 minutes had elapsed since. That meant one of two things: Angus was either in the throes of unleashing an eye-watering stench in the public loo, or he'd made a side trip to the airport bar to replenish his spent fluids. Talk about picking your poison.

Malcolm, at least, stood fast by Gavin's side. On the walk in from the short-term car park, it occurred to them they didn't know what John's daughter looked like. And unless she'd studied her father's photos, Kate probably wouldn't be able to pick them out of the crowd either. So Gavin, ever resourceful, took it upon himself to chat up one of the limo drivers in position to intercept his passenger, offering a pound coin in exchange for one of his placards. But the driver, visibly moved by the tale, waived off the remuneration. He even volunteered to fill in the name.

"M-C-M-A-L-O-N-A-N," he said, reading his handiwork. "How dae ye pronoonce tha'?"

"MAC-uh-LOH-nan," said Gavin. "I's Irish. Though Kathleen is an American, like her father. We go back 20 years, at least. Ye've been a great help."

"Think nothin' o' it," said the driver. "I's a terrible business."

Gavin, meanwhile, squinted to make out the monitor.

"I' says her plane is on the groon," he said. "She shoould be oot any minute noo."

The odd couple refocused on the doorway. Through it passed the usual cast of characters: a fragile silver-haired husband and wife appearing to hold each other up; a pack of amped teenagers dressed in matching orange T-shirts, apparently on some sort of overnight school-related adventure; the obligatory business warriors, smartly dressed, briefcases in one hand, mobile in the other. And then.

"Wait," said Gavin. "Tha' one. Coold be her."

"Who ye talkin' aboot?" asked Malcolm.

"Two o'clock," said Gavin. "Youngish woman. Dark broon hair, borderin' on black. Creamy Irish complexion. Aboot five-foot-six, Ah reckon. Attractive but, strangely, unaccompanied. An', ba her attire, clearly nae on a business trip. Looks tae be lookin' for someone."

"Yer goin' all Sherlock on me, Gavin. But aye, Ah dae see her," said Malcolm. "An' Ah also see the mannerisms. Look a' the way she stands: free hand on her hip an' the left foot slightly in front o' the right. Remind ye o' someone?"

"Noo tha' ye mention it," said Gavin. "There's definitely a lot o' Mac in her. Well done Dr. Watson."

"Ah seem tae have a knack for readin' body language," said Malcolm. "Ma misspent youth as a boxer, Ah guess."

Just then the woman in question, having thoroughly scanned her new surroundings, decided to make a move. It soon became clear that she had Malcolm's sign in her sights. He braced himself as she accelerated with each succeeding step, as if a tractor beam had locked onto her coordinates and was pulling her in.

"Kate McAlonan," she said, reaching out to shake Malcolm's hand. "Are you with Machrihanish?"

"Na' wi' but o'," said Malcolm. "Ah'm Malcolm, one o' yer father's friends."

"So you're not the driver?" she said with a hint of condescension. "I saw the sign and thought they'd sent a driver."

"In a manner o' speakin', they did. This is yer driver. His nemme's Gavin," said Malcolm.

"Gavin? Oh, right," said Kate. "We spoke on the phone."

Gavin, unbeknownst to him, shifted into Royal Bank of Scotland mode. "Please accept oor sincerest condolences, Miss

McAlonan," he proclaimed. "Ah trust ye've had a safe journey."

"Safe? Yes. Uneventful? Not exactly," said Kate. "But I'll live."

Malcolm cringed. "Unfortunately yer father will na'," was the thought that flashed through his head.

"Baggage claim is this way," said Gavin.

"Oh, I have everything I need right here," said Kate. "I practically live in airports. It's all carry-on all the time for me."

"Efficient," said Gavin. "Ma wife, uh, Ah mean, ex-wife, cooldn't survive a week wi' anythin' less than a full-sized steamer trunk."

"A week?" said Kate, startled. "I'd only planned for a day or two. How long could this take?"

Now it was Gavin and Malcolm's turn to be caught unawares.

"Very difficult tae say," said Gavin. "Another o' yer father's friends, Dr. MacKenzie, has been in Tarbert wi' the authorities all mornin' tryin' tae sort tha' oot. We figured tha's wheer ye'd wanne go next."

"Yes, the sooner the better," said Kate. "I appreciate your help. Really, I do. But I need to be on my way to New York by Wednesday, at the latest. Got a client there who's spinning in circles. But we have the rest of today and all of tomorrow, a good 36 hours, right?"

Gavin and Malcolm hesitated, taking it—and her—all in.

"Aye, tha's right. We'll dae oor best," said Gavin, finally. "We just need tae collect the other member o' oor foursome an' we can be on oor way."

It'd now been 30 minutes since Angus' last sighting, so Gavin and Malcolm knew right where to find him. The banker led the way up to the airport's second level while the boxer, yet always the gentleman, commandeered Kate's bag. As they stepped off the escalator, Gavin spotted the outline of their ring leader's beefy frame in the distance, hunched over the bar, a pint of Guinness in his thick right mitt. Angus, however, didn't see them coming.

"On yer feet, big man," said Malcolm. "Theer's a lady present."

"Oh forgive me," said Angus, struggling to pull himself upright. Clearly, this was not his first round. "Welcome tae Scotland, Kate. Ma nemme is Angus. I's a shame tha' 'tis under such sorrowfool circumstances."

"Uh, thank you, I guess," said Kate, who heard a jumble of vowel sounds, virtually no consonants and—as far as she could tell—only one fully formed word: her name.

"Allow me tae translate," said Gavin. "Angus said he's glad ye're here, but he's saddened ba the reason."

"Well if he did, he used a lot more words than that to say it," said Kate.

"Ah'm paraphrasing just a wee bit, in the interest of tahm," said Gavin. "Dinna worry if ye dinna understand him. I's taken me nearly half a lifetahm tae become flooent in Angish."

"Aye, ye're in very good company," said Malcolm. "Ah recently came across an interview wi' Tom Watson. He's been playin' gowf heer since 1975. Won five o' our Opens, what ye call the British Open. Only the great Harry Vardon has won moor. Yet Watson admits he canne understand a word we say. Says he needs a translator. I's shockin'."

"Tom Watson?" said Kate. "Wasn't he that old guy who almost won the British, uh I mean, Open a few years back?"

"Aye, tha's right," said Gavin. "A' Turnberry. Tha's na' so far from Machrihanish, as the crow flies. Broke oor hearts."

"And my dad's, apparently," said Kate. "Don't know if he ever mentioned it, but Tom Watson was one of his heroes."

"Only a couple hundred tahms," said Angus.

"Dad had dinner with him once, when he was filling in for the golf writer at the *Chronicle*. Said it was one of the highlights of his life."

"Oh, Ah am such an eejit!" said Malcolm. "Ah apologize for bringin' it up, Kate. Ah knew, but forgot."

"No, no. It's alright," she said, softening if only for a moment. "I'd almost forgotten myself, until now. It's a happy memory." Then, a beat or two later, "Wish I had more."

Kate looked down. Gavin checked his watch. Malcolm shifted his stance. The gears of the conversation had ground to a sudden halt. It took Angus, in his well-lubricated state, to get them moving again.

"Can Ah buy ye a beer, Kate?" he asked slowly and with, for him, a reasonable facsimile of proper diction.

"Hey, I got that!" said Kate, regaining her composure. "Thank you, but no. I don't drink on Mondays. And if I did, I wouldn't drink before dinner. And if it were dinner, I wouldn't have a beer. A glass of wine, perhaps. Or, preferably, a Cosmo. But not a beer. I'm not into beer."

"Na' intae beer," repeated Angus, pausing to let the odd sequence of words rattle about in his brain. "Apparently ye dinna git tha' gene from yer father. As far as he was concerned, this stuff makes the woorld go round. Ah'm inclined tae agree, though Ah'm still conductin' ma research."

"I'm sorry. I plead jet lag. Could you repeat that?" asked Kate.

"Ah'll explain later," said Gavin. "If we head oot noo, Ah believe we can catch the Dunoon an' Tarbert ferries on oor way back. Might na' save us much tahm but 'twill definitely shorten the drive."

"Yer the captain o' this ship, Gavin," said Angus, polishing of his pint. "Anchors away!"

A Land as Bizarre as Oz

Gavin redirected the Jag toward the town of Greenock, about 20 miles west of the airport, where—after too short a stretch of divided motorway—a maze of narrow surface streets would eventually lead them to Gourock and the jumping off spot for the first of their two ferry rides.

That gave Kate time to take stock of her situation. She congratulated herself for holding her own during the initial exchange in the terminal, thanks largely to sheer bravado. But now, as an uneasy silence paralyzed the passengers, she couldn't stop the foreignness of it all from bubbling up to the surface.

Fewer than 48 hours ago, all was right in her carefully constructed world—with the possible exception of that lame indiscretion with Steven that she'd have to clean up when this was behind her. She was surrounded by her things: the Boxster, the beachside condo, the business trip to New York, maybe even a Lakers' playoff game if she could come up with a creative way to swing it.

Then, out of nowhere, she'd been bushwhacked by an emotional tornado and, like Dorothy Gale, had been transported—against her will—to a land as bizarre as Oz. Now she was making her way on a not-so-yellow brick road to an emerald golf course called Machrihanish accompanied by stand-ins for the Scarecrow, the Tin Man and the Cowardly Lion. Yet these three escorts, when they opened their mouths, sounded more like the Lollipop Guild—especially the big one. Kate never much identified with Dorothy who, in her opinion, put too much faith in the men in her life—real or imagined— to rescue her. But she did agree with the displaced Kansan about one thing: There really is no place like home.

If Gavin hadn't insisted on picking her up in Glasgow, Kate would have simply rented a car and made the drive herself, doing what she could to wrest some measure of control over her predicament. Still, even she had to admit that being chauffeured by a local in an XJ wasn't such a bad way to go. Perhaps there was more to these country bumpkins than she'd first thought. She could only hope.

"We're cuttin' it a wee bit close, but Ah think we'll make it," said Gavin finally, mostly to restart the stalled conversation.

"Ah ha'e complete confidence in ye, Gavin," complimented Angus, completely out of character. Previously, in the car park,

Gavin and Malcolm were similarly caught off guard when Angus had surrendered his front passenger seat to Kate and retreated to the second row with Malcolm.

"Geez, Ah woonder how long this will last?" thought Malcolm. The ex-boxer's body language skills confirmed that Gavin was wrestling with the same question.

"So, I'm familiar with the concept of a ferry, at least the American kind," said Kate, deciding to join in. "But perhaps you could explain what *you* mean by that."

"In this instance, Ah'm feerly certain we're both on the semme page," said Gavin. "We drive oor car ontae a boat an' it takes it, an' us, across a body o' water, in this case a loch, wheer we roll off ontae dry land an' continue on oor way."

"Boat?" asked Kate. "Define boat."

"Bigger tha' a dingy, smaller tha' the QE II," said Angus, making an intentionally restrained attempt at joke. "I's standard operatin' procedure aroond heer. Nothin' tae worry aboot."

"And this loch business," followed up Kate. "Smooth sailing, right?"

"Moor often tha' na', aye," said Gavin. "Is theer a problem?"

"Probably not," said Kate. "It's just that, well, I do have some history when it comes to boats. Seems I'm susceptible to motion sickness. But I've learned to overcome it."

"Drugs?" blurted Angus.

"No," said Kate, betraying a chuckle. "I looked it up on the Internet."

"Aye, tha's how 'tis done," interjected Malcolm. "Wha' did ye find?"

"Well, I had just watched or, I should say, tried to watch, a movie that was shot with a hand-held camera. You know, the kind that bounce all over the place."

"*The Blair Witch Project?*" said Malcolm. "Tha' movie scared the bejesus oot o' me."

"Not that one but you get my drift," said Kate. "Anyway, halfway through, I thought I was going to lose it. So I put my head down and tried to follow along by listening to the dialogue. It took me two days to fully recover from those miserable two hours. Had me wishing, instead, that I'd gotten it out of my system and been done with it."

"Noo theer's a feelin' tha' Ah dae know somethin' aboot!" said Angus. "But, Ah must confess tha', in ma case, the infliction is usually self-induced."

"Well, in my case, it had me wondering, 'Why did that happen?' And, 'Was there a way to prevent it?' said Kate. "So I Googled it."

"Ah woulda' just Guinnessed it masel'," joked Angus, morphing back into his wisecracking self.

"Hadn't thought of that, but OK," said Kate. "Anyway, turns out the body has two ways of sensing motion: the eyes and the inner ears. If the two don't agree with one another, your digestive system basically freaks out."

"Semme thin' happens wi' too much single malt," said Malcolm.

"Well if you were in a bar, I guess you could stop drinking," said Kate.

"Ye would guess wrong," said Angus.

"Huh?" said Kate, just when she thought she was getting the hang of Angish.

"Ne'er mind him,'" said Gavin, relieved that Kate had taken the lead. "Please continue."

"Turns out there's not much you can do about the disconnect in a movie," said Kate. "You're just sitting there and your inner ears are saying, 'Not moving.' But your eyes are saying, 'You're crazy! We're bouncing around all over the place.'"

"Soonds like the Machrihanish clubhoose aroond midnight," said Angus.

"Put a sock in i', Angus," said Gavin.

"Anyway, you *can* minimize the effect on a boat," said Kate. "You just establish the horizon as a point of reference, then notice how the boat is moving relative to it. That way your eyes and ears stay in sync."

"An' tha' works?" asked Gavin.

"Yeah, I've gotten to be pretty good at it," said Kate. "I took a cruise along the Mexican coast during a reunion with my sorority sisters last year and I was perfectly fine."

"Well then, this little jaunt shoold be a walk in the park for ye," said Gavin. "Theer's really nothin' tae it."

"Tha' explains it!" exclaimed Malcolm.

"Explains wha', X-man?" said Angus.

"Why Mac, every tahm we brought up the ferries, always insisted on makin' the long up-an'-ower drive tae Machrihanish," said Malcolm. "It would appear, Kate, tha'—when it comes tae this particular unpleasantness—ye are yer father's daughter."

"Really?" said Kate. "My dad got seasick, too? I didn't know that about him."

"But a' least ye dinna inherit his addiction tae beer," said Angus. "Ye'll be relieved tae know tha' ye won't find yersel' prayin' tae the porcelain gawd on tha' account."

"Oh, Angus, must ye?" said Gavin.

"No, it's OK, Gavin," said Kate. "I usually don't understand what he's saying, so he can't offend me. And, fact is, even if I did catch every word, it would take a lot to set me off. I've developed a pretty thick skin over the years."

"So ye're immune tae Angus' super powers?" said Malcolm. "Ye're goin' tae fit in just fine ower heer, Kate. Ye really will."

"Kind of you to say, Malcolm," she replied. "But I'm not looking to fit in. I'm looking to do what's needed to be done and, well, to be done with it. So if these boats will speed up the process, then I say, 'Bring 'em on!' I'll tough it out if I have to."

"As ye wish," said Gavin, as he noticed that *his* stomach was starting to feel a bit queasy. "Tha's the Dunoon ferry on-ramp, straight ahead an' right on tahm."

Three States o' Bein'

Bernard, Donald and Ewan gathered in the clubhouse for lunch, though they hungered as much for each other's company as they did for Margaret's cooking after a morning left to their own devices.

"Any woord?" asked Margaret as Bernard paid for the trio's beverages at the bar. "They shoold be on theer way back ba noo."

"Aye, Gavin texted me tae confirm tha' Kate arrived safely," he said. "He ended it wi' a smiley face."

"Gavin uses emoticons?" snickered Margaret. "He dinna strike me as the type."

"Emoti-whats?" asked Bernard.

"Tha's wha' those little doodads are called," said Margaret. "As the caretaker o' this place, Ah dae ma best tae keep up wi' the latest technological developments. But 'tis a ne'er endin' battle, Ah'm afraid."

"Aye, well, on tha' front, put me doon as a pacifist," said Bernard. "As a man o' letters, Ah must confess tha' Ah take the spellin' habits o' today's text-happy youth as a personal affront. Makes me feer for the future o' our very language, it does. Dinna git me started!"

"Indeed," said Margaret. "Let's na'."

"Anyway, 'tis probably somethin' Gavin's daughter taught him," said Bernard. "The thing is, the smiley face wasn't exactly smilin'. Was more a look o' sheer panic, wi' a wide slit o' a mouth flashin' a full set o' teeth. Not sure wha' tha' means."

"Well, ma guess is he's just a wee bit anxious," said Margaret. "He's probably afraid he won't know wha' tae say tae her. And, at the semme tahm, he's probably afraid Angus will say the wrong thing tae her. An' then there's Malcolm. He could go either way. I's a tricky situation."

"Aye, indeed 'tis," said Bernard. "Probably best tha' we got tae hang back an' hold doon the fort."

Meanwhile, Donald and Ewan chose seats with an unobstructed view through one of the clubhouse's picture windows. The table before them was set with wooden placements, each depicting a different scene from Scotland's golfing past, that served as oversized coasters to steaming bowls of potato leek soup. Soon the spread would be joined by three plates of chicken curry on a bed of white rice, the kitchen's entree of the day. Funny how a little duress can drum up such a big appetite.

Bernard rejoined them, deftly delivering three pint glasses without spilling a drop.

"So Ewan, how's the course lookin'?" asked Bernard, choosing not to go *there*, at least not to start.

"I's in fine nick. Perhaps the best Ah've e'er seen it," said Ewan, relieved at his friend's line of questioning. "Given the rough winter, Ah was expectin' the turf—especially on the greens—tae be a wee bit threadbare. But the surfaces are rollin' true. Ye hit the put, ye make the putt."

"Tha's a shame," said Donald, surprisingly on point. The smaller the circle, it seems, the more likely he is to stay in sync with the conversation. "Ah was countin' on poor conditions as one o' ma excuses for ma poor gowf. Guess Ah'm goin' tae have tae dig a bit deeper intae ma bag o' tricks, assumin' we decide tae actually play some matches."

"Oh, we will," said Bernard. "Ah'm sure John woold've wanted it tha' way."

"Ah hope yer right, Bernard," said Ewan. "It woold be a shame tae miss this opportunity. Ah mean, Ah dinna think any o' us is in a hurry tae rush back home. Yet we're all at a loss aboot wha' tae dae next. The agenda has always been so refreshin'ly simple heer. An' noo 'tis not."

"Indeed," said Bernard. "Tha's one of the things we love aboot this place an' this week. Theer's basically three states o' bein' at Machrihanish: the playin' o' the gowf, the drinkin' an' conversin' after the gowf, an' then the sleepin' it all off after the drinkin' an' conversin' after the gowf. Then we wake up tae a new day an' start all ower again."

"Aye," said Ewan. "Like tha' movie *Groundhog Day*. I's a beautiful thing."

"Well, no matter wha', Machrihanish is still a beautiful place," said Donald, once again right on point. "Ah spent most o' ma mornin' on the beach. Fabulous place, especially when the tide is oot. Exposes all manner o' thin's tha' the waves wash ashoor, thanks tae the underlyin' currents. Did ye know tha' the icy water we soak oor feet in at the end o' a 36-hole day travels thousands o' miles tae git heer, nursed along ba the Gulf Stream?"

"Ah ha' no idea, Donald," said Ewan, the words escaping his mouth before his internal editor had a chance to delete them. Once Donald was engaged, Ewan and Bernard well knew, a nerdy lecture would soon follow.

"Oh, aye 'tis a fascinatin' phenomenon," said Donald. "It starts its journey in the balmy Caribbean, then tracks aloong America's eastern seaboard before bendin' northeast aroond the Grand Banks o' Newfoundland, wheer it breaks up intae various swoorls, one o' which—known as the North Atlantic Drift—continues on tae these shores."

"OK, we git it," inserted Bernard. "But…"

"Ponce de Leon, the Spanish explorer, was the first tae write aboot it, way back in the 16th century," continued Donald without skipping a beat. "An' would ye believe Benjamin Franklin, o' American colony fame, was the first tae map it, in the late 1700s?"

"Wheer does he git this stuff?" Ewan asked Bernard, out loud. But Donald plowed on.

"While the local surfers wooldn't think o' bravin' these waves wi'out a wetsuit, the water is actually warmer tha' it shoold be, helpin' tae moderate oor climate," he said. "Though, Ah shoold warn ye: The latest computer models suggest global warmin' coold stop the Gulf Stream in i's tracks, in which case Scotland coold end up lookin' an awful lot like Greenland. We're pretty much a' the semme latitude, dinna ye know."

"Tha', actually, Ah did know," said Bernard. "An' did *ye* know, Donald, tha' yer soup's gettin' cold?"

"Oh, right ye are, Bernard," said Donald, snapping out of his self-induced spell. "Ah must admit tha', sometahms, Ah dae tend tae lose sight o' wha's right under ma noose."

"Nae need tae apologize, Donald," said Bernard. "Ye aren't the only one a' this table who suffers from tha' affliction."

With that, Bernard, Ewan and Donald agreed unanimously, and without uttering another word, to take refuge in the unambiguous joy of consuming hot food on a suddenly cooling day, pausing between bites to read the agitated sky. But they didn't need eyes to see that a pair of storms, one by land and another by sea, was fast approaching, locked on a collision course. The three men could feel it in their guts.

Your Basic Triple Whammy

Gavin felt it, too. The sky was clear when his foursome left the airport. But as they passed through Greenock, he couldn't help but notice that a thick gray blanket had materialized overhead seemingly out of nowhere, like some sort of meteorological magic trick. The uncharacteristically calm weather was deteriorating at an accelerated clip as the Dunoon ferry pushed off in Gourock with the Jaguar and its crew safely aboard.

The banker's first instinct was to remain in the parked car, but his passengers outvoted him. Like the Johnny Jump-ups on taxiing jets who never wait for the pilot to turn off the seatbelt sign, all three immediately unbuckled and braved the elements.

Angus set off in search of the bar. Malcolm beat feet for the gents. And Kate twisted and turned Gumby-like amid the tightly packed grid of vehicles until she broke free to an open patch of metal decking near the ferry's bow.

At first, Kate managed to fix her gaze on the farther shore just six miles to the west, intent on completing the 20-minute journey with her senses—and her Heathrow breakfast—fully intact. But Lunderston Bay's churning blue-green water, where the Firth of Clyde and Loch Long converge, clearly had other plans. One moment, the bow would rise up while the stern sunk down. Then, violently, the roles would reverse with, at most, a nanosecond of sweet equilibrium in between. As if the liquid teeter totter weren't enough, a thick bank of low clouds drifted into position, obliterating the horizon from view. And before she knew it, Kate found herself, quite literally, soaking in the scenery. It was your basic Scottish triple whammy.

"Are ye sure ye dinna wanne stay in the Jag?" asked Gavin, who had retraced Kate's footsteps after he spotted the incoming squall. "This will pass. But ma guess is na' any tahm soon."

"No, it's OK," shouted Kate above the surf's roar, determined to ride out the bucking bronco. "I'm much better off in the fresh air, even if my jacket is no match for this rain. So, is this what you people call smooth sailing?"

"Ma apologies," he said, struggling to keep his balance. "Bad timin', Ah'm afraid."

"Yeah, well, I shouldn't be surprised. I've been on quite the roll lately, basically from the moment I returned your call," she said, practically spitting out the words through half-clenched teeth.

"Aye," he said, bracing himself against the gunwale. "Truth be told, we're all oot o' sorts. Daein' our best tae muddle through."

"Stiff upper lip and all that, right?" she said.

"Our friends tae the south might put it tha' way. But yes, we're keepin' mostly calm an' carryin' on. Tryin' tae play it one shot at a tahm," he said, relieved that the wind had begun to decrease as the rain increased. He'd happily made that trade many a time while knocking it around in his waterproofs at Machrihanish.

"Sounds like something my dad would say. Never missed a chance to make a golf reference. Just one of his many quirks that kind of drove me crazy," said Kate as she relaxed her hold on the ferry's railing.

"Well, he *was* crazy aboot the gemme, even if it dinna always return his undyin' affection," said Gavin.

"Or maybe he was just plain nuts," she said, wiping the rain drops from her eyes. "Feeling a little whacked out myself at the moment."

"Kind of hard for us tae pass judgment," he said, cinching his jacket's zipper against his chin. "He seemed perfectly normal tae us. Which means either tha' he really was normal or, more likely, tha' the whole lot o' us is off oor rockers. Guess ye'll have tae decide tha' for yersel'."

Just then a rogue wave slapped hard against the side of the ferry, momentarily knocking it off its slow but steady path toward Dunoon. Kate, naturally athletic, re-clenched the railing and, in one motion, lowered her center of gravity and adjusted her stance. Gavin, caught unawares, instinctively grabbed hold of Kate.

"Oh for fuck sake!" he blurted, quickly backing out of the bear hug and latching onto the boat's capstan. "I beg your pardon."

"No harm, no foul," she said, far more amused than annoyed. "But look at you!"

"Excuse me?" said Gavin.

"It's your face," she said. "That shade of red reminds me of my Porsche. Makes for a good warning light in this storm, though."

"How embarrassin'," shuddered Gavin. "Though, in fairness, Ah canne help but notice tha' your complexion is decidedly devoid o' color. Are ye all right?"

"Not entirely, but I'll survive," she said, straining her eyes in a futile attempt to connect with even one small still point amid the whiteout. "We're almost there, right?"

"Aboot half way, Ah reckon," said Gavin. "This headwind is slowin' oor progress."

Kate grimaced. Having completed a triathlon or two, she's well acquainted with the concept of "The Wall," where your mind must convince your body that you really can go the distance—no matter how seductively your body argues to the contrary. But in her experience, those moments of truth had always come when the end was nearly in sight. Gavin's guestimation on the balance of the ferry crossing didn't meet that qualification. Not even close.

Meanwhile, Gavin scanned the deck in search of Angus and Malcolm. Not another soul stirred out in the open, which made him wonder why he was still with Kate in the ship's bow, getting pummeled. Though a staunch proponent of chivalry, even Gavin would acknowledge that the lost art has its limits. The knights were brave. But they weren't stupid.

"If 'tis OK wi' ye, Ah think Ah'm goin' tae return tae the car," he said to the back of Kate's head as she clung to the railing and stared into the mist.

She didn't reply.

"Hey Kate, Ah'm takin' cover in the Jag!" shouted Gavin, assuming she hadn't heard him.

This time she did react. But, alas, it wasn't words that came spewing from her mouth.

She's On Scottish Tahm Noo

Kate slouched in the front seat of the Jaguar that, now, was a passenger on the second ferry, the one that bridged the gap between Portavadie and Tarbert across Loch Fyne. Since the first crossing, she'd had about an hour's drive along a twisting back road that, at times, narrowed to a single lane, to recover. Not surprisingly, it wasn't nearly enough—not even with the window rolled down in the rain, much to the dismay of Gavin and his car's leather seats. Now though, the sky had cleared and the breeze had subsided. So while Kate might not be feeling much better, it was unlikely she'd feel worse—at least not when it came to her digestive system.

Meanwhile the three men, sensing Kate's need for some

space, climbed a narrow ladder and took in the view from this smaller ferry's afterthought of an upper deck. The fishing village of Tarbert, their destination and also their dread, beckoned in the distance.

"So Gavin, have ye had any communication wi' Alister since we left this mornin'?" asked Angus.

"Aye," said Gavin. "He's been in direct contact wit' the procurator fiscal, a Mr. McIntire. He's runnin' the show. Given the circumstances, a post mortem examination is required. But they've been havin' a wee bit o' trouble trackin' down a pathologist who can complete the task."

"Ye'd think they'd be able tae find someone in Campbeltown," said Malcolm.

"Apparently na'. But accordin' to ma last text from Alister, a wumman in Edinburgh was bein' fetched ba private plane. Tae speed things up, they've made special arrangements tae land on the runway a' the old Royal Air Force base they shut doon a few years back."

"The one tha's visible from the 10th tee?" asked Angus.

"Aye," said Gavin. "Hopefully she'll be theer soon, if she's na' already. Soonds like 'twill take another 48 hours, at least, after tha' afore the legal requirements are settled."

"So we're talkin' through Wednesday, a' the minimum," said Malcolm. "Have ye informed Kate?"

"Dinna see the point," said Gavin. "Especially na' in her current state."

"Aye," said Angus. "She's on Scottish tahm noo, whether she likes it or na'."

"Ah'm going wi' na'," said Malcolm.

Just then, a metallic creak stole their attention. Kate was climbing the ladder to join them.

"So, is this the 'He-man Women Hater's Club' tree fort or can anybody come up here? joked Kate.

"A 'Little Rascals' reference from someone yer age? Ah'm impressed," said Malcolm. "Welcome back tae the land o' the livin'."

"Are you kidding?" she said. "Thanks to my dad, I was practically raised on 'Our Gang.' Other kids got Burt and Ernie. I got Spanky and Alfalfa. Yet another of my dad's little obsessions."

"Sounds like a guid trade tae me," said Angus.

"You could be right," said Kate. "Funny the things you remember. So, is that Tarbert?"

"Aye," said Gavin. "Closin' in on it. Won't be long noo."

"That's the best news I've heard in quite awhile," she said. "Hopefully I can pick up a cell signal over there. New York's probably wondering what happened to me. In the meantime, think I'll find the ladies room. Try to freshen up."

Gavin, Angus and Malcolm watched as Kate descended the ladder, still not quite sure what to make of her. Nearly 20 hours of arduous travel had brought her within eyeshot of what would likely be the most heart wrenching moment of her still young life. Yet she displayed the nonchalance of a college student in search of a double shot of espresso to help her rally after pulling an all-nighter. There seemed to be two possible explanations: Reality, like Klingon photon torpedoes aimed at the Starship Enterprise, had so far bounced harmlessly off her powerful shields. Or, worse yet, the slings and arrows had in fact managed to hit their mark, but Kate simply refused to acknowledge the wound.

Women, in general, had always been somewhat of a mystery to these three and, for that matter, most of their Scottish brethren. After all, even Augusta National, a real-life "He-man Women Hater's Club," had acquiesced and admitted female members, beating St. Andrews to the punch. But Kate? She had them impersonating Joe Pesci in Oliver Stone's *JFK*: "She's a mystery, wrapped in a riddle, inside an enigma."

"Back tae the car, boys," said Angus. "'We'd best be bailin' ootta this boat."

Mr. McIntire, I Presume?

Kate was granted at least one of her wishes: Tarbert proved to be a cellular oasis amid the Scottish hinterlands' technological desert. That allowed Gavin to connect with Alister, who texted directions to the police station where he'd been holed up since dawn. And it gave Kate a chance to check her email, though that exercise—a pricey proposition for an American-based iPhone on foreign soil—proved pointless. Not a single missive of substance appeared amid the flood of Facebook updates, Linkedin requests and ever-present spam.

"How is that possible?" she thought, double-checking her

in-box. After all, hadn't an eternity passed since she'd left civilization? Half-baked Einstein aficionados, though, might have explained that the expanse of space between Los Angeles and the Argyll penninsula had warped her perception of time. It was still early on a Monday morning back home. She hadn't missed a thing.

One brief text message, however, did manage to cut through the clutter.

"U should B safely on the ground by now," wrote Joe. "Hang in there. Got your back."

Kate's first instinct was to reply. Instead, she hesitated, unconsciously using the time difference as an emotional buffer. Joe sent the message hours ago, when he was still up and about. Now, he was either sleeping or scrambling to catch an early-morning flight to New York. Either way, the last thing he needed was a text message from her that he'd feel compelled to read and acknowledge. It's not that it was inconvenient for her to respond now. But it would be better to wait until it'd be more convenient for him, she rationalized.

While Kate conducted this internal debate, Gavin pulled into the police station's car park. They had arrived.

"Ye, obviously, arc Kathleen," said Alister, who had spotted the Jaguar and rushed out to greet its occupants. "Ye must be exhausted."

"And you must be Dr. MacKenzie," she replied. "The guys said you'd be here."

"Please call me Alister," he said. "Ah've had quite the frustratin' mornin' masel'. Ah'm afraid the wheels toorn very slowly in these small towns, much more so than ye're used tae in the States, tha's for sure. Gavin, if ye'd like, Ah can take it from heer. There's nae point in all five o' us millin' aboot. Ah'm afraid we'd only owerwhelm theer tiny waitin' area."

"Are ye sure, Alister?" replied Gavin.

"Absolutely," said the doctor. "You chaps head back tae Machrihanish. Track doon Bernard, Ewan and Malcolm. Make sure they're na' gettin' in Margaret's hair. Ah'll walk ye through this, Kate. Will make me feel like Ah'm daein' somethin'."

"Thank you," said Kate. "You've all been very kind."

"Think nothin' o' it," said Gavin, relieved. "An' dinna worry aboot makin' arrangements for the night, Kate. We'll take care o' tha' for ye. Let's plan tae rendezvous at the clubhoose for dinner, say aroond 7."

"Aye, Kate," said Angus. "Will give me another chance tae make guid on tha' drink offer."

"By then, I might willingly accept," said Kate.

"Even if 'tis a Monday?" said Angus.

"Even if," she said.

Alister escorted Kate into the station that, from the outside, looked more like someone's modest home than the set for *Law & Order*. Once inside, he motioned to the receptionist who, without a word, disappeared and soon returned with a gentleman in her wake.

"Mr. McIntire I presume?" said Kate, receiving his handshake.

"Aye, Ms. McAlonan," said McIntire. "Ah'm the procurator

fiscal who's been assigned tae yer father's case. Please accept ma condolences for yer loss."

"So you're certain it's him?" asked Kate.

"Ah'm afraid so, beyoond all reasonable doubt at least," he replied. "Though we'll need ye tae address any doubt tha' might be unreasonable."

"Is he here?" parried Kate without missing a beat.

"Nae," said McIntire. "Ah came heer tae be briefed ba the local police, who have completed theer investigation o' the accident site. Meanwhile, yer father's body has been transported tae the Mid Argyll Community Hospital. I's the nearest facility capable o' conductin' the examination."

"Please tell me I won't have to board another ferry to get there," said Kate.

"Na' at all. I's aboot a 20-minute drive north o' heer on the A83, in the town o' Lochgilphead."

"Ah can take ye theer," said Alister. "I's literally wi'in a short iron o' the Lochgliphead Golf Club, appropriately enough. Wha's the latest on the pathologist?"

"The last Ah heard she was on the groon at the old RAF base," said McIntire. "Shoold be on her way tae Lochgilphead ba noo. Seems doubtful, though, tha' she'd be able tae dae much taeday. But ba taemorrow this tahm, she'll ha'e completed her exam. An' then ba Wednesday, ma work shoold be done an' we can release the body tae a funeral director o' yer choosin'."

"Wednesday?" said Kate. "I need to be on a plane to New York by then. Any way we can speed this thing up?"

"Sorry tae say, but nae," said McIntire. "The steps are set in stone. Ah assure ye we're daein' every thin' we can tae expedite matters. Ah can only imagine how difficult this must be for ye."

"No offense, but it feels like I'm stuck in a nightmare that grows increasingly bizarre with each passing second," said Kate. "The sooner I can wake up the better."

"Yer nae alone theer," said Alister.

"Well then, as my dad would probably say, time to play our next shot," said Kate.

Oh, Papa

The community hospital, built within the past 10 years, stood out against a backdrop of drab stone-and-masonry structures that hugged the shore of Loch Gilp, no more than an inlet off the expansive Loch Fyne. Kate, who'd spent too many of the past 24 hours in a seated position, dispensed with the chairs in the reception area and remained standing, mentally tracing the cloud patterns visible through the large skylight that comprised much of the room's 20-foot ceiling. Alister, meanwhile, flashed his medical credentials at the front desk and made the necessary inquiries.

"It appeers Dr. Urquhart, the pathologist, has also just arrived," he said after rejoining Kate. "They're gettin' word tae her tha' we'd like tae meet."

"As soon as possible?" said Kate.

"Aye, but she might need a bit o' tahm tae sort things oot," said Alister. "Are ye hungry? Looks like they have a cafeteria."

"Starved, but wary of reloading," said Kate. "Don't know if Gavin texted you, but the first ferry ride didn't exactly go smoothly."

"Well then, how aboot a simple cup o' tea," said Alister. "As yer resident physician, tha' woold be ma prescription. Ah'll let them know wheer tae find us."

"How quintessentially British," said Kate. "I believe I'll take you up on that offer."

As they made their way to the dining area, Kate couldn't help but size up Alister as if he were a client and this was a business transaction. Unlike Angus, he was tall and trim. Unlike Malcolm, he was slightly built but still subtly athletic. And unlike Gavin, he seemed more at peace in his own skin. In some ways, he appeared younger than the other three, his age betrayed by a head of pewter hair in fast retreat. Mostly, he had an air of authority about him, as if he'd been down this road before. Given his profession, he probably had.

Kate did her best to match Alister's calm exterior. But, she confessed to herself, she was doing a poor job of emulating his rock-solid interior. There were simply too many unknowns. Hopefully, he could provide some clarification.

"So, Alister, I know I'm here to identify my dad's body. But what, exactly, does that mean?" asked Kate as they sat on opposite sides of a small table, twin cups of Earl Grey brewing in front of them.

"Well, tha's largely up tae ye," said Alister. "In the movies, someone in a white lab coat generally pulls back a sheet just long enough for the loved one tae establish recognition, then quickly puts it back. In the reel woorld, 'tis a bit moor involved than tha', especially at a modern facility like this one. Typically, ye start in a waitin' area. From theer, Dr. Urquhart will invite ye intae a counselin' room, wheer she'll dae her best tae prepare ye for wha's tae come next. From theer, ye'll advance tae the viewin' room, which is separated from wha's called the bier room ba a large window. I's somewha' like a hospital nursery wheer people can see the newborns but canne touch them, as a precaution given theer still developin' immune systems. In this case, the glass divide is moor for the benefit o' the viewer tha' the viewee."

"OK, I get that," said Kate, holding onto the white porcelain mug for warmth.

"Ye can stay as long, or as short, as ye choose," continued Alister. "Theer should be a chair in the viewin' room if yer knees git a wee bit wobbly. An' ye should have direct access tae a loo, uh, just in case."

"Already been there, done that," said Kate between sips.

"Noo, if tha's all too clinical for ye, a technician, maybe Dr. Urquhart, will escort ye through a door tha' leads directly intae the bier room," said Alister. "Ye're welcome tae touch the body if the spirit moves. Again, the staff will follow yer lead. But Ah will say this: Dependin' on how things unfold wi' the funeral director, this coold be the last tahm ye see yer da'. So, in ma mind, 'tis na' a moment tae be rushed. But again, tha's entirely yer call."

Just then, over Kate's left shoulder, Alister made eye contact with a female doctor and waved her to their table. Kate turned and looked.

"Ms. McAlonan an' Dr. MacKenzie?" said the middle-aged, heavy set woman with salt-and-pepper hair. "Ah'm Dr. Urquhart. We're ready whene'er ye are, ma'am."

Kate gulped down another swig of her rapidly cooling beverage, then slowly set the clinically generic mug—adorned only by the hospital's logo—back down on the table.

"Yes, thank you," she said. "No reason to delay on my account."

"Dr. MacKenzie can accompany ye if ye wish," said Dr. Urquhart.

"No, that's not necessary," said Kate. "He's already gone above and beyond. I'm ready."

With that, the two women left Alister to his tea while they made their way to the mortuary. When they arrived, Kate was at least somewhat relieved to find it much as Alister had described it.

"Please, take a seat," said Dr. Urquhart as she closed the door between the waiting room and the counseling room.

"So, have you begun the post-mortem?" asked Kate, doing her best to keep the conversation going.

"Ah've only had tahm for an initial look," said the doctor. "The complete exam will need tae wait until taemorrow. But, if Ah could ease yer mind, ye'd ne'er know from lookin' at the body tha' yer father was in a car accident. The police report confirmed tha', thankfully, he was drivin' a late-model vehicle equipped wi' several airbags tha' inflated on impact. Ah'll know more ba this tahm taemorrow. But ma instincts tell me tha' the accident dinna cause his death. Rather, it seems moor likely tha' his death caused the accident. Did he ha'e any history o' heart trouble?"

"Not that I was aware of," said Kate. "Though, to be honest, he never shared his medical history with me, among other things. He was a very private man."

"Ah'm sorry, but 'twas a question tha' needed askin'," said Dr. Urquhart.

"No need to apologize," said Kate. "You're just doing your job."

"Aye, tha's true," said the doctor. "Na' tha' it e'er gits any easier. Dae ye ha'e any questions for me?"

"None that you're likely to be able to answer at this point," said Kate. "If you don't mind, I'd just assume we get on with it."

"Aye, o' course," said Dr. Urquhart. "Follow me."

Dr. Urquhart led Kate into the next chamber, an institutional white room that, clearly, had been intentionally softened with overstuffed lounge chairs, a vase filled with fresh-cut pyramid orchids and light fixtures fitted with dimmed incandescent bulbs that suffused the space in a warm glow. An internal window, covered with a beige mini-blind, dominated the far wall. Kate stared in its direction.

"Aye, yer father is on the other side o' tha' window," said Dr.

Urquhart. "When ye're ready, simply open the blind. Ah'll be waitin' in the counselin' room, if ye need me. Take as much tahm as ye need."

Kate heard the door close behind her and, moments later, swore she could hear her heart beating, and at a quickening pace. She'd always prided herself on her ability to control her emotions, whether it was on the athletic battlegrounds of her school days or in the Fortune 500 boardrooms of her adulthood.

The same held true on the golf course. Unlike her father, or Joe for that matter, golf was just a game to her, not an endeavor of epic proportions. For them, it seemed, every swing defined their intrinsic worth. A good shot confirmed their goodness; a bad shot, well, meant they were fundamentally flawed. For her, the three-second exercise was just physics: the action of a club striking a ball; the reaction of the ball flying toward a target. That detachment gave her a decided edge on her opponents. She could focus laser-like on execution, while the true believers contended not merely with the shot at hand but also with the nefarious demons that always lurked just below the surface.

Perhaps that's why she naturally gravitated to the pre-2009 Tiger Woods, whose aura of invincibility intimidated those prone to backing away from the big moments—the same aura that evaporated the moment he smashed his SUV into a fire hydrant and a tree on an ill-fated Thanksgiving night. Meanwhile, her father's role model was Tom Watson, who never apologized for wearing his heart on his polo shirt's sleeve.

Now, in this moment of truth, Kate was the one who quivered. And she didn't like it. Not one bit. The only consolation: no one was there to witness the slip.

Tapping into a discipline she'd learned in yoga classes, Kate took a few deep breaths and, haltingly, steadied herself. Then she stepped forward and, like a fearless child who cannonballs into a cool pool on a hot summer's day, opened the blind in a single continuously flowing motion.

She gasped.

Audibly.

Several seconds passed before her conscious mind came to, reminding her to keep breathing. But she didn't need to be prompted to maintain her visual focus. For someone who'd never seen a dead body, let alone her father's, she was powerless to look away.

First things first: It was definitely him. There was no mistaking that profile, dominated by a sizable yet symmetric nose, complemented by a protruding chin and bushy eyebrows, and topped with naturally wavy and luminously white hair. All that was missing was his piercing blue eyes, now permanently hidden from view.

Kate's finely tuned mind tried to take it all in and, simultaneously, compartmentalize the data. But for the first time in her carefully choreographed life, it simply wasn't up to the task. Like an overloaded computer in need of a stiff shot of control-alt-delete, her brain locked up. That freed her natural instincts, that for so long had lain dormant, to fill the void.

It wasn't that her body had begun to convulse uncontrollably, overcome by grief. For that matter, her eyes barely formed a tear. Rather, it was the simple fact that she was no longer consciously dictating her actions. Some unseen outside agency was pushing buttons on a remote control, directing her movements, inducing her right hand to grab and twist the knob that opened the door to the bier room. In the same manner, this Svengali repeatedly shifted one foot in front of the other, until Kate stood next to her father as he lay motionless on a cold stainless steel gurney, his body partially draped with a stark bleached sheet.

Dr. Urquhart spoke the truth. There were no obvious signs of trauma. In fact, the casual observer might conclude that her father was in a recovery room, not a mortuary, and simply still under the influence of general anesthesia after a routine removal of an appendix or some other nonessential organ. But Kate, so close she could detect the still faint whisper of Old Spice, his go-to cologne, was no casual observer. The eerie lack of movement was irrefutable. This, she thought to herself, is what death looks like. And no amount of poetic spin would ever again convince her that it bore even a remote resemblance to deep and peaceful sleep.

The puppet master wasn't quite done with Kate yet, however. It forced her to not merely look at her dad's body but to really see it, to fully absorb its unique details. Such as the moles that formed a small constellation on his right cheek. The broad shoulders. The slim arms permanently dyed from the biceps on down with a golfer's tan. And the runner's legs, similarly hued from mid thigh to ankle, with matching scars on both knees—war wounds from a tumble on concrete during an evening's jog.

And then there were his hands: his connection to the world,

whether they clacked a keyboard while earning a living at the newspaper or grasped a rubber-and-cord Golf Pride grip while pursuing his passion on the course. Strong, gentle, steady hands. The same hands that held Kate close to his chest when she was just an infant, that guided her when she took the first pumps of her bike's pedals without training wheels, that applauded her game-winning hit when her high school softball team clinched its league championship, that signed the checks that put her through college. The same hands that, in the end, dialed the cellphone in an attempt to connect with her one last time.

"Oh, Papa," she whispered, as if he might hear.

Without thinking, Kate reached out and held her father's left hand in hers. She could feel the calluses—along the lower extremity of the index finger, at the base of the ring and pinky fingers and across the pad of the hand—etched by a lifetime of golf played, Freddie Couples-style, without a glove. Then she walked to the other side of the gurney, grasped her father's right hand and was surprised to find it was the final resting place of what had been her father's wedding ring. Her parents had discovered it together in the seaside holiday town of Lahinch during an engagement trip to Ireland, its silver trinity knot weave worn but still intact after all these years. Funny how she'd never noticed it since the divorce, though it must have been there all along.

Kate allowed the moment to linger, gently caressing her father's right hand in both of hers, in no hurry to let go.

Gradually, though, the distinct sense that she was no longer alone seeped into her consciousness. Kate raised her head and looked back through the window, where she saw Dr. Urquhart observing her as she observed her father. Like the June gloom marine layer that invariably surrenders to an irrepressible Los Angeles sun, her out-of-body experience had dissipated. Kate, somewhat reluctantly, regained full control of her faculties.

The moment had passed. But Kate knew that the memory would linger. In the presence of death, she had never felt more alive.

"Ah hope Ah dinna startle ye," said Dr. Urquhart as Kate made her way back to the viewing room. "Ye were in heer for quite a long tahm. Ah just wanted tae make sure ye were OK."

"No, I'm alright. Thank you. You've been very considerate. I can go now," said Kate, gently embracing the pathologist. "And oh, for the record, that *is* my dad. Beyond a shadow of a doubt."

Ye Were His Pride an' Joy

"So, *this* is Machrihanish?" asked Kate, shattering the silence and catching Alister off his normally impenetrable guard.

His American passenger had fallen fast asleep soon after they'd begun the 45-minute drive south on the A83. Alister, though, didn't take it personally. Kate's father had always required a round of golf, out in the elements, to fend off the effects of jet lag on his first day in the country. His daughter, meanwhile, had been cooped up in various modes of transportation, had barely eaten (and expelled most of what she had consumed en route), then had been forced to confront—quite literally face to face—an unspeakable loss. A lesser human would have waved the white flag long ago.

As such, Alister didn't have the heart to roust Kate when McIntire texted him instructions to stop by the police station on their way back through Tarbert. The procurator fiscal had an update: The police had released custody of John's personal effects, which had survived the crash fully intact. So Alister took matters into his own hands and quietly loaded the belongings into his Vauxhall's boot while Kate continued to rest peacefully.

"Aye, so ye're awake?" replied the good doctor as he negotiated the final bend in the B843 that led to the clubhouse. "Actually, the flagsticks ye see theer belong tae the wee coorse, a 9-holer tha', originally, was set aside for the ladies. Most o' the big coorse isnae visible from the road."

"That's a relief," she said. "Awful long way for someone to come to play golf, only to find a course that, well, excuse me, could double as a cow pasture."

"Well, theer is farmland immediately adjacent tae the wee course an' parts o' the big coorse, for tha' matter," said Alister. "But Machrihanish is indeed a proper linksland. 'Tis well worth the effort required tae get heer, Ah canne assure ye o' tha'."

"Guess I'll just have to take your word for it," said Kate. "But, I have to say, the first impression isn't exactly wowing me."

"We'll have tae git ye out theer, assumin' ye're up for it," said Alister. "Give ye a chance tae experience the coorse for yersel'."

"Doubt I'll have time for golf," said Kate. "This isn't exactly spring break in Myrtle Beach."

Alister considered a reply, but instead focused his energies on threading his sedan into one of the few remaining openings in the clubhouse car park.

"We're heer," said Alister.

"So soon?" joked Kate, momentarily refreshed. "That was easy!"

"Not sure wha's been arranged for ye. But Ah'm guessin' we'll find oot inside," said Alister, leading the way toward the clubhouse's side door. But Margaret beat them to it, walking out to greet them before they'd advanced more than a step or two.

"Welcome tae Machrihanish, Kate," said Margaret, opening her arms and taking Kate in as if they'd known each other forever. "Ye've had a very long journey. But consider yersel' home noo, dear. Ye're among friends heer."

"Thank you," said Kate, surprised she didn't feel the least bit compelled to recoil and reestablish her personal space. She'd almost forgotten what it felt like to be surrounded by a maternal embrace. "It's been quite the adventure."

"Well, theer's nae need tae go any further," said Margaret. "Gavin has already put yer bag in ma guest room, just a' the top o' the stairs. Ye can rest theer noo if ye'd like. Or, if ye're hungry, Ah can fix ye a plate o' food. An', this bein' Scotland, the bar is always open. Wha' we might lack in creature comforts, hopefully we can make up in hospitality."

"Actually, at this point, a shower and a change of clothes would probably feel like a trip to a five-star spa," said Kate.

"If ye're willin' tae dispense wi' the hot rocks an' mud wraps, Ah dae believe Ah can arrange tha' for ye," said Margaret. "Just walk thi' way."

As the two women headed in, Alister returned to the Vauxhall, opened the boot and began offloading its contents: a black backpack, a small silver hard suitcase and a golf bag still wrapped in its puncture-proof travel cover. Kate shot him a glance, but the significance of the items didn't register with her. If she'd had a thought, it was that the bags belonged to Alister—an assumption apparently confirmed when the doctor motioned to her to carry on.

Inside, Margaret led Kate up a dark and narrow staircase to a landing, then down a short hallway and through an open door that led to a small room dominated by a twin bed on one side and a Victorian dresser on the other. In between, natural light poured through a dormer window that, Kate soon discovered, offered an elevated perspective of the first hole.

"So that must be the beach my dad told me so much about," she said, following the roll of the waves as they converged with the shore.

"Aye," said Margaret. "Oor pride an' joy. Ah'm afraid the view is the room's only redeemin' feature, howe'er. Nae exactly the Savoy noo, is it?"

"Seems very cozy to me," said Kate. "It's very generous of you to open up your home like this to a complete stranger."

"Stranger?" said Margaret. "*We* might be strangers tae ye. But yer father told us so much aboot ye ower the years, ye're hardly a stranger tae us. Ah almost feel like Ah watched ye grow up like one o' ma own, if the guid Lord had been so inclined."

"My dad talked about me, here?" asked Kate.

"All the tahm," said Margaret. "Ye were *his* pride an' joy, dinna ye know?"

"No. I didn't," said Kate. "But it's a nice thought."

"Well, Ah know he always wanted tae bring ye heer," said Margaret.

"I guess he got his wish then," said Kate, cooly.

The comment, and even more so Kate's harsh tone, knocked Margaret back on her heels. Certainly, Kate didn't mean it quite the way she'd said it. Odds are, it was just the stress and fatigue talking. Probably shouldn't read too much into it, reasoned the steward. Best to move on to more concrete matters.

"So, aboot tha' shower," said Margaret. "Ye'll find the bathroom tae yer left, at the end o' the hall. Tha's a fresh towel on yer bed. Ah need tae go downstairs an' git the kitchen crew goin' on dinner, so ye have the whole palatial estate tae yersel'. As ye might say in California, *mi casa es su casa*."

"Spanish with a Scottish accent?" said Kate. "Excuse me, but I can't help but feel like Alice after she fell down the rabbit hole. This trip just keeps getting curiouser and curiouser."

"Aye, indeed. Ye're na' oor only new arrival taeday. Ah'll have a convention o' Swedish dentists clammorin' for theer supper if Ah dinna git on wi' it."

"Swedish dentists!?" thought Kate. But before she could mouth the words, Margaret had already spun around and descended the stairs—leaving the American to her lonesome.

Noo Tha's a Gowf Hole!

While Kate was getting situated, Alister had been evaluating various strategies for schlepping John's bags from the car park to the clubhouse. Just when he'd nearly surrendered to the notion that he'd have to make more than one trip, he spotted Ewan emerging from the black-and-white arched entryway of the Ugadale.

This once stately but now sagging Victorian hotel, just a lob shot over a low stone wall from Alister's current position, had long served as the group's home away from home during their annual reunions. Its origins date back to the late 1800s when the spot was occupied by a small guest house known as the Pans Hotel, a nod to Machrihanish's decidedly grittier past when coal, extracted from a nearby mine, heated huge pans of seawater and produced salt through evaporation.

A fire in 1898 gutted the Pans, but the ornate Ugadale Arms Hotel soon arose, Phoenix-like, on the site. In the Gilded Age, it became the accommodation of choice for city-dwelling captains of industry and their families in search of fun in the seaside's warm summer sun. But the Ugadale's glory days, alas, were short-lived—a victim of the Great Depression and, in 1932, the suspension of a rail line that, in its heyday, carried passengers from the port town of Campbeltown to Machrihanish Bay and, at the end of their holidays, back again.

The Ugadale changed hands several times in the seven decades since, each time sinking more deeply into a state of irretrievable disrepair. The current owner, trying her best to make a go of it, had kitted out the rooms as self-catering flats and offered them up at bargain rates by the week. Though their significant others would never have set foot in the ungainly death trap (not that they'd ever be invited), the Ugadale suited the eight men on golf holiday just fine. In fact, over the years, they'd developed an odd affection for the drafty old barn with its brittle wiring and convoluted plumbing—somewhat akin to Mary Hatch's relationship with that abandoned mansion in Frank Capra's classic movie *It's a Wonderful Life*. After marrying George, Mary painstakingly restores the money pit into the Bailey family dream home. Just imagine that house within a short walk of the Bedford Falls Country Club's first tee and the logistical advantages soon reveal themselves, in all their minimalist glory.

"Perfect tahmin'," shouted Alister across the car park, securing Ewan's attention. "Yer younger muscles would be a big help heer."

"Is this wha' Ah think 'tis?" said Ewan as he grabbed hold of the covered golf bag.

"Aye, 'tis John's. All o' these things are, or Ah should say, were," said Alister. "I's up tae Kate wha' happens tae them noo."

"His daughter?" said Ewan. "So she's heer?"

"Aye," said Alister. "Margaret has taken her in."

Alister climbed the stairs to Margaret's flat with Ewan in tow and knocked on the jam of the open door.

"Hello?" he said tentatively. "Kate, are ye heer?" The gentle gurgle of running water at the end of the hall was the only reply. "Must be in the shower already. Let's leave these things in her room an' be on oor way."

Down below, the two men retreated to the safety of the dining room and sidled up to the bar. Bernard, Donald and Malcolm had already beaten them to the punch, staking claim to the room's largest table. Through the side window, they spotted Angus and Gavin, who had embarked on the brief hike from the Ugadale and would soon join them.

"Wha' canne Ah git ye?" asked Margaret.

"Guinness, Ewan?" inquired Alister.

"Aye, Doc. Cheers," said Ewan.

"Make tha' two pints," said Alister. "Wha' a day, Margaret. All yer wee chicks have returned tae the roost."

"Aye, ye're eight strong again," said Margaret. "Hopefully ye're newest member will be doon soon."

"Well, if she's delayed, she canne claim tae be stuck in Los Angeles' infamous traffic," joked Alister.

"Na'," said Margaret. "But Ah get the strong feelin' tha' she'd rather be theer than heer."

"Ah fear ye're right aboot tha'," said Alister. "For her father, Machrihanish was very much a case o' love at first sight, certainly at first swing. But the daughter? The charms o' this place seem tae be lost on her."

"Aye, tha' was ma sense o' it as well," said Margaret. "Perhaps it will be an acquired taste, like John an' single malt. As Ah remember it, he stuck exclusively tae the beer his first yeer or two."

"Beer!?" blustered Angus, barging in on the conversation. "Kate doesn't seem tae have much interest in tha' either. Just boggles ma mind, given tha' she's Mac's flesh an' blood."

"Wi yer mind, tha's na' sayin' much," said Margaret. "Give the poor gurl a chance. She's been through the ringer."

"Aye, tha's true, Margaret," said Gavin, joining in. "All day, Ah've been tryin' tae put maself intae her shoes. Unlike Cinderella, 'tis not a good fit."

"Ah suppose ye're right Fauntluhroo," said Angus. "We all need tae reserve joodgment."

"Speakin' of reserve, the boys have saved us a prime island location amid a sea o' Swedish dentists," said Alister. "I dinna know aboot ye, but Ah'm several degrees beyond peckish."

"Na' tae worry, Doc. Eight plates of neeps an' tatties are on the way," said Margaret.

"Ah Margaret, yer a wumman after ma own stomach!"

replied Alister.

The seven men took their places around the table, reestablishing the same basic configuration they'd formed three days earlier—including the one empty chair waiting to be filled. But they struggled to recapture the same feeling.

"So, gentlemen, Ah trust all o' ye are up tae speed on the latest," said Angus. "Mac's daughter has arrived an', it woold appear, will be amongst us most likely through the week, though Ah dinna know if she realizes tha' just yet. Theer's really na' much we can dae noo but provide moral support. The important details are in her hands an' those o' the local authorities."

"So wha' *are* we goin' tae dae wi' oorsel'es all week?" interjected Malcolm. "Ah've worked too hard for this holiday tae go back tae the daily grind just yet."

"How does a round o' gowf sound tae ye?" answered Angus.

"Too soon?" asked Gavin.

"Na' a' all," said Angus. "And Ah'm quite confident Mac would agree. We're all hurtin', make no mistake aboot tha'. But Ah canne think of a better medicine than goin' at each other on the links for a pound nugget or two. Dae ye concur, Doc?"

"Aye, Ah dae indeed," said Alister. "Heer we are, seven grown men on a gowf holiday, an' we're na' playin' gowf? I's na' healthy tae hold in all of tha' repressed energy. At the risk o' gettin' all technical on ye, the testosterone is bouncin' aroond inside us, inflictin' damage tae our internal organs an' such. We need tae release the pressure valve. Take oot oor frustrations on oor gowf ba's, na' oor ga' bladders."

"Theer ye ha'e it, laddies. Doctor's orders," said Angus. "So, Roy Boy, Ah heer ye already availed yersel' o' the gemme's healin' powers."

"Aye," said Ewan, the lanky redhead. "Ah hope Ah wasn't oot o' line."

"Na' at all, ma guid man," said Angus. "Ah woold ha'e been right theer wi' ye this mornin' if Ah coold. But ma instincts told me tha' Fauntluhroo needed a wing man."

"Well, ma initial thought was tae just dae the 12-hole loop. Ye know, playin' oot tae the 6th hole an' circlin' back at 13," said Ewan. "But as Ah was puttin' oot on the 6th green, Ah could hear the 7th callin' oot tae me. Like the Sirens, i' was. An' Ah'll admit, Ah was as powerless as poor old Odysseus tae resist. The 7th is ma favorite hole on the coorse, wi'out a doubt."

"The 7th?" said Bernard. "Only a stick like yersel' would say such a thin'. For us mere mortals, Bruach More—i's given nemme—is a dragon's lair wheer fine young roonds, like virgins, go tae die."

"Aye, yer right aboot tha'," said Angus. "Starts with a semi-blind drive tha' ye absolutely have tae hit it on the button."

"Agreed," said Bernard. "But the tee shot is child's play compared wi' the fully blind approach. Ah know in ma mind that Ah have tae fully commit tae tha' aimin' post, hard against tha' imposin' dune on the right. But in the depths o' my soul? Fear an' tremblin'. Even the slightest bit o' a slice an' i's bye-bye Bridgestone. Way too penal for ma tastes. Nae, for ma money, the best hole on the coorse is the 8th."

"Really?" said Ewan. "Tae me tha's just a bomb-an'-gouge

affair. Kinda' like the 6th."

"Well, tae me i's an embarrassment o' options," said Bernard. "The brave can take the Tiger line doon the left, across a yawnin' chasm. Pull tha' off an' ye're rewarded wi' a short-iron approach up tae the highest point on the gowf course, which is quite helpful given the small margin for error on tha' shot. Land short and yer ba' will roll back down the hill, practically right to yer feet. Land on top o' tha' exposed surface an' ye risk boundin' ower the back an' doon the other side. So the shorter the club in yer hands for tha' shot, the better yer odds o' pullin' it off."

"Aye," said Ewan. "Just bomb the driver an' gouge oot a wedge. Nae bother."

"Well, tha's na' an option for the wee hitters among us," continued Bernard. "We git tae avail oursel's of the generous landin' area tae the right. Tha' leaves a longer approach, probably wi' a middle iron, tha' must be struck wi' the utmost precision. But it can be done."

"Aye, an' if Ah buy enough Big Lotto tickets, Ah can win the jackpot an' retire," joked Malcolm.

"Ah'd say yer odds on the 8th are slightly better," responded Bernard. "An' when ye dae hit an' hold that green, theer is nae better feelin' in gowf. Ye hardly notice the extra effort required tae scale the summit. Ye git tae line up a birdie putt. And ye git tae take in a full panoramic perspective o' the links from tha' perch, relieved tha' ye dinna sully yer scorecard wi' a big number. Tha's why i's called Gigha, for i's excellent view of the island of the same nemme, one of the Hebrides. Noo tha's a gowf hole!"

"Ye make a strong case for the 8th, Bernard," said Gavin, jumping into the fray. "But Ah say the 13th is the best. I's certainly the most underrated."

"The 13th!?" said Angus. "Tha' hole is possessed."

"Ah dinna say 'tis the most enjoyable," said Gavin. "But it just might be the best. Theer's na' much tae the tee shot when the wind's at yer back. But when 'tis blowin' stiff in yer face? Another matter entirely. If ye fail tae make it up on level ground, yer second shot, usually from an uneven lie, is always in danger o' gittin' gobbled up ba tha' hidden cross bunker aboot 30 yards short o' the green."

"Ah must admit tha', Ah sometahms forgit aboot tha' hazard, until Ah walk up an' find ma ba' in it," said Bernard, the resident scribe. "Leads me tae toorn the 13th hole's nemme into a verb, as in, 'Once again, Ah got Kilkivan-ed!'"

"Well, ye could git conservative an' lay up short o' the bunker," said Gavin. "But then ye're left wi' a mid-range bump-and-run shot up an' ower a false front—the kind few o' us ever practice. If ye dinna clear the crest, yer ba' will roll back off the puttin' surface, wheer ye git tae try it all ower again, albeit from closer range."

"An' wi' a flat stick, at least," interjected Angus.

"True. Unless, Gawd help ye, yer approach starts movin' sideways, due tae wind or faulty technique or some combination o' the two. Then, odds are, one o' two greenside pot bunkers will snare ye. Havin' said all tha', strike a solid drive an' a well-judged approach tha' lands just short o' the crest an' pops gently ower, an' ye could just as easily walk away wi' a birdie. Talk aboot drama! The 13th, gentlemen, is links golf at i's finest."

"Spare me the drama," said Angus. "Ah much prefer holes tha' let ye belt it off the tee wi'oot undue threat o' retribution. The 1ˢᵗ hole kinda fits tha' description."

"If ye dinna mind playin' off the beach!" said Malcolm.

"Mind? Ah've practically patented tha' shot," fired back Angus. "But, in truth, it was the 14ᵗʰ tha' Ah was thinkin' o'."

"Castlehill?" inserted Bernard. "The longest par 4 on the coorse?"

"Aye, tha's the one," answered Angus. "Loads o' room off the tee, even for a thrasher like me. And theer's nae point in holdin' back on the second shot either, nae wi' a fairway riddled wi' hollows. Grip it an' rip it! That's ma motto."

"Which is why *oor* nickname for *ye* is Ravishanker, wi' an emphasis on the latter hauf!" said Alister. "I's certainly got nothin' tae dae wi' yer ability tae play the sitar!"

"Such shockin' language, an' from a professional man nae less," said Angus. "Ah'll happily answer tae Ravi if it provides ye wi' a wee bit o' amusement. But the S-word? Like Harry Potter's nemesis, 'tis gowf's dark an' sinister spirit who shall na' be named."

"Tell that tae Armitage," said Alister.

"Who's Armitage?" said Angus.

"The brand name emblazoned on the urinals in the gents," said the doctor. "Just look doon the next tahm ye're takin' care o' yer business. I's right theer: 'Armitage Sh…'"

"Dinna say it!" implored Angus. "I's the semme as castin' an evil spell, Ah tell ye."

"OK Ravi, Ah'll let it pass," said Alister. "But Ah canne let this discussion end wi'oot an appreciation for the pure genius o' the 5th hole."

"Punch Bowl?" said Bernard.

"Aye, tha's i's nemme," said Alister. "An' when i' gits a wee bit blowie oot theer, you'll swear tha' someone's spiked the punch! 'Tis the only true dogleg on the coorse which, Ah contend, makes i' such a stern test. I' tempts big hitters like Ewan tae cut the corner an', potentially, drive the green an' be puttin' for eagle. But all manner o' nastiness awaits those who boldly go wheer few gowfers ha'e successfully gone afore."

"Ah ha'e personal experience wi' both outcomes," said Ewan. "But tae me, the risk is worth the reward."

"Nae tae the faint o' heart—or is tha' sane of mind?" responded the good doctor. "We aim for the center o' the fairway, ideally wi' a touch o' a draw. But use too much club an' ye'll run through the bend an' intae the cack. Conversely, use too little an' ye risk settin' up a long approach from an awkward sidehill lie. Noo, even if ye successfully execute the tee shot, yer work is far from done. Ye'll still need tae choose the right club an' the proper trajectory tae get yer ba' tae stop on the same level as the pin on this two-tiered green."

"One o' the most demandin' approaches on the course, Ah'll grant ye tha'," said Gavin.

"Aye," said Alister. "An' woe be tae any player whose second shot sails tae the right o' the puttin' surface, wheer it drops off hard an' fast rather than blendin' gently intae the surroundin' terrain. Ye'll be facin' a Sophie's choice for yer third shot: a high-risk lob off a tight lie, a runner up tha' grass wall with yer putter, or somethin' in between. The possibilities are virtually endless. Ah believe Ah could play tha' hole, an' only tha' hole, every day for the rest of ma life an' Ah'd never tire o' it. 'Tis absolutely brilliant."

"Aye, well, tha' hole i's possessed, too, just like the 13th," said Angus. "Wha' aboot ye X-man? Ye've been awfully quiet taenight."

"Just tryin' tae learn from everyone's many yeers o' experience," said Malcolm. "Compared wi' ye, Ah'm still crawlin' on ma hands an' knees up a steep learnin' curve. But Ah dae find it interstin' tha' ye've completely left oot Machrihanish's par 5s which, in ma opinion, are just as maddenin' as the two-shotters."

"Ye make a good point, Malcolm," said Bernard. "There's nae let up at this place, except maybe Lossit—the short an' anticlimactic 18th."

"Consider the 10th, ma old friend Cnocmoy," continued Malcolm. "Ah've learned the hard way tha' the percentage play off the tee is right center, givin' ye a view o' the green oot in the distance through the gap in the dunes. But if Ah git greedy an' have eagle on ma mind, then Ah've got tae wield the big stick an' try tae split tha' gap."

"Well, tae paraphrase the Guid Book, i's harder for a big hitter tae thread the needle o' the 10th than i' is for a rich man tae get intae heaven—or somethin' like tha'," said Bernard.

"Soonds aboot right tae me," said Malcolm. "Ower swing

an' pull yer tee ba' left o' the gap an' ye're left wi' a blind second shot tae a fairway tha' never seems tae flow the way ye think it does."

"Aye," said Alister. "After all the yeers Ah've been playin' heer, ye'd think Ah'd have tha' landin' area permanently etched in ma brain. I's some sort o' optical illusion."

"Indeed. The 10th is mostly aboot the first an' second shots. But the 12th hole? I's the third shot tha' sets tha' par 5 apart. Ah've noticed tha' most greens tend tae slope from back tae front. But the 12th falls away from ye. All ye can see is the front edge o' the dance floor."

"An' just the top o' the flag, even wi' the tallest pin on the links," added Ewan.

"Are ye sure aboot tha', Ewan?" questioned Bernard. "Ah dae believe the stick on the 2nd would give it a run for its money."

"Guid point, Bernard," said Ewan. "Would make a good Quiz Night question, assumin' we git tae dae tha' this yeer."

"Still a possibility," said Angus. "But we digress."

"Aye, we dae," said Malcolm, slightly annoyed. "If Ah could continue, Ah know the approach tae the 12th is na' a difficult shot. If the wind be favorable, ye should have nae more than a wedge in. But 'tis so visually disorientin' tha' i's hard tae swing away wi' complete an' total confidence. Ah canne tell ye how many tahms Ah've gotten a wee bit tentative, shortened up ma arms—T. rex-style—an' watched ma ba' roll intae one o' those two frontin' pot bunkers. Ye know, the ones tha' bear a family resemblance tae the Spectacles at Carnoustie. I's a bloody mind game, tha' 12th hole is."

"Ye'll git nae argument from me," said Bernard. "Though ye'd think they coold come up wi' a more poetic nemme than Long Hole."

True to form, Donald had yet to weigh in. His six friends, sensing they'd dominated the conversation at his expense, simultaneously pressed their internal pause buttons, creating an opening for the septuagenarian to step up and be heard.

"So, wha' say ye, Don-Don?" said Angus, somewhat reluctantly inviting the elder statesman to mount his soapbox.

"Well, since ye asked, Ah'd ha'e tae say tha' ma favorite hole is the Hut," said Donald at last.

"The par 3?" said Gavin.

"Aye," said Donald. "Machrihanish has four one-shotters. But, as Ah see it, the 15th is ba far the best. 'Tis riddled wi' five pot bunkers, three short an' two greenside on the right."

"Aye, but better tae miss it theer than left," said Alister.

"Ah was just gettin' tae tha'," said Donald. "Wander in tha' direction an' ye'll find yersel' in the deepest an' most treacherous hollow at Machrihanish, maybe anywheer in Scotland. At most, the hole's only 166 yards long. But i's diabolical. Yer effective landin' area is, maybe, 20 feet wide. An' ye'd best git the distance right or it won't matter how straight ye hit it. Amazin' how a simple 3 can toorn intae a nightmarish 6 in the blink o' an eye."

"Ah know the feelin'," said Angus, intentionally regaining control of the conversation. "An' if the 15th leaves ye buggered, the 16th—a brute o' a par 3—becomes even more intimidatin'. A strappin' 232 yards from the back o' the tee an' it plays much longer than tha' intae the prevailin' wind."

"A tough hole? Aye, theer's nae question aboot tha'," said Bernard. "But one o' Machrihanish's best? Rorke's Drift? Ah dinna think so."

"Well, Ah know at least one person who woold completely agree wi' ye," said Malcolm.

"Who might tha' be?" asked Angus.

"Why Mac o' course!" said Malcolm. "Ah'm sure we all rimember wha' happened tha' first tahm he played the 16th."

"Aye," said Angus. "Talk aboot yer big chopper. Duck-hooked his tee shot intae the deep stuff just off the tee an' needed six more swings just tae git his ba' out. Looked like he was wieldin' a sickle, na' a gowf club."

"Wha' he needed was a turbocharged weed whacker," said Malcolm. "Ah canne rimember his score…"

"It was a 14," said Bernard, ever the group's fact keeper.

"…but Ah'll never forgit the look o' despair on his face," continued Malcolm. "Ah think he was afraid tha', after tha' display o' utter futility, we'd want nothin' more tae dae wi' him."

"Little did he know tha' we've all been brought tae oor knees ba the vagaries o' links golf, in particular as 'tis expressed at Machrihanish," Bernard. "He dinna forfeit his membership in the club tha' day. He earned it."

"Aye, indeed," said Angus. "And Ah think we can all agree on at least one moor thin': 'Tis high tahm we renewed *oor* playin' privileges. Shall we reconvene on the first tee in the mornin' boys, ready for battle?"

"Aye!" replied the choir.

The hearty Guinness-fueled banter revived the seven friends' spirits. But it also distracted them from the small matter of a seat at their table that, four hours after the not so little rascals had gathered, had remained vacant.

Fortunately, Margaret's motherly instincts were still fully operational. So after deputizing a waitress to hold down her post at the bar, she ascended the stairs to check on her flat mate. From the hallway, Margaret could see that the guest room door was open and the ceiling light on. But she sensed no movement. One glance inside revealed why: Kate, fully dressed and fetal positioned, had fallen asleep atop the bed's comforter.

Margaret made her way carefully to the window, stepping over a black travel cover, a red golf bag and its related paraphernalia, splayed about the carpeted floor. Silently, she drew the blind, turned down the light and reached for a quilt that hung on the back of the room's only chair. Then, just as she was about to insulate Kate against the evening's chill, Margaret noticed something odd in the young woman's clutches.

"Tha' looks like a gowf club," thought the older woman. "A Hobbit-sized gowf club."

Searching for a Connection

Kate didn't wake up so much as she grew gradually aware that she was no longer asleep. Still on the bed snuggled in Margaret's handiwork, she tried to read the daylight that oozed through the window's translucent blind.

"Mid-morning already?" she guessed. "I was even more exhausted than I thought."

And then, Kate's taskmaster self pushed aside her nurturing self, with the latter failing to muster even a modicum of resistance.

"Oh my God!" said the worker bee, calculating the time difference between Scotland and New York. "I missed my window to call the office. But I can check email. Where did I ditch my phone? This room's a mess!"

Kate's pulse eased slightly when she found her purse and, within it, her iPhone. But it surged again when she saw that the device wasn't tethered to a cell signal. Even more surprising: It was only 5 a.m.

"How is that possible?" she wondered. "The sun's already up. Maybe I'll find a connection outside."

Kate shed the quilt and replaced it with a sweater she extracted from her carry-on. Then she laced up her running shoes, hid her hair under a crumpled Olympic Club hat she found in her dad's golf bag and tiptoed down the staircase. Not a soul stirred on ground level, a stark contrast to the raucous merriment that had rattled her room's floorboards the night before. A phone check revealed that the clubhouse dining room was wired for Wi-Fi. But that pathway to the Internet was password protected. She wasn't about to wake Margaret now to get the code.

Instead, Kate made her way through the side door and wandered about the now empty car park, alternately looking down at her device and up at a mixed but relatively stable sky, as if she could spot the longed-for radio waves as they shimmered between breaks in the clouds. Every so often, one bar—at times even two—would flash on the touchscreen. But, like a mirage, the graphic would vanish the moment she made a move to refresh her inbox.

Undeterred, Kate pushed on in her quest. She crossed the road that fronted the clubhouse and followed the brick path that led past the practice putting green on the left, the 1st tee on the right and toward the pro shop straight ahead. But that hut-like structure, with a regiment of aluminum two-wheeled trollies standing at attention on one side and a solitary wooden park bench stationed along another, was in full lockdown mode. Nobody home.

Kate, though, was far from alone. Rather—standing now where the turf gave way to a jumble of rocks and the beach a few feet below—she was thoroughly gob smacked: stretching out before her, as far as her eyes could see, was a broad tableau teeming with abundant and varied life. All manner of water fowl bobbed on the placid ocean's surface, including shelducks, elders, scoters, gadwalls, puffins and plovers. Whimbrels, terns, gulls and white wagtails floated lazily in the air above. Seals slumbered on the slowly warming sand. The ever-present oyster catchers waded amid the tide pools. And way out in the distance, where the merger of sky and ocean created the illusion of a fixed horizon, a pair of dolphins played.

Yesterday, at first blush, Machrihanish Bay had looked to Kate like just another meeting of land and sea. Ho hum for a Californian. But now, up close and personal, she was mesmerized. The more deeply she absorbed the stunning foreground, the more her need to check her email receded into the background.

After a good long look, Kate turned 90 degrees to her right and thought to herself, "I've been here before." Whether it was a bona fide deja vu moment or simply the cumulative effect of the wide-angle photo that hung on the wall above her father's desk, Kate swore the view from Machrihanish's first tee was as familiar to her as if she'd played the course a hundred times. But now she had the power to step into that image and discover, at long last, what lay beyond it.

She gave the clubhouse a glance, then, a bit self consciously, descended the small slope that led from the 1st hole's tee to its fairway. Though the grass was tightly cropped, the sandy soil underneath seemed to put a spring in her step. It was almost as if the linksland was a porous membrane that allowed an unseen energy source from deep within the Earth to pass through— revitalizing all radiated in its flow. Complemented by a salty ocean breeze, these vibrant emanations turned the simple act of walking into an exhilarating experience.

Rejuvenated, Kate picked up the pace, stretching her travel-weary legs. Then, roughly 200 yards into her walkabout, she caught her first glimpse of an authentic Scottish pot bunker, the kind her dad had told her so much about. Four such pits guarded the right-hand rough of both the 1st and 18th holes, which ran parallel to one another but in opposite directions.

"Note to self," thought Kate. "Steer clear of these off the tee. Both tees."

Striding on, she soon set foot on the opening green. From her American frame of reference, the surface was massive. Also foreign to her was its eclectic mix of relatively level ground and wildly undulating slopes.

"Pin placement is everything here," noted Kate. Her competitive juices had started to flow.

And then she discovered the simple perfection of links golf routing. Kate had been weaned mostly on courses built since the 1970s, whose primary purpose was to pump up the value of their surrounding real estate. To maximize the number of homes that overlooked the greenery, designers of such layouts were forced to impersonate contortionists, snaking the routing to and fro amid the gated communities. Often, this created large distances between the previous hole's green and the next hole's tee. That made these monstrosities virtually impossible to walk. And that, in turn, necessitated the use of motorized carts (the Scots call them, somewhat dismissively, buggies) and a network of concrete paths upon which to drive them.

Thankfully, Old Tom had not been similarly constrained a hundred years earlier when Machrihanish's founding fathers hired him to transform their original 12-hole course into a full 18. So he placed the 2nd hole's tee a mere 10 paces to the left of the 1st hole's green. And while the club had recently purchased a handful of buggies, primarily to extend their oldest members' playing days, there wasn't a mini interstate freeway system in sight. As Nancy Sinatra might have put it, this course was made for walking.

So Kate kept hoofing it, and soon came upon a deep and fast-moving stream that cut across the full width of the 2nd hole roughly 230 yards from the tee. The burn, as it's known in the local vernacular, flows from the farmland to the east into the ocean to the west. If the club ever dredged this watery grave, they'd undoubtedly excavate enough errant golf balls to stock the modest practice field wedged between the beach and the 2nd hole's left-hand margin, clearly marked with white out-of-bounds stakes. Until then, the range would remain strictly

BYOB (Brin' Yer Own Ba's).

Kate crossed the burn by way of a footbridge, then climbed one of the course's largest dunes atop of which, appropriately enough, she laid eyes on one of the course's largest greens. If Kate had given the script on the marker back on the tee a closer look, she might have learned that the 2nd's given name is Machairinnean, a relic of ancient gaelic that harkens back to when the Scots and Norse duked it out for control of this rugged coastline. During Machrihanish's construction, laborers reportedly excavated human remains on this spot where, it's believed, the Battle of Machair Innean was waged in the 10th century. Today's warriors wield golf clubs, not Viking swords. But that doesn't mean the 2nd has had its fill of casualties. Far from it.

"Very tricky hole," thought Kate. "Par would be a good score here."

Kate easily found the tee for the 3rd hole, just past the green for the 2nd. But the 3rd's putting surface was nowhere in sight. Thankfully, a red-and-white marker post led the way, so Kate followed. As she approached the wooden barber pole planted at the crest of a hill, the terrain seemed to part like a theater curtain—revealing a big-sky vastness that, quite literally, took her breath away.

"Whoa!" said Kate out loud.

Then, as if choreographed by a Hollywood director, the sun pierced the clouds, bathing the snowless globe in a brilliant amber aura. From this vantage point, Kate could see the 3rd hole's green, its white flag fluttering in the breeze. But her attention soon drifted beyond that point, out toward the sea and the island of Jura. For the next 30 seconds, Kate held still, simply taking it all in. Then she fished her phone out of her pocket, not to check for a cell signal but to try to preserve this display of natural beauty in digital bits and bytes.

That's when she heard something. Or thought she did. Kate spun around, but saw no one. She did, however, spy the top of a maintenance shed tucked into a hollow to her left. Odds are, she deduced, the grounds crew was inside, gearing up for their day by commiserating over the previous night's football match. They're early risers, right? That makes sense.

Kate shook off the distraction and reengaged with the view. But as she prepared take another snapshot, she heard it again. Or, more accurately, felt it. Slightly more emphatic this time. But still no more than a whisper, really. Soft but distinct. More presence than voice.

Where is this coming from, thought Kate? Definitely not the shed. Someone on the beach behind the green, perhaps? From Jura? But that's crazy. The island is miles away. Must be in my head. Hallucinating on fresh air. Or an empty stomach. Or something. Kate strained to dial it in, resisting the urge to suspend her disbelief.

But, try as she might, she couldn't shake its grip, whatever *it* was.

Then, at last and out loud, Kate said:

"Gratitude. *Gratitude?* What the heck?"

But there was no explanatory reply. Just the whir of the wind and the lyrical wake-up call of the skylarks nesting in the marram-covered dunes along the hole's borders.

Kate, though, didn't curse the silence. Quite the opposite. A sense of contentment enveloped her, somewhat like Margaret's quilt, but with a luxuriousness that transcended the material world, that existed beyond the spoken word, that felt—well, somehow—eternal. For a few fleeting seconds, there was no separation. All of it—time, space, thought and emotion—was one. And Kate, who for so long had waged war against her brokenness, voluntarily laid down her weapons. Safe and secure in this larger than life landscape, she was whole again. And for once, her inner cynic didn't immediately burst the bubble and point out, like a know-it-all, that the moment—no matter how life-affirming—wouldn't last. This time, graciously, that pedantic pipsqueak stood down.

Overcome, Kate's knees buckled and she fell, gently, first into a seated position and then prone on her back in the still dewy grass. She closed her eyes, but the lids couldn't contain the tears that streamed down her cheeks. Tears of relief, not sorrow. A downpour that cleanses, not destroys. A letting go, not a holding back. A vulnerability, not a weakness. A sweet surrender, not an indignant defeat.

Kate remained motionless but emotion-filled for several minutes, right up until a voice shattered the solitude. But this voice, quite clearly, was of this world—not some alternative reality, or whatever it was that she'd heard or felt or experienced. Or was it something, more simply, that she'd remembered?

"Excuse me, ma'am, are ye OK?" said the greenskeeper, who had spotted Kate when he wandered out along the service road that connects the course and the maintenance shed.

Kate, only momentarily startled and with eyes still shut, replied: "Never better!"

Freudians Have a Field Day

Given the choice, Kate's spirit would have willingly remained at rest in the center of the 3rd hole's fairway. But her flesh? It was weak or, at least, in dire need of attention. For starters, it had been more than 24 hours since she'd consumed solid food. And, at the risk of putting too fine a point on it, it had been nearly 12 hours since she'd used a bathroom. Some things simply can't wait.

Kate retraced her steps to the 3rd hole's tee. Then, from that elevated vantage point, she noticed that shifting over to the 17th, rather than heading back down the 2nd, would be the more direct route home. Besides, a small structure to the right of the 17th green looked suspiciously like the facilities she so desperately desired. But when she arrived there, after semi-jogging her way up the 370-yard par 4, her bladder's prayers, alas, were not answered. It's not that the shack didn't exist for her desired purpose. Rather, the foul odor inside confirmed, in no uncertain terms, that it did so in a decidedly medieval manner. Apparently, links courses—or at least this one—are not equipped with modern plumbing.

So Kate carried on, now with a renewed sense of urgency. Downshifting into a flat out run, she dispensed with the 314-yard 18th, found a shortcut across the road shy of the 1st tee, then continued through the car park and directly to the ladies room on the clubhouse's ground floor.

"Aye, so theer ye are," said Margaret as she watched Kate zip by. "An' theer ye go."

Kate, relieved on multiple levels, circled back to greet Margaret, who was busy restocking the bar.

"Good morning, Margaret!" she exclaimed.

"Well, my, guid mornin' tae ye as well," replied the stunned steward. "When Ah dinna see ye in yer room, Ah was a wee bit concerned. But apparently, Ah had nae reason tae fear."

"Sweet of you to say but, no, I'm feeling much better now. More than that, really. I've had the most amazing morning," said Kate.

"'Tis shapin' up tae be a crackin' day, tha's for sure," said Margaret.

"I do have one request, though," said Kate. "If it's not too much trouble, I could go for some breakfast. So sorry that I missed dinner last night."

"Oh nae bother," said Margaret. "After all ye've been through, theer's nae need tae explain. Ah'm sure ye needed tae rest."

"Well, that's true," said Kate. "But I had every intention of joining everyone. Until I found my dad's things, that is."

"Right," said Margaret. "Alister mentioned tha' he'd made a delivery tae yer room."

"To be honest, it caught me off guard," said Kate. "I thought the police still had everything."

"Oh tha' man!" said Margaret. "Ah thought ye knew. He should have warned ye."

"It's OK," said Kate. "It *was* all a bit much at first. But I'm OK now. More than OK, really. And very grateful to have so much to remember Papa by. Huh, there's that word again."

"Wha's tha' ye say, dear?" asked a puzzled Margaret.

"Oh, never mind. I'll tell you later," said Kate.

"For heaven's sake, here Ah am blabbin' away an' yer in need of a full Scottish. Some kind o' host Ah am."

"A full Scottish?" replied Kate.

"Aye, love, that's breakfast ower heer. The works. A full Scottish will toorn ye intae a full American, guaranteed," said Margaret.

"Aye, soonds guid," said Kate, playfully trying her Scottish accent on for size.

"Aye, indeed!" said Margaret. "Come wi' me."

Due to her single-minded focus on the way in from the course, Kate didn't notice that her father's friends had gathered around the pro shop and were preparing to head out onto it.

But they had no such difficulty spotting her.

"So tha's Kate?" asked Bernard of Angus.

"Aye," said the big man. "Have tae admire the dedication tae her exercise routine, Ah guess. But if Ah dinna know better, Ah'd say she's daein' everthin' in her power tae avoid us."

"Who can blame her?" joked Bernard. "Clearly, she's a much better judge o' character than her father. For some inexplicable reason, he actually foond this motley crew irresistible."

"Like a moth tae a flame," said Angus.

"So wha's the gemme taeday?" inquired Malcolm, inserting himself into the two men's conversation.

"Two fourba's for the matches," said Angus. "Ah pulled nemmes ootta hat tae select the teams. Everyone can pitch in a pound coin for an individual Stableford. Any side bets are strictly up tae ye."

"Uh, Ravi, Ah'm a words man, so correct ma math if Ah'm wrong, but Ah believe two tahms four equals eight," said Bernard. "An' theer's only seven o' us."

"Ah'm well aware o' tha' fact, Monkey Boy," said Angus. "So Ah took the liberty o' invitin' Angelo tae join us this mornin'."

"Angelo!? An' he agreed?" said Bernard. "From wha' Ah've observed, he tends tae keep tae hi'sel'."

"Aye, 'tis true," said Angus. "But under the circumstances, he was actually quite honored tha' we woold consider includin' him. He had some very nice thin's tae say aboot Mac."

"Well, Ah'm fine wi' it," said Bernard. "Ah jus' hope the others agree."

"They'll git ower it," said Angus. "We're playin' gowf. Oot

heer, we're all equal in the eyes o' the gemme."

News of the substitution soon migrated to the practice green, where Donald and Gavin were fine-tuning their putting strokes, and to the unauthorized practice tee behind the pro shop, where Ewan was belting shag balls into the Atlantic. As Bernard had feared, the response was decidedly mixed. It wasn't that they disliked the man so much as they didn't know quite what to make of him. He was a foreigner in their eyes, in more ways than one.

For starters, Angelo wasn't a Scot. He was an Italian. He had washed up on these secluded shores nearly 20 years ago and, to this day, none of the locals could say with any conviction exactly why. The story is told that he'd fled his home country under questionable circumstances, having run afoul of the law or, even juicier, the Mafia. But that's little more than hearsay. What is genuinely agreed upon is that he arrived with just the clothes on his back and one prized possession—a small leather bag that, suspiciously, he never leaves out of his sight. Whenever anyone asks him about it, he deflects the inquiry with the same stale joke: "This issa muh man purse. Issa all the rage in Italy."

Angelo lives frugally, almost hermit-like, in a tiny teepee structure in a caravan park a couple miles north on the B843. Still, everyone at some point needs money. But, try as they might, the townsfolk couldn't figure out what the man did to earn any. He didn't have a job. Heck, when he first turned up, he didn't even have golf clubs. So Colin, Machrihanish's teaching pro, graciously put together a mixed bag of cast off sticks, gave him a few pointers, and sent him on his way. In response, Angelo spent seemingly every waking hour either on the range beating balls or on the course honing his skills. Golf, a game he claims he never tried in Italy, had become his *raison d'etre*.

A couple of years into this monotonous routine, a rumor had rippled through the tightknit community that Angelo was going to make a run at earning his playing privileges on the European Tour's senior circuit. If true, it would have confirmed that the man was, in point of fact, completely and thoroughly daft. But now, well into his 70s by most people's estimations, that dream—assuming it ever existed—had long since evaporated. Yet Angelo pressed on, perhaps convinced that he's just another 10,000 swings from cracking the code.

Angelo arrived at Machrihanish as he does every morning, by way of the Campbeltown city bus that stops just up the road from the first tee. All seven men turned and, instinctively, sized him up as he approached: About six-feet tall, big boned and rail thin, a deeply lined face leathered by too many hours in the Scottish sun—protected only in part by an unkempt moustache—and atop his head a thick crop of steel wool that no hat could possibly tame. If not for his waterproofs worn shiny at the knees and elbows, a faded blue pencil bag stuffed to overflowing and slung from his broad right shoulder, and his ever-present satchel strapped tight to his left, he could easily be mistaken for Jack Nicklaus' long-time caddy of the same name.

"*Buongiorno!*" said Angelo as he made his way up the path. "Issa beautiful mornin' for the gowf, no?"

"Aye," said Gavin en route from the practice green to the 1st

tee. "Thank ye for joinin' us, Angelo. John woold be touched."

"No, no," said Angelo with a wave of his hand. "It'sa me issa honored. Mr. Mac was good man. 'Ee be missed. God rest 'is soul."

"Aye, tae be honest, we all ha'e mixed feelin's aboot playin' taeday," said Gavin. "But we're na' sure wha' else tae dae wi' oorsel'es."

"You do right thing," said Angelo. "This game save me. I know that. For sure. Without golf, where I be?"

"Well, then, Ah'm glad ye're heer. An' Ah hope ye came ready tae play," said Gavin. "Ba the luck o' the draw, we're partne's this mornin'. An' we're in the first group off, wi' Ewan an' Angus. Shall we?"

"I do muh best, Mr. Gavin," said Angelo. "You know that."

It's often said that golf doesn't build character, it reveals it. Similarly, examining someone's golf swing, many believe, is akin to peering into the depths of that player's soul. If true, armchair Freudians would have had a field day watching this collection of misfits make the first of what would be, for most of them, well more than 80 such attempts until they circled around and putted out on the 18th green just 120 yards away.

After the toss of a coin, it fell on Gavin to set the big wheel into motion. While Ewan is far and away the group's most talented player, Gavin is arguably its most polished. Though a member at Machrihanish, he plays most of his golf at Western Gailes, a top-drawer links in Northern Ayrshire that's often pressed into service as a venue for Open Championship qualifying. Gavin never deluded himself into thinking that his game could rise to that lofty level. But that doesn't stop him from participating in Western Gailes' weekend amateur competitions on a regular basis and, most years, making a run at its club championship—though, for some reason, he's yet to break through and claim the top prize. The net effect of such high class seasoning is a game that, while it might not overly impress in any one element, is rock solid in all of them.

As such, none of his friends were the least bit surprised when Gavin's rhythmic and graceful motion with the driver propelled his ball comfortably over the beach on the left and well inside the pot bunkers to the right, at least 240 yards down the heart of the fairway.

"Position A-1, Fauntluhroo," said Angus. "Ah suppose Ah'll have tae git used tae watchin' tha' all day."

"Ah suppose ye will!" said Gavin, the perfect start setting loose in the normally measured man more than the hint of a boast.

"Nice shot, Mr. Gavin," said Angelo. "I try follow."

If Gavin's swing exuded cultured refinement, Angelo's technique screamed mad scientist. He set up to the ball with a noticeably open lower half, his front foot pulled 6-8 inches away from the target line. But his upper half was square to the intended flight of the ball, thus pitting his body against itself. To compensate, Angelo employed a sharp bend at the waist and let the grip end of his club hang low. While Gavin's swing was all about angles and levers, Angelo's was all about his hands. They started the move away from the ball. They initiated the move down from the top. And, at the bottom, Angelo's still fully cocked wrists unleashed like a compressed spring, the clubhead exploding through the hitting area with a whir.

The timing, thought Gavin, has to be perfect for that sort of self-styled approach to work. And in this instance, it was: Angelo's ball started out high and to the right, then drew gracefully back toward the center of the fairway, coming to rest within five yards of Gavin's.

"*Bellissima!*" exclaimed Angelo. "Tat's why we play tis game, no?"

"Aye," said Angus. "We're all very happy for ye, Angelo. Noo if ye'll please step aside, Ah'll show ye how thi' is really done."

Angus' natural athleticism, though dulled by the years and the Guinness, was still apparent as he approached his teed up Titleist. Everything about his set-up looked to be on point and on plane. Just wind it up and let it go, right? Not exactly. True to his nature, Angus' body spun around with the subtlety of a cement mixer, his driver's steel shaft dipping well past parallel on the way up before racing to close the gap with his torso on the way back down. Perhaps sensing the disconnect, Angus' body popped its chute and slowed abruptly mid-downswing. That sent his arms and hands, and by extension the clubhead, shooting across the finish line at impact, the face of the driver smothering the ball and snapping it hard, low and left.

Reflexively, Angus' right hand let go of the grip, like a pilot who, sensing his aircraft is in a nosedive, pulls back on the stick. But in Angus' case, it was much too little and tragically too late. All eight men watched, some in horror and some in hysterics, as the big man's white pebble skittered across the beach, ricocheted off several rocks like a pinball and, finally, screeched to a halt on the wet sand 180 yards away.

"Oh for fuck sake!" cried Angus.

Then, without missing a beat, "Ah suppose Ah'll have tae git used tae watchin' tha' all day!" said Ewan, his partner.

Angelo, strangely stoic, apparently didn't get the joke. But the other five Scots most definitely did, breaking out in a chorus of laughter that—just 24 hours earlier—they couldn't have imagined they'd ever share again.

"Always entertainin', Angus," said Malcolm. "Ah dae believe ye coold sell tickets."

"Ma only wish is tha' I had a front-row seat when ye hit yer openin' tee shot, X-man," replied the big man. "Apparently ye haven't heard o' this little thin' called karma."

"Ye mean wha' goes aroond comes aroond?" said Malcolm. "If ye put enough spin on it, an' Ah have nae doubt tha' ye have it in ye, tha' woold apply to yer gowf ba'! Ye might want tae wear a helmet, Ravi."

Ewan, doing his utmost to suppress a snicker, assumed center stage. He took a few leisurely waggles, just one look at his target and then, without hesitation, started into his motion. And oh what a swing! Effortless but powerful. Balanced yet flowing. Unhurried yet, when it matters most, fast. Very fast. Titanium smashed into urethane and, as if cycled around the Large Hadron Collider, his golf ball screamed through the cool morning air on a disastrously aggressive line—for anyone but Ewan, that is. His yellow Srixon, defying gravity, easily carried the hazard and bounded down the fairway to within a mere bump-and-run shot of the green. The prodigious blast had traveled some 330 yards.

"Mamma mia!" gasped Angelo. "How many strokes you give us? More please."

"We'll be OK, partne'," said Gavin. "Ba the time we make the toorn back home at the 10th tee, Ewan will be so exhausted from searchin' for Angus' wayward shots in the cack, he'll beg us tae quit the gemme. Ah just hope we dinna have tae carry them in. Perhaps we shoold take a buggy, Angus?"

"Tha's awfully bold talk from a mild mannered banker, Fautluhroo," responded Angus. "I say we play it oot an' see wha' happens."

With that, the first foursome was on its way down the first fairway, a mere three days behind schedule. Once they'd played their second shots toward the green—actually, Angus needed a third to fully extricate himself from the beach—the remaining four golfers giddily moved into position to take their cuts. Their best-ball match: Alister and Donald vs. Bernard and Malcolm.

The lanky doctor had the honor and responded with an equally languid swing. Alister rarely hits it far. But he almost always hits it in the right place, having thoroughly sorted out his strategy for each hole before setting foot on the course.

His partner Donald followed, his lack of confidence in his game betrayed by a Sergio Garcia-like grip and regrip twitch and a display of happy feet that would have made Steve Martin proud.

"This is gowf, for Gawd's sake, not the freakin' ballet," said Malcolm, anxious to get started. "Hit yer ba' a'ready."

At long last, Donald did pull the trigger, though not fully. The clubface came through impact wide open, imparting a left-to-right slice spin that sent his ball safely away from the beach but toward the 18th green. No chance of reaching the 1st in regulation from there.

Then, as Donald leaned down to pick up his tee, he froze. An even more dumbfounded look than normal spread across his face.

"Oh for heaven's sake," he said finally. "Ma shoes."

"Wha' aboot 'em?" asked Malcolm.

"Theer ma street shoes. Ah forgot tae change intae ma gowfin' spikes," said Donald. "Ye boys carry on. Ah'll catch up wi' ye. Thank guidness the Ugadale is so close ba."

The other three men, conditioned over the years to expect these Don-Don moments, responded with little more than a collective shrug and continued about their business while Donald scurried back across the road.

Next up was Bernard. Like Alister, he was anything but a big hitter. But like Ewan, he first picked up a club at a young age and still possessed a well-developed short game—a weapon that earned him a spot on his secondary school's golf team. His challenge? Silencing his conscious mind that, as a writer, is wired to observe, question and analyze everything that moves, and much that doesn't. That makes it difficult for his unconscious body to do what, after all these years, it knows perfectly well how to do.

The first shot of every round is particularly problematic for Bernard. The first shot of a golf holiday? Even more so.

Invariably, he will read too much into it—for good or ill—setting the tone for everything to follow. Fortunately, Bernard came into this particular reunion with his game on a bit of a roll. So he was able to quiet his inner chatter long enough to let his compact swing go, unfettered by negative thoughts. He put his tee ball safely into play, though still at least 200 yards from the putting surface.

That left just Malcolm, an athletic fast learner who, on a good day, could outplay Angus, Bernard, Alister and Donald and hold his own with Ewan and Gavin. But on a bad day? Such tales are best left untold in mixed company.

In a word, it's about tempo for Malcolm. Let it happen and it does. Try to force the issue and it blows up. All of it. To mushroom cloud proportions.

What will this round bring?

"Ayeee!" yawped Malcolm barbarically as he watched his drive, a tightly controlled power fade, drift from the margin of the hazard back toward center cut, then hit the linksland running until it had trimmed a full 250 yards off the stout par 4. "Tha', ma guid chappies, was wor' the wait."

The Truth Will Set Ye Free

Kate was famished. But something on the plate of food that Margaret placed in front of her on the steward's kitchen table caused her to freeze, with knife and fork poised for the attack.

"Excuse me Margaret, but what the heck is *that*?" she asked, gesturing in the general direction of a dark purple goo molded into the shape of a 5/8th-scale hockey puck.

"Oh, aye, tha' woold be the black poodin'," replied Margaret as she added some fresh water to a small vase of bluebells that served as the table's modest centerpiece.

"OK, let's try this again: what the heck is black pudding?" said Kate.

"Just a mix o' oatmeal, onions, spices an', well, pork blood," said Margaret. "Standard issue for a fry up. Give it a go."

"You had me right up until blood," said Kate. "No offense, but I'm going to start with the eggs and, uh, Canadian bacon, and work my way up to it."

"Nae offense taken," said Margaret. "Ah watched yer father poosh his black poodin' aroond his plate on more than one occasion."

"He used to say, 'No one ever goes to Scotland for the food,'" said Kate. "But I have to say, this breakfast is hitting the spot. Completely burying it, more like. Thank you, Margaret."

"Ye're most welcome, deer."

Margaret circled back to her cramped kitchen's counter, where the electric kettle had begun to crescendo to the boiling point. In the time it took her to fill a white porcelain tea pot with hot water, drop in a fresh bag of English Breakfast and bring the brew and two matching red toile cups to the table, Kate's Full Scottish had already been halved. The pudding, however, remained unscathed.

"Guid appetite," said Margaret. "So glad yer enjoyin' it."

"Oh, yes. Thank you again," said Kate.

"Once more intae the breach," said Margaret, marveling at how Kate laid waste to her breakfast with the same reckless abandon that William Wallace, aka Braveheart, dispatched Scotland's English oppressors back in the 13th century.

Finally sated, Kate set down her cutlery and took up her tea.

"Uh, Margaret, I was wondering if I could ask you a question?" she inquired.

"Certainly, love. Wha's on yer mind?"

"Well, last night on my way in and again this morning on my way out, I couldn't help but notice all of the photos on your hallway walls. There's a very handsome gentleman in many of them, some with you by his side and some only of him. I was just wondering…"

"…who tha' is?"

"Yes. Please excuse me if I'm prying."

"Nae, 'tis OK. Tha' woold be Ian, ma husband. Ah lost him tae cancer. Moor tha' 15 yeers ago noo."

"Oh, forgive me, Margaret. I *was* prying, wasn't I."

"Na' at all. Don't git me wrong. Na' a day goes ba tha' Ah dinna thin' o' Ian. But enough tahm has passed tha', noo, the memories, for the most part, fill me wi' joy na' sorrow. We had 23 wonderful yeers taegither. Tha's far moor tha' most people. Ah consider maself very blessed."

"I can see that. I only wish I could feel it, for my dad. That might sound cold, especially for someone like you who's so warm-hearted. But, full disclosure: There's just an emptiness inside. A nothingness. A numbness."

"Ah can see tha'."

"It's that obvious, isn't it? I'm sure the guys, when they picked me up in Glasgow, expected me to be grieving. Deeply. I mean, my dad had just died! But that's not what I was feeling. Made me think something was wrong with me." Then, half a beat later, "Do you think there's something wrong with me?"

"Nae, Ah dae na'," said Margaret. "Tha's just yer natural defenses daein' everthin' they can tae protect ye from the hurt. Ah went through tha' phase masel' right after Ah lost Ian. An' Ah had some tahm tae prepare, though, in the end, theer's really nae way tae prepare for the reality o' death—Ah dinna care wha' anyone tells ye. Ye, on the other hand, had nae warnin'. I's na' surprisin' tha' yer feelin' shell-shocked."

"So this is…normal?"

"Aye. Ye have nothin' tae apologize for. We all ha'e tae come tae terms wi' a tragedy like this in oor own way. Only ye know wha's right for ye. Nae one else can possibly know tha' for ye."

"Thank you for saying that, Margaret. It is such a relief. I feel like I've been disappointing everyone. And I honestly don't want to do that. You've all been so kind. But, the simple fact is, I didn't want to get on that plane in LA. I didn't want to be here. I didn't want to be doing this. I just wanted to live my life. I'm sorry to say this, but it's the truth."

"And the truth will set ye free," said Margaret. "Dinna e'er apologize for speakin' yer truth."

"Well then, it's also true that, during the short time I've been at Machrihanish, something has begun to stir inside. Kinda hard for me to put into words."

"Just give i' a try, dear. Will help tae put a nemme tae it."

"Well, it's not sadness so much. It's definitely not anger, though I could certainly make a case for being angry. I don't know. When I think about it, the word that comes the closest to describing it is, I guess…regret."

"Regret? Noo theer's a toxic emotion. Thi' probably isnae the tahm, dear. But when 'tis, Ah truly hope tha' ye can let tha' go. Take it from someone who's been theer: 'tis nae use, wha'soever."

"Should be easy for me. Fact is, I decided very early on in my life not to let setbacks slow me down."

"I believe it. Yer father regaled me wi' yer many accomplishments. An' at such a young age. Ah know ye dinna think i's true, but he really was so very proud o' ye. An' ye should be proud o' yersel'."

"Well, I'm starting to think that maybe, just maybe, I've learned that particular lesson a little too well. Here's some more truth for you: I've had more than one boyfriend refer to me as the Queen of Denial."

"Oh my!" said Margaret, stifling a giggle.

"Hey, I used to laugh it off, too," continued Kate. "But now, I'm finding that even her royal highness has her limits. I don't know what it looks like from the outside. But from the inside? I'm a tangled mess. And I don't have a clue how to untangle it."

"'I's only been a few days, dear. Truth be told, Ah needed a few yeers after Ah lost ma Ian tae git my feet back under me. An' it might ha'e taken e'en longer if Ah hadn't foond ma way tae this place."

"So you weren't born and raised here?"

"Guidness nae. Ah'm a city gurl. Grew up in Edinburgh. Went tae university theer. Tha's wheer Ah met Ian."

"Oh, a college boy!" said Kate, relieved to be shifting the focus back on Margaret. "Now there's a feeling I *can* relate to."

"Well noo, this was nae youthful fling, Kate. Ah'm talkin' aboot love at first sight. Head ower heels, stop the presses, thunderbolt city love."

"You're joking, right? Everyone knows that only happens in Disney movies."

"This is nae joke," replied Margaret, a wee bit more forcefully. "Wha' Ian an' Ah had taegither was very real. Ah can honestly say tha' we were crazy aboot each other from the day we met until the day we parted. Noo i's ma toorn tae speak *ma* truth."

"Oh Margaret, I'm sorry," said Kate. "Sometimes my cynicism gets the best of me. I didn't mean that."

"Nae bother. Ah realize tha' when it comes tae afeers o' the heart, Ian an' Ah were the exception tae the rule. But, Ah ha'e tae say, yer reaction does kinda beg the question."

"What's that?"

"Ha'e ye e'er been in love, Kate?"

"Love? Now there's a complicated concept."

"Only if ye make it so."

"Well, if you're talking about strong physical attraction, then, yes, there've been a few of those. And they weren't complicated. At least not at the start. But in love? True love? The kind you speak of? Can't contribute much to that discussion. In fact, I'd just assume we didn't go there, if you don't mind."

"Oh dear, so noo Ah'm the one who's pryin'."

"See there. I *knew* it was wrong of me to ask you about the photos!"

"Well, Ah dinna say tha', exactly. But perhaps it woold be best if we changed the subject."

"I'm definitely down with that."

"But apparently na' doon wi' the puddin'," said Margaret

with a laugh.

"I'm sorry. I've been known to faint at the sight of blood. So the thought of eating it, well," said Kate. "Perhaps you could tell me how you got from Edinburgh to Machrihanish. Was it for the golf?"

"Gowf? Contrary tae popular belief, na' everyone who lives in Scotland plays the gemme. If ye ask me, anyone who does is at least slightly daft. Take Angus, for example."

"More than slightly, if you ask me," joked Kate.

"Ye'll git nae argument from me on tha'," replied Margaret.

"Then why *are* you here?"

"Ah needed a job. An' a change o' scenery. Plain an' simple. After Ian passed, Ah just had tae get away from the city. I's like tha' song, 'Ah'll be lookin' a' the moon, but Ah'll be seein' ye,' crooned Margaret."

"Very nice," said Kate.

"Ah just love those auld ballads," said Margaret. "They dinna write 'em like tha' anymore. Anyway, as Ah was sayin'…

"…and singing…"

"…durin' those dark tahms, Ah was seein' Ian an' oor life taegither in Edinburgh at every toorn, day an' night. So Ah went online. Cast a wide net. Tha's when Ah saw tha' Machrihanish, oot in the hinterlands, was in need o' a steward. So Ah applied for the job an', against all odds, they offered it tae me."

"Wow! I just assumed you'd been here your whole life. You seem so, well, how can I put this? Settled."

"Surprises me, too. A' first, Ah thought it was just a transitional move. But noo? Theer's naewheer else Ah'd rather be. Ah'll stay as long as they'll ha'e me. Once this place gits intae yer blood, theer's nae gettin' it oot.

"Kind of like the puddin'?"

"Aye. Theer's just somethin' aboot Machrihanish. I's hard tae explain."

"Sounds like something Papa would say. Of course, it would sound a wee bit different coming from him."

"Indeed. Yer father loved this place, Ah dare say e'en more tha' we dae."

"Well, selfishly, I wish that hadn't been true. The way I saw it—experienced it—Machrihanish stole my dad away from me, time and again. I couldn't help but feel that he loved it more than he loved me."

"Oh, ye should ne'er say tha'! 'Cause it simply isnae true. But Ah dae believe yer father's loyalties were divided. An' he strooggled mightily wi' tha'. He wanted tae be heer. An' he wanted tae be wi' you. A' some point, Ah think he decided tha' ye were better off livin' yer life. So he decided tae live his. Which meant comin' back heer, yeer after yeer. Given all yer success in school an' yer career, perhaps he was right."

"Perhaps. It's just that, now, those things don't seem to matter to me nearly as much as they did a few days ago. I can't stop thinking about all those times when my dad and I were out of sync with one another. When he reached out to me and, I'll admit, I pushed him away. When I really needed him, and he just wasn't there. When he was on the road with the Giants. Or over here with the boys. Or physically present but emotionally distant. Those rare moments when we fully opened up to each other are so precious to me now. But there could have been more. There should have been more. And now there is…no more."

Kate reached for her tea as her eyes began to well up. Margaret hesitated for a second or two, not quite sure if words or a hug were the appropriate response. Instead, she split the difference, taking Kate's free hand in hers.

"I's OK, dear. Let it oot. I's no use holdin' it in."

"I know," said Kate, taking a deep breath. "I'm getting there. I'm one tough nut to crack, I'm afraid."

"All in due tahm then," said Margaret. "Life is a strange an' maddenin' thing, Ah can assure ye o' tha'. Theer's nae makin' any sense o' it. All ye can dae is take it as it comes. Be grateful for the joys it brings. Grateful for the lessons it has tae teach ye. And be grateful, even, for moments like this, that shatter yer heart intae a million pieces. Wha' choice dae we have?"

"Grateful. Yes. That's the word. And the choice," said Kate, softly.

The younger woman, aging before her Scottish mother's eyes, put down her cup and added that hand to the three that had already melded into one at the center of the table. Silence, except for the surf's distant roar as it drifted through the kitchen's open window, filled the space between them.

After a while, Kate said, "Margaret, would you be willing to tell me more about Ian? I'd really like to know the truth about him. And you. And this epic love you speak of. And about which, apparently, I know nothing."

"Ah'll make a deal wi' ye," said Margaret. "Ah'll tell ye

aboot Ian an' me if ye'll tell me aboot tha' miniature gowf club ye we're cuddlin' like a teddy beer last night."

"Oh that!" said Kate with a snicker. "Funny story."

"Then Ah dae believe we'll need tae brew some moor tea."

His Most Prized Possession

While Kate and Margaret huddled above, the clubhouse below had taken on the deep calm of a Benedictine monastery, what with the seven Scots and one Italian getting an early start on the course and the Swedish dentists filling out the tee sheet behind them. But it didn't take long for that silent space to morph back into the convivial confines, once Angus and his cohorts had cycled through the locker room in the back, paid their respects to the gents and regrouped at the bar.

"So Angus, care for a wee swally?" asked Gavin.

"Dae ye really have tae ask?" replied the big man.

"Right, pint o' Guinness, brunch o' champions."

"Cheers, Fauntluhroo."

"Think nothin' o' it," responded the banker. "After all, Ah'm usin' yer money tae pay for the bevvies."

"If ye were a true gentleman, ye woulda' given yer ill-gotten gains to yer partne'. Angelo played like a man possessed."

"Ah'll admit Ah was a wee bit concerned when ye announced the pairin's. But Angelo ended up carryin' me, na the other way aroond. Definitely na' my A-game oot theer taeday."

"Ah think tha' was ma C-game," said Ewan, who joined the conversation late, apparently having more business than his buddies to attend to in the loo. "Ma apologies, Ravi. Ye deserved a better partne' than tha'."

"Thin' nothin' o' it, Roy Boy," said Angus. "It was guid just tae git out on the coorse an' knock it aroond, even if the coorse ended up knockin' us aroond."

"Aye," said Ewan. "Angelo certainly showed us all a thin' or two. Makes me wonder wha' ma gemme woold be like if Ah dinna ha'e a day job, an' a mortgage, an' kids, an' responsibilities an' etcetera, an' Ah coold just beat ba's all day."

"Well, ye'd probably break par e'ery tahm oot," said Angus. "But ye'd also be livin' in a wooden teepee in a caravan park, scroungin' aroond for shillin's just tae git ba."

"Funny thin' aboot tha'," said Ewan. "When Ah went tae hand Angelo his winnin's, he refused tae accept. Said the mornin's stroll aroond the auld links wi' us was moor than plenty reward, in an' of i'sel'."

"Well guid on him then," said Gavin. "He might na' have been born on this soil, but Ah dae believe, ba noo, he's earned his stripes as an adopted Scot. Speakin' of Angelo, why isnae heer wi' us?"

"Ah invited him in, but he begged off," replied Ewan. "Said he wanted tae head doon too the practice field an' work on his knockdoon shots. Noo tha's a man who's dedicated tae his craft. Ye got tae admire him for tha'."

Just as the three men were about to choose a table and order some food, the second wave landed on the beachhead. There was no mistaking Malcolm's deep baritone voice as it bellowed from the back hallway.

"One more woord aboot yer ruminatin's on strin' theory, Donald, an' Ah'm goin' tae use reel strin', not theoretical, to boond an' gag ye. An' Ah'm startin' with yer mouth!" boomed Malcolm.

"Ma, ma! Any o' ye laddies wish tae wager how tha' match toorned oot?" proffered Angus.

"Clearly, the auld man got the best of the X-man, in moor ways tha' one," said Ewan.

On cue, the four men entered, stage right: Malcolm, his face flush from the fresh air and heated conversation; Donald, eyes down, but his true feelings betrayed by the hint of a sheepish grin; Alister, beaming and with his right hand resting lightly on his partner's shoulder; and Bernard, shaking his head in disbelief.

"So how'd it go, boys?" inquired Angus, tweaking the already tightly wound Malcolm.

"Ah'd rather na' talk aboot it," replied Malcolm. "Ah've endured enough blather in the past four hoors tae last me 'till Boxin' Day."

"But Malcolm, ye have tae admit it *was* a woonderful match," said Bernard. "Came doon tae the 18th. If Ah'd made ma birdie putt, we'd ha'e salvaged a halve. An' tha's after we were dormie wi' three tae play."

"Aye," said Alister. "Ah was convinced tha' ye were goin' tae sink it, Bernard. We limped across the finish line, tha's for sure."

"Wi' the non-stop runnin' commentary tae go wi'it," added Malcolm. "Next tahm we're in the semme foursome, Donald, remind me tae pack ear plugs in ma golf bag. Ye drive me absolutely batty, ye auld numpty!"

"Ma apologies, Malcolm," said Donald. "I's just tha' ah have all these ideas cogitatin' in ma brain. Ah canne seem tae keep them from leakin' oot. The least Ah can dae is git ye a bevvy."

As these four friends joined the other three at the bar, an eighth man appeared, ghost-like, out of the shadows. But this was no apparition, say, of Old Tom Morris come back to give the living a fright. And the ethereal being was clearly not a golfer, nattily attired in black suit, white shirt and blue tie, his face clean shaven and his hair combed neatly into place.

Alister bravely stepped forward to greet him, or it.

"Mr. McIntire," said the doctor. "Ah dinna expect tae see ye heer."

"Well, Ah been tryin' tae call ye on your moby, but Machrihanish is apparently off the grid," said the procurator fiscal. "So Ah figured Ah'd dae this the old-fashioned way an' meet wi' ye face-tae-face. Thankfully, the drive from Tarbert was quite pleasant."

"Guid tae heer," said Alister. "So Ah assume ye have news for us, an' Kate."

"Aye. Is she heer?"

"Aye, though na' sure exactly wheer at the moment. Perhaps Ah could git a message tae her for ye."

"Na' exactly ba the book. But under the circumstances, Ah think tha' woold expedite matters. Ah know she's pressed for tahm."

"Aye. So wha's the latest?"

"The pathologist, Dr. Urquhart, has completed her examination an' determined the cause of death: acute myocardial infarction."

"So 'twas a heart attack," said Alister, translating for the others.

"Aye. Accordin' tae Dr. Urquhart, theer was probably nae warnin'. Theer was nothin' Mr. McAlonan coold ha'e done. She's certain he was already gone afore the accident occurred. So he probably dinna suffer much."

"Ah guess we can take some comfort in tha'," said Alister.

"Aye, indeed," said McIntire. "Ma work is nearly done noo. Ah can release the body tae Ms. McAlonan taemorrow. Dae ye know wha' she has planned?"

"Ma guess is she hasn't thought it through tha' far," said Alister.

"Well, generally a' this point in the proceedin's, a local funeral director steps in. Ah can recommend one in Tarbert, if tha' woold be helpful."

"Perhaps," said Alister.

"Wait, Ah have an idea," said Malcolm, who like his friends had hung on every word that passed between the solicitor and the physician. "Ma wife, Ah mean ex-wife, had family tha' lived in Campbeltown. So unfortunately, ah attended moor tha' one funeral heer ower the yeers. Ah can strongly recommend Sloan an' Sons. Theer closer ba tha' Tarbert. An', in ma experience, they handle such matters wi' the utmost delicacy an' professionalism. Ah can talk wi' Kate aboot it, as soon as she makes an appearance."

"Tha' sounds like a plan, then," said McIntire. "Dr. MacKenzie, ye have ma number. Hopefully ye can find a way tae call from heer once ye've sorted oot the details. Again, my condolences tae all o' ye on the loss o' yer friend. I's tragic, truly tragic."

And with that, the well-dressed apparition disappeared into the car park, leaving the seven men to once again engage with the reality they'd managed to escape all morning on the course. Without a word, they assembled around one of the dining room's two large round tables, set back into an alcove comprised mostly of windows for an optimal view. But for now, the friends had little interest in looking outward.

That's when Margaret and Kate waltzed in, practically arm in arm, sharing a private laugh.

"Oh ma!" exclaimed Margaret as she sized up the circle. "It must ha'e been a very bad day for the gowf. Wha' a bunch o' sour pusses."

"Yeah, it's just a game, gentlemen," added Kate, mirroring Margaret's playful tone. "It's not life and death, don't you know."

None of the knaves at the round table responded. Kate's poorly timed comment, coming on the heels of the black-suited ghost's visitation, felt like piling on.

Gavin, finally, decided to speak for the group.

"Looks like the two o' ye ha' had a guid mornin'," he said.

"Aye," said Margaret. "Amazin' wha' a little gurl talk can dae for a, well, gurl."

"And a little golf talk, Margaret," added Kate. "Don't forget about that."

"Aye," said Margaret. "Kate showed me some o' John's belongin's. Ah never realized how much ye coold learn aboot a person ba wha' they carry in theer gowf bag."

"Including this!" said Kate, waving what appeared, at first to the men, to be some sort of magic wand. "This, laddies and fair lassie, is my father's very first golf club."

"Lemme see tha'," said Angus, Kate's gesticulating apparently having broken McIntire's spell. "Well Gawd help me, this is indeed a real golf club. I's got a 3-iron head, a True Temper steel shaft an' a Golf Pride rubber grip, a very dry an' crusty one a' tha'."

"But 'tis so small," said Malcolm. "Got tae be no more than 30 inches long, e'en stubbier tha' ma shortest putter, an' have at least a dozen in ma growin' collection tae choose from."

"Yeah, well my great grandpa, my dad's dad's dad, who emigrated to America from Ireland—from the little town of Ballymoney, to be exact—had this custom made for my dad," said Kate. "My papa said his papa wasn't really into golf. But his grandpa was, so he wanted to get his grandson started in the right way. I'm pretty sure my dad was seven when he first hit a plastic golf ball with it. Then, when he was somewhere around 12 or 13, he got to set foot on a real golf course. So he used this club as his first putter."

"He woulda' needed tae position his hands well ahead o' the ba' tae square up the face an' putt wi' tha' thin'," said Ewan. "Looks tae have aboot 20 degrees o' loft."

"Perhaps tha' explains why Mac always had a lot o' forward press in his puttin' stroke," said Alister. "Probably started wi' this club, or more accurately, clubbette."

"Well, at some point," continued Kate, "he replaced it with a real putter and mounted this clubbette, as you say, on a wall in the den of the house I grew up in. One day, when he was at work, I snuck in there, took it down and used it to dig out a little garden for myself in our backyard. I was five or six at the time. I vaguely remember my mom being mildly upset that I'd messed up a small patch of the lawn. But I'll never forget the moment my dad came home and found his club caked in mud. He went absolutely ballistic! I've never seen him so angry, before or since. I learned the hard way that this was his most prized possession. So I never touched it again, until last night that is."

"So tha' explains why ye were a no-show for dinner," said Alister.

"Yes," said Kate. "Kind of stumbled down memory lane and, after a while, was too mired in the past—not to mention too exhausted—to find my way back."

"Hold on a second," interjected Angus. "Did ye find this wee stick in yer father's golf bag?"

"Uh-huh," said Kate. "It was stuffed down near the bottom. You'd never see it unless you were looking for it."

"So tha' means Mac was carryin' aroond 15 clubs wi' him all this tahm?" said Angus. "Tha' changes everythin'. Ah demand a recount!"

"What?" said a puzzled Kate.

"The rules o' gowf limit ye tae just 14 clubs," explained Gavin. "If ye hav' more than tha', ye incur a penalty. In match play, which is oor preferred mode ower heer, tha' would mean loss o' hole for every hole ye play wi' extra clubs, up tae a maximum o' two holes per match. Moor often tha' na', tha's enough tae change the final outcome."

"And you guys would actually throw the book at him for that, because of this child's plaything?" asked Kate.

"Na'. But Ah woold ha'e enjoyed more tha' a wee laugh at his expense tryin' tae," said a smiling Angus. "It was a missed opportoonity. Tha's the offense, if ye ask me."

"Oh, I hear you on that," said Kate. "I'm sure Papa would have enjoyed mixing it up with you, too."

"Uh, Kate, Ah hate tae change the subject, but theer's some thin's tha' we need tae take care o' regardin' yer father," said Alister. "Mr. McIntire was heer. Ye just missed 'im."

Kate took her father's club back from Angus, wrapped her hands around the hardened rubber in a classic Vardon overlap grip and gave the 3-iron a waggle or two, careful not to take a divot out of the clubhouse's velvety blue carpet.

"It's OK, Alister," she said, suddenly subdued. "As long as I have this magic wand in my hands, there's no darkness that can defeat me. Where're we at? And what needs to happen next?"

"Tha's ma gurl," said Margaret, reaching out to gently touch Kate's face. "Ye're far from alone, deer. We'll all git through this taegither."

The Firm of McAlonan and McKinlay

The seven men, even those who'd lost their morning matches, were anxious to return to the course for an afternoon round. After all, they had a lot of swings to make up for. But more than that, what they truly desired was to reestablish the proper balance between their private playground amid the dunes and, well, pretty much the rest of creation.

It's that sweet separation that makes golf so endearing and, admittedly, so addictive. It stakes out a world within the world, where—on the first tee—they hand you an unblemished scorecard and all manner of new and wonderful experiences are suddenly possible. Then, 18 holes and who knows how many shots later, you circle back to where you started, with the invitation—as well as the inclination—to start all over again.

Clearly, golf isn't about the destination. You move about a vast expanse of open land yet never actually get anywhere, geographically speaking. So by process of elimination, the game must be all about the journey. Perhaps that's why some of its adherents—most notably those who worship at the altars of Shivas Irons and Bagger Vance—liken it to the inward path traveled by the eastern mystics. So does that mean it's the sports world's equivalent of *Seinfeld*, the show about nothing? Guess again. Golf is, in equal portions, absurdly simple and unfathomably deep, not unlike that 19th century children's rhyme we all learned in kindergarten: "Roll, roll, roll your ball, gently on the green. Merrily, merrily, merrily, merrily—life is but a dream."

Unfortunately, while the friends ate, drank and bantered inside, the conditions outside had become a nightmare.

"Ah sure hope the Swedish dentists remembered tae pack theer waterproofs," said Angus, peering through the clubhouse windows, streaked with rain. "Those poor bastards are gettin' a right nasty peltin'."

"Aye," said Malcolm. "If Ah've learned anythin' aboot links gowf, 'tis tha' ye always come prepared for the worst tha' Mother Nature can throw a' ye, no matter how benign the conditions when ye set oot."

"Safe tae say the afternoon's festivities ha'e been canceled?" inquired Gavin.

"Ah'm afraid so," answered Angus.

"That's a shame," said Kate, who mingled amongst the men,

meeting Bernard, Ewan and Donald for the first time. "You know, I was actually toying with the idea of joining you out there. I have nothing on my schedule until tomorrow morning at 10, when Malcolm and I have an appointment at Sloan and Sons. And I have a full array of gear up in my room…"

"…that, wi'oot a doubt, yer father would encourage ye tae put tae guid use," said Bernard.

"That's what I was thinking," said Kate. "So there's no chance this will blow over? It kind of looked like this on the ferry yesterday and, within the hour, it was clear again."

"Nae this tahm, Kate," said Gavin. "Tha' bit o' weather we encountered crossin' Lunderston Bay was just a wee shower. This is a steady rain tha's likely to stay wi' us through the night. Wish Ah coold be moor encouragin'."

"Well, maybe tomorrow afternoon then," said Kate.

"Consider it done," said Angus, pleasantly surprised that the young woman had begun to transform into a fully-fledged human being. In fact, he swore that, at times, glimpses of John even managed to break through. Margaret must have given her a good talking to, he thought. "I's high tahm ye got yer first taste o' gowf the way it was meant tae be played."

"So if there's no golf, what's next?" she asked.

"Kitchen duty for me," said Gavin. "We plan oot every detail o' this week months in advance. This was always ma night tae whip up a big batch o' chili tae feed the whole crew. Ye're moor than welcome tae join us. Angus an' Ah will be acceptin' dinner guests at oor luxurious Ugadale flat a' hauf past seven."

"Chili?" said Kate, slightly incredulous. "You cook, Gavin?"

"Aye," said Gavin. "Ah've developed a wee bit o' a repertoire. Ah find it tae be a relaxin' change o' pace from the stresses o' the bankin' woorld, when Ah ha'e the tahm. And, thanks tae tha' storm, Ah definitely ha'e tha' this afternoon."

"Well, you've got me beat then," said Kate. "I'd offer to help, but I can barely boil water. I'd only be in your way. I'd love to partake, though."

"We'd love tae have ye," said Gavin as he zipped up his jacket and donned his cap. "Come on, Angus. Ye might na' make much o' a sous chef. But a' least Ah can count on ye tae chill the beer."

Gavin and Angus weren't the only ones who abandoned the shelter of the clubhouse in search of counter-programming. Malcolm recruited Alister and his Vauxhall to make the drive to the Tesco to restock their flat's larder, though no one would have been the least bit surprised if a side trip to the Burnside, a slightly seedy Campbeltown pub, was added to their agenda. Donald retreated to the flat he shared with Bernard to pick up where he'd left off in a book that claimed to prove the existence of multiple universes or, more simply, multiverses.

And Ewan, who would have bunked with John if everything had gone according to plan, went in search of Angelo in hopes of finishing a discussion on radical swing theories that they'd started on the course. The redhead had this sneaking suspicion that the Italian ex-pat, in his relentless pursuit of perfection, had stumbled onto some magic move, maybe even Hogan's mysterious "secret," that could turn the human body into the flesh-and-blood equivalent of Iron Byron. That club-wielding robot, engineered to emulate the great Byron Nelson's machine-like swing, is used by golf's equipment makers to push the envelope on the latest technology and by golf's governing bodies to ensure they don't burst the bubble. Ewan, stubbornly clinging to the dream of turning golf into his day job, just couldn't resist the urge to seek out the mad scientist and attempt to pick his eccentric brain.

Meanwhile, Margaret returned to the clubhouse's main kitchen and began playing catch-up on her chores, the penance for having spent most of the morning with Kate. Thanks to Gavin, she wouldn't have to prepare an evening meal for the Scots. But the Swedes? They'd be in desperate need of nourishment after slogging through the worst of the weather.

Bernard, though, lingered in the mostly empty dining room, accompanied by his thoughts and his ever-present journal. Kate, not wanting to be alone, approached him.

"Boy, this place sure cleared out in a hurry," she said jovially. "Was it something I said?"

"Oh, na' a' all, Kate," said Bernard, a bit too seriously. "We're just a flock o' odd birds tha' canne seem tae sit still on a wire for too long before flyin' off tae dae somethin', anythin' really, tae pass the tahm. Ower the years, each o' us has developed his own way o' dealin' wi' the rainouts."

"So what's your strategy," asked Kate.

"Well, like yer father, Ah write for a livin'," he said. "So when Machrihanish is socked in like this, Ah take it as a sign from above tha' Ah have permission tae indulge maself in readin' a guid book or scribblin' in this one. Wha' else can ye dae?"

"So you're a sports writer, like my dad?"

"Na'. Nothin' as glamorous as tha'. Ah make ma livin' as a corporate communications consultant. Some o' 'tis internal: employees, retailers, tha' sort o' thin'. Some o' 'tis external: media relations, executive speechwritin' an' the like."

"I'm in advertising. Different side of the same coin."

"Aye. I's guid, steady work. Ah'm grateful for the income. An' on a guid day, it can be very fulfullin', a' least on an intellectual level. But doesn't dae much for the soul, if ya know wha' Ah mean."

"I believe I do. Not sure, exactly, why I chose advertising for my profession. The money's good, I will say that. But when I really stop and think about what I'm doing, I can get a little depressed."

"How's tha'?"

"Well, at its essence, our job is to convince people to buy the things our clients are selling. More, more, more. Always more. So in a very direct way, I'm helping to feed the consumption beast."

"Aye, an' i's insatiable."

"Exactly. I've fallen prey to it myself, I'll admit."

"As have we all."

"Well, in the back of my mind, though, I'm aware that what I'm doing—what we're all doing—just isn't sustainable. I mean, the last thing the planet needs is more stuff. Yet we keep making it and selling it and buying it. It's really hard to stop. Like we're all addicted."

"Which we are. But wha' can we dae?"

"Most of the time, I choose not to think about it. Which, I suppose, isn't sustainable either."

"Nae i's na'. When ye git tae be ma age, ye canne help but woonder if theer's somethin' else ye should be daein' wi' yer life. Yer father an' Ah talked aboot this very subject on moor tha' one occasion, especially in the last yeer or two."

"Really? I always thought he loved his job."

"He started oot lovin' it. But he lamented tha' the newspaper business he broke in wi' nae longer existed. Tha' it had become all aboot the bottom line, na' helpin' tae create a moor informed public. The travel was also startin' tae wear on him. Theer's nothin' moor depressin', he'd say, than wakin' up alone in some generic hotel room in some generic town, only tae spend yer tahm tryin' tae extract some deep meanin' oot o' the actions an' cliches o' some half-educated pituitary case who's makin' millions just because he can throw a baseball 95 miles per hour."

"Wow! He said all of that?"

"Moor or less in those words, aye."

"But Papa loved baseball."

"Aye, he did. Almost as much as he loved gowf. But he hated the business o' it. An' the monotony. Trust me, he was countin' the days 'til retirement, when he coold leave tha' woorld behind an' lose hi'sel' fully in this one."

"That I believe."

"Ah'll let ye in on another little secret."

"What's that?"

"Yer father an' Ah talked aboot collaboratin' on some writin' projects o' oor own. Gowf-related, o' coorse."

"What did you have in mind?

"The ideas weren't fully formed. But we were thinkin' aboot a website or blog or some such. Express oor thoughts on the true meanin' o' the gemme. Git back tae the heart o' it. Before buggies. Before cell phones. Before GPS devices an' laser range finders. Before six-hour roonds which, for the most part, we've managed tae hold the line on ower heer."

"Hmmm…you've just described my reality when it comes to golf. That's the game I play."

"Well, i's na' the gemme we play. And i's na' the gemme yer dad enjoyed playin'. He believed, an' Ah definitely agreed wi' him, tha' gowf as we knew it—as he believed the woorld needed it—was fast becomin' an endangered species. An' he felt compelled tae use his skills an' influence in the publishin' woorld tae try tae dae somethin' aboot it. Unfortunately, tha' work has noo been left undone."

"But *you* could take up the cause, Bernard. It's obvious just how passionate you are about it."

"Aye, perhaps. But Ah was never the natural born leader tha' yer father was. Tha's why we woold ha'e made such a guid team taegither. Oor personalities complemented one another perfectly. Noo? Ah just dinna know if Ah can dae this wi'oot him."

"That's entirely up to you. If you believe, deep in your heart, that you were born to do this, then you should do it. You *must* do it."

"Tha' soonds like somethin' yer father woold say."

"Because he did. To me. On more than one occasion. Not that I always listened."

"Well, Ah'm willin' tae consider it," said Bernard. "Ah certainly need somethin' moor tae live for, professionally, tha' writin' yet another press release."

"Just like I could use something more than leading another client by the hand through some pseudo crisis."

"Wha' are ye sayin'? Dae ye wanne work on this, too. Wi' me?"

"Is that what I said!? Well, you know, maybe. I'm 32 years old. I've never done a spontaneous thing my entire life. Perhaps this is the time, and the place, to start."

"Tha' would be bloody amazin'! Yer father woold be so proud."

"And, no doubt, shocked! Look, I'm not quite ready to throw all caution to the wind here. But I am willing to explore our options, see where we might go with this."

"Ah canne ask for moor tha' tha'"

"Huh."

"What's wrong?"

"This idea just came to me. In the spirit of spontaneity, I'm thinking I should share it with you, right here and now."

"Please dae."

"OK, I'm just talking out loud here, but what if we turn the blog into a conversation between you and me? Traditional Scottish male golfer debates the true nature of the game with modern American female golfer. That could be interesting.

And fun!"

"Ah like tha'. Ah like tha' a lot. An' Ah like the way ye thin', Kate. Ye know, theer's more o' yer father in ye tha' ye realize."

"I'm starting to get that. So, partner, what do you say? Want to shake on it?" said Kate.

"Well OK then," said Bernard, reaching for Kate's right hand. "I say the firm of McAlonan and McKinlay is back in business!"

Pot Bunkers and Black Holes

The next three hours whooshed by while Kate and Bernard brainstormed their budding collaboration. At some point, Margaret made an appearance and asked if they'd like a pot of tea. But Kate, who got an early start to this action-packed day, was in need of something stronger.

"I realize this is one of the world's few remaining Starbucks-free zones, but I could really go for a big cup of java right now," she said.

"Ah think Ah can manage tha' for ye," said Margaret. "We aren't limited tae just one delivery system when it comes tae caffeine, dinna ye know."

In truth, Kate probably could have gotten by just fine without the artificial stimulant. She and her new business partner fed off each other's divergent perspectives like a battery's positive and negative poles, generating more sparks between them than they ever could have produced on their own.

Their first order of business: What should they call this new thing they were bringing to life?

"I was thinkin' 'The Odd Couple,' started Bernard.

"Too dated. How about 'He Said, She Said?" countered Kate.

"Perhaps," parried Bernard. "But tha' dinna say gowf tae me."

"Gotchya. So maybe something along the lines of, say, 'Up and Down.'"

"Or 'Ham and Egg.'"

"'Ham and Egg?' As in a Full Scottish?"

"Na', as in well-suited partners in best-ba' match play."

"Not familiar with it. I'm strictly stroke play myself."

"Guid heavens! We really are comin' a' this from different perspectives."

"I know. That's the beauty of it!"

And so the conversation continued, with both Kate and Bernard, each in his or her own way, coming to the conclusion that while this might be work, it felt suspiciously like play. At minimum, the distinction between those two modes of existence had become decidedly blurry.

Then, out of nowhere: "Can tha' be right!?" exclaimed Bernard, glancing down at his watch. "'I's really haulf past seven?"

"Oh right," said Kate. "Gavin and his chili."

"We'd best git ower theer. If we stand up Angus we'll ne'er heer the end o' it."

Though the Ugadale was just a short walk from the clubhouse, Kate raced upstairs to grab her father's Gore-Tex rain jacket as protection from the persistent precipitation. Bernard, similarly wrapped, waited for her by the side door and, as they stepped outside, invited Kate to join him under his oversized golf umbrella. Then, when they were half way across the car park, Kate's cell phone, tucked in her pants pocket, broke forth in a berserk barrage of buzzing and bleeping.

"What the heck?" said Kate. "I'd pretty much given this thing up for dead."

"We must have walked over 'The Spot,'" said Bernard.

"The spot?"

"Aye. I's the lone square foot in all o' Machrihanish wheer the cell signal manages tae break through. Someone really needs tae mark it wi' an X."

"That would have come in handy this morning," said Kate, fumbling for her phone. But before she could enter her passcode and triage the incoming, the city bus pulled to a stop in front of them—the high-pitched hiss of its air brakes diverting her attention.

The door opened and out popped Ewan, accompanied by an older gentleman she didn't recognize. Bernard made a move to greet them, so Kate, rather than lose the shelter of his brolly, stuffed her phone back in her pocket and remained in lockstep.

"Guid evenin' Angelo," said Bernard. "So ye've come tae

sample yer partner's cookin'?"

"*Ciao*," said Angelo. "Ewan say OK. Mr. Gavin make big pot, no?"

"Aye," said Bernard, as the group slowly shuffled toward the Ugadale, carefully navigating the puddles that had formed in its semi-circle gravel driveway. "Ah'd be surprised if we touch bottom. Plenty tae go aroond."

"Who is your friend?" asked Angelo.

"Oh, pardon me," said Bernard. "Allow me tae introduce Kate. She is John's daughter. Kate, this is Angelo."

"I honor to meet you, Miss McAlonan," said Angelo. "I like your father very much."

"So *you're* the guy from Italy," she said. "Very nice to meet you."

"*Si*. You hear me?"

"From my dad. He said your life would make a great story, one that I think he was hoping to tell."

Bernard and Ewan gave each other a look.

"Really!?" said Angelo. "We had good talk. But no much to it, I think. I live simple life."

"Na' simple when it comes tae gowf," said Ewan. "Yer swing theories are fascinatin'. Unorthodox, but utterly fascinatin'."

"I try things," said Angelo. "Some work, *si*. For while. But some no work. Ever. That's the golf, no?"

Ewan jumped ahead to open the hulking hotel's over-sized door and the other three took advantage of his courteous gesture, stepping out of the rain and into the Ugadale's darkened foyer.

"What's that sound?" asked Kate as Ewan closed the hatch

behind them.

"Oh, tha' woold be the Ugadale's high-tech weather trackin' system," said Bernard. "I's also known as the skylight tha' illuminates the staircase leadin' tae the upper levels. When we're in oor flats in the wee hours o' the mornin', woonderin' wha' the playin' conditions are going tae be like tha' day, we dinna have tae look oot a window. We just listen for the peltin' on the plexiglass, hopin' all's quiet on the gowfin' front."

"Aye, an' check this oot Kate," said Ewan leading her through a door to the right and into a cavernous hall topped with at least a 20-foot ceiling. "Back in the day, this was a grand ballroom, wheer the rich an' famous woold gather in all theer finery for some highbrow socializin'."

"Noo?," said Bernard. "'Tis wha' we call the *un*-dryin' room, wheer we scatter oor gowf belongin's aboot after we've had a guid soakin' on the coorse. I's mostly a pointless exercise, though."

"Aye. Only a daftie woold expect his grips tae dry oot in this drafty!" joked Ewan.

The responding laughter reverberated off the Ugadale's sagging plaster walls as the foursome ascended the stairs to the third floor landing. At the other end of the hall, Angus and Gavin's flat awaited, its open door beckoning and The Beatles' "Long and Winding Road" blaring.

"So guid of ye tae join us," said Gavin, a tad sarcastically. "Ah was aboot to send oot the search party."

"Sorry Gavin," said Bernard. "Kate an' Ah ha'e spent most o' the afternoon workin'."

"Workin'?" said Gavin.

"Aye, Ah'll explain later. But na' until Ah've had ma first round o' chili."

"That sounds good to me, too," said Kate.

"So yer appetite has been fully restored?" asked Gavin.

"Oh yes," said Kate. "My stomach, along with most of the rest of me, is starting to settle in nicely, if I say so myself."

"Glad tae heer it. Allow me tae git ye a bowl," said Gavin as he dashed off to the kitchenette.

The rest of the gang clearly enjoyed a sizable lead in this particular event, having claimed the few available chairs and accessorized them with half-empty chili bowls and mostly empty beer bottles. Angus, Alister and Malcolm formed a tight circle, talking amongst themselves. Donald, as is his wont, orbited from a distance like the moon. So Kate, emulating Apollo 11's Eagle spacecraft, came in for a landing while she waited for Gavin to return.

"So, did you have an enjoyable afternoon, Donald?" she inquired, naively.

"Aye. Quite pleasant. And quite educational," said Donald.

"How so?"

"Hard tae explain in a few words. But the short answer is that theer's a lot moor tae reality tha' meets the eye."

"Hmmm, that's funny. You don't strike me as the type to fall for all that New Age mumbo jumbo."

"Oh, Ah'm na'. Quite the contrary. Wha' Ah was referin' too was the theory tha' moor than one universe exists, just like theer's moor than one planet in our solar system an' moor than one star in oor galaxy. Extrapolate the precepts o' the latest physics an' theer's every reason tae believe theer's moor than one universe. In fact, as ma hero Carl Sagan might say, theer coold be billions an' billions of 'em."

"Oh that's just what I need," Kate jested. "I kinda have my hands full with just this one universe that we're living in right now. Hard to wrap my head around much more than that, if you know what I mean."

"Understood."

"That's not to say I'm completely clueless on this subject. I took an Intro to Astronomy class to fulfill my science requirement in college. Surprisingly, I kind of got into it."

"Is tha' so? Then perhaps ye're familiar wi' the concept o' black holes."

"Vaguely. It's been more than 10 years."

"Well, Ah have ma own personal theory aboot black holes…an' pot bunkers."

"Come again?"

"Pot bunkers? Is tha' wha' Ah heard ye say, Donald?" said Gavin as he handed Kate a bowl of chili, heaped high with grated cheddar and chopped onions.

"Aye," said Donald. "Dae ye e'er notice how pot bunkers function just like black holes?"

"Wha' the heck is a black hole?" said Gavin.

"I's a cosmological oddity, formed when a dyin' star collapses in on i'self," said Donald. "It becomes so tightly compacted—imagine the entire mass o' the sun contained wi'in the city limits o' Campbeltown—tha' it creates a super powerful gravitational force tha' even light canne escape. Anyway, Ah have come tae the conclusion that black holes an' pot bunkers are twins separated at birth."

"Ah woold expect nothin' less from ye, Donald," said Gavin.

"Think aboot it," continued Donald. "Most pot bunkers are actually quite small when it comes tae the strict boundaries o' the sand pit. But theer effect is far greater, extendin' out tae theer event horizon, just like wi' a black hole."

"Event horizon?" said Kate, who had begun to split her attention among Donald's astrophysics lecture, her dinner and the new arrivals on her cell phone. "I used to know what that meant."

"Well then, allow me tae refresh yer memory," said Donald. "When it comes tae pot bunkers, the event horizon is tha' line tha', if yer ba' crosses it, ye just know tha' gravity is goin' tae take ower an' tha' ba' is goin' tae roll right intae the hazard. The same applies tae interstellar space. Any matter or energy tha' wanders wi'in range o' a black hole's prodigious gravitational field is goin' tae git sucked in. Theer's nae stoppin' it. The parallels are inescapable."

"As are most pot bunkers if yer ba' winds up hard against the face," said Angus, who had wandered over to help Gavin free Kate from Donald's verbal clutches. "Ye know Don-Don, most o' the words tha' flow oot o' yer mouth—an' theer are so many tae choose from—only confirm tha' ye are, indeed, a first class eejit. But, as much as it pains me tae admit it, in this particular instance, ye just might be ontae somethin'."

"Why thank ye, Angus. Sorry tae disappoint," said Donald,

unintentionally making a joke that, against all odds, had his audience laughing with him rather than at him. "Theer's moor wheer tha' came from."

"Dinna push yer luck," said Angus. "We have ye on a strict one-lecture-per-night quota."

Meanwhile, Kate had set down her bowl, stepped aside from the conversation and become fully engrossed in the little bits of light that flashed across her phone's screen.

"So sorry to eat and run, Gavin. The chili was wonderful," she said. "But I really need to find The Spot again."

"Ah dinna think ye wanne be wanderin' aroond in the car park noo," said Gavin. "If Ah'm hearin' the skylight right, i's still pissin' doon pretty guid oot theer."

"It can't be helped. It's business time in America," she said.

"If ye must," said Gavin.

"I'd rather not," said Kate, "but I think I should."

"Then may Ah suggest ye trouble Margaret for the password tae the clubhoose Wifi," said Gavin. "At least tha's a safe haven."

"Wish I could say the same about New York. Looks like all hell is breaking loose back in the real world."

A Soft Spot for the Underdog

"**R**eally! That's it?" said Kate as she typed P-A-S-S-W-O-R-D into her iPhone's WiFi screen.

"Make it complicated an' people, startin' wi' me, forgit," said Margaret. "Besides, wha' dae we ha'e tae hide?"

"Good point," said Kate, as she tried to ramp back up to business speed. How odd, she thought to herself. In just three days, what had been her world now seemed strangely alien.

Her first instinct was to respond in writing. But the complexity of the issues and the fuzziness of the sequencing left her uncharacteristically uncertain that her reply would hit the mark. Better to speak with Joe directly, she reasoned. Sort it all out in real time. After all, now that she was equipped with a free

Internet connection and the Skype app Ewan recommended that she download, an extremely long-distance phone call was not only viable but also affordable. She had the technology.

Four rings later, just as Kate was about to hang up and try again, Joe answered.

"Hi, Joe Kinney here," he said.

"Joe!" exclaimed Kate, a bit more forcefully than she'd intended. "It's Kate. Can you hear me?"

"Katie! Beaming you in loud and clear. Everything OK in Scotland?"

"We're getting there. This is some place. Lot's to tell you."

"I'm all ears."

"Before we go there, what the heck is going on in New York? I scanned the email threads."

"Oh that. Looks worse than it is."

"Are you sure?"

"Yep, nothing to worry about. Yesterday's crisis really. We've got a handle on it now."

"Well, there's a break in the action on this front. I could jump in and help if you need me."

"Not necessary. That particular storm has passed. Though, I'll admit, you dodged a doozy. By the way, from now on, your client shall be affectionately known as Hurricane Jack."

"Oh, God! Definitely diva material. I should have warned you."

"No worries. It's why we get paid the big bucks, right?"

"Well, if it's any consolation, I've had my fill of storms, too. In fact, I'm looking out the clubhouse windows as we speak and the rain is coming down. Sideways."

"Whoa!"

"Yeah, fortunately I have my dad's golf gear to protect me."

"Oh, right," said Joe haltingly. "So it's confirmed?"

"Yes, as of yesterday," said Kate. "I meant to text you. The connection's been hit and miss. Mostly miss."

"No need to explain. Are you OK?"

"For the most part. I've had my moments. I'm sure I'll have more. But my dad's friends have really taken me in. They're a funny lot."

"Funny as in strange? Or funny as in, well, funny?"

"Both. I'm beginning to understand why my dad fell in love with this place. And these people. Everything feels bigger here. More connected. More alive."

"Interesting choice of words."

"Yeah, kind of ironic, given the circumstances."

"Wish I could be there to experience it with you."

"Maybe some day. I have this sneaking suspicion I'll be back."

"Gotta be better than New York."

"No doubt. You really *are* a good man, Charlie Brown!"

"Well, you really are a good daughter. I'm sure your dad would be very proud of you right now."

"You aren't the first person who's said that recently. I just hope it's true."

"You'll know, deep down inside—no matter what anyone else has to say about it."

"Thanks."

"Hey Katie, it's been great to hear your voice. But I gotta run. I can hear old Hurricane Jack, picking up strength down the hall. I just want you to do one thing for me."

"Sure. Anything."

"Check out this email I'm about to send you. While we've been talking, I've been searching. I found a link you'll definitely want to click on."

"OK, I'll look for that. Thanks, Joe."

"Hang in there, kid. Still got your back. Peace, out."

Kate closed down Skype and pulled up her inbox, this time zipping past the derailed train that, Joe assured her, was already back on track. Instead, Kate zeroed in on the message at the top of the list, with a subject heading of "READ THIS!" that practically demanded to be opened. Then she followed Joe's shared link to the online home of the *San Francisco Chronicle.* Her father's employer, it seems, had honored him with a full-on obituary:

Bay Area Sports Writer Dies in Scotland

SAN FRANCISCO -- Award-winning *Chronicle* staff sports columnist and Giants beat writer John Patrick McAlonan, known for a penetrating insight that revealed the private humanity of San Francisco's most famous and beloved athletes—when his rapier wit wasn't cutting their public personas down to size—died last Friday near Tarbert, Scotland. He was 62.

Local authorities confirmed the death on Tuesday after an autopsy, stating that McAlonan suffered a heart attack and then lost control of his vehicle en route to Machrihanish Golf Club. He was a long-time international member of the club and vacationed there each May for many years.

McAlonan came to the Chronicle 23 years ago after a seven-year stint covering mostly Stanford athletics for the *San Jose Mercury News*. Prior to that, he developed his distinctive writing style in Idaho, first at the *Idaho State Journal* in Pocatello and then at the *Boise Statesman*.

In a *Chronicle* article written when he won an Associated Press award for his incisive profiles, McAlonan said that while he admired the athletic prowess of the superstars, he "naturally gravitated to the grinders who dug out a career for themselves, in spite of their modest talent."

"Hey, I'll admit it: I have a soft spot in my heart for the underdog," he said. "In part, that's because I grew up in Cleveland, the city of loveable losers. But if I'm honest, it's also because I always considered myself an underdog, too. As a teenager, I longed to follow in the footsteps of Jack (Nicklaus) and Arnie (Palmer). Strolling down the fairways of the PGA Tour was the dream. But I soon realized it was little more than that. Thank God I was more adept at turning a phrase than swinging a golf club. Otherwise, I would have starved."

McAlonan's tutelage in the fine art of athletic failure continued at Northwestern University, where he earned an undergraduate degree from the Medill School of Journalism. The football team's combined record during his four years in Evanston? A woeful 3-40-1.

"I covered the team for the student newspaper my junior year," said McAlonan. "I should have received college credit. It was basically a creative writing class. I mean, how many different ways can you say that you got clobbered? I dispensed with the usuals, then had to invent a few more to make it through the season.

"Let me put it this way," he continued, "the highlight that year, if you can call it that, was the opening game against Illinois amid a sweltering heat wave the first Saturday in September. It ended in a scoreless tie, with players on both sides of the line of scrimmage essentially inert before we even made it to the fourth quarter."

Appropriately enough, McAlonan's favorite memory from his college days was also sports-related.

"On those rare warm spring Chicago afternoons, my friends and I would ditch class, hop on the El and sneak into the Wrigley Field bleachers for a couple of bucks," he said. "This was back when they only played day games. What a joy! That's when I really became smitten with baseball. Looking back, that was probably the turning point that led me to where I am today."

McAlonan said he was "in awe" of John Schulian, a sports columnist at the *Chicago Sun-Times* while he was at Northwestern. Other tutors, whether in person or from afar, included Jim Murray of the *Los Angeles Times*, Dan Jenkins of *Sports Illustrated* and Bernard Darwin of *The Times* of London.

As for baseball, he credits Duane Kuiper for "graciously serving as a mentor in the finer points of the game." Best known as the Giants' play-by-play announcer, Kuiper was a second baseman for the Cleveland Indians during McAlonan's formative years. To this day, he is the only player in Major League Baseball history to have a career spanning more than 3,000 at-bats and yet hit just one home run.

"Needless to say, we had a lot in common," said McAlonan. "But then, while both Kuip and I were covering the Giants, they went and won the World Series. Three times in five seasons! I don't know about him, but I'll admit that I didn't know quite what to do with myself."

Asked to sum up his approach to sports writing, McAlonan turned the microscope on himself and offered this observation: "In the long run, it won't be the action on the field that we remember—or that really matters—but the people who brought it all to life. That's what fascinates me. Why do they do what they do? Why do they give so much of themselves, so much of their lives, to what is—in the final analysis—just a game? For the pros, the easy answer is the money. But I'm convinced it's something far richer. More sublime. It's the promise of finding *that* gold that keeps me digging."

While writing about baseball was his vocation, playing golf—in particular Scottish golf—was definitely his avocation.

"The auld country! That's my true home," he said, presciently. "When I retire, I'm going to move there and play every day, rain or shine. Get back to the business of working on my game. If it still exists, that's where I'll find it. I can feel it in my heart."

McAlonan is survived by a daughter, Kathleen May McAlonan, 32, of Los Angeles.

Kate set down her iPhone and stared into the darkness as her father's words reverberated in her mind. In the two days since she'd viewed his body, she'd managed to push his passing largely into the periphery, distracted by the new surroundings and the curious people who inhabited them. But now, in the silence of the vacant clubhouse, reality had returned front and center. And once again, she felt his loss—perhaps more acutely than at any other moment during her ordeal.

Maybe that's why, instinctively, she reached for her mobile device and calmly retrieved her list of voicemail messages. Her father's last missive was still there, right below Gavin's. And, just as she'd left it on the 777—hurtling across the Atlantic at an altitude of 30,000 feet—the recording remained unplayed. Its emotional weight and power, at least as Kate imagined it, was still fully intact.

So perhaps now, in this solitude and with both of her feet planted firmly on Scottish linksland, it was finally time to press the play button. Was this, as her father might have put it, her next shot?

Kate let the question float into the void.

"Not yet," was the voiceless reply. "But soon. Very soon."

"It's just that, I miss you Papa," countered Kate. "I really, *really* miss you."

"I know. I miss you, too."

Sloan and Sons

The next morning—which broke clear, bright and mercifully calm—found Kate once again in the front passenger seat of Alister's Vauxhaul. But this time Malcolm, not the country doctor, was at the wheel, making the six-mile drive from Machrihanish to Campbeltown for their scheduled meeting with the funeral director at Sloan and Sons.

"So this is the big city in these parts," said Kate.

"Aye, if ye consider a population of 5,000 a city," said Malcolm.

In its Victorian heyday, the former royal burgh thrived on fishing, shipbuilding and—most significantly as far as Malcolm was concerned—whisky distilling. At one point, it boasted more than 30 purveyors of the country's liquid gold, leading its proud inhabitants to dub Campbeltown the "whisky capital of the world." Today, only three distilleries remain, though a high tech wind turbine company—an early proponent of the hoped-for renewable energy boom—is doing its best to keep the locals gainfully employed and off the UK dole. The beat goes on, though to a decidedly different rhythm.

"Thank you for doing this, Malcolm," said Kate. "I'm sure you'd much rather be with the guys out on the course. Truth be told, I'd rather be there, too."

"Aye," said Malcolm. "We dae wha' we must dae. Though, Ah shoold confess, Ah ha'e nae prior experience when it comes tae matters such as this."

"That makes two of us then," said Kate.

Malcolm brought the car to a stop in front of the Sloans' modest gray stucco two-story building, jumped out and raced around to open Kate's door, but she was too quick for him.

"Very thoughtful of you Malcolm, but not necessary," said Kate. "I was born and raised in the land of self-service. Which, if you ask me, is just another way of saying no service."

Kate's comment, though, couldn't stop Malcolm from opening and holding the door to the funeral home for her. He might have been raised in a laborer's household. But thanks to a mother who longed for more for her son, the manners of an aristocrat were deeply ingrained.

Inside, it took a few seconds for the odd couple's eyes to adjust to the dimly lit entryway. Their ears, though, had no trouble picking up the first movement of Gabriel Fauré's "Requiem" being piped through invisible speakers. Both focused their gaze on the receptionist's desk, left unattended except for two unlit candles. Just as Malcolm was about to step forward and peer around the counter, a middle-aged man emerged from a darkened side hallway.

"Greetin's," he said, extending an open right hand to Malcolm. "Are ye wi' the McAlonan family?"

"A friend o' John, yes," said Malcolm. "This is his daughter Kathleen."

"Welcome," said their host. "Ah am Mr. Sloan. Please accept ma deepest condolences on yer loss."

"Thank you," said Kate. "And thank you for meeting with us on such short notice."

"Na' at all. We're heer tae serve," he said. "May Ah invite ye tae join me in ma study? We can speak privately theer."

Kate and Malcolm followed Sloan toward the light that filled the open door at the end of the hallway. Along the way, they couldn't help but notice the traditional religious icons that adorned the otherwise drab walls: celtic crosses, a montage of Madonnas, a collection of crucifixes and a trove of trinity knots—the latter transporting Kate back to the mortuary, when she held her father's right hand and spotted his Irish wedding ring. The surprise connection nudged Kate slightly off her stride, causing Malcolm—who was following closely behind—to nearly stumble into her.

"Oh for fuck sake," he said, softly but distinctly. "Sorry father, please excuse my rough language."

"Oh, Ah'm na' a priest," said Sloan. "Truth be told, Ah'm

not even a Christian."

"Really!? But then wha's wi' all o' this?" asked Malcolm, gesturing to the walls.

"Target marketin'," said Sloan. "One must cater tae one's customers, doesn't one?"

"Uh, aye, Ah guess one does," said Malcolm. "Just ne'er thought aboot it like tha'. A' least na' for yer line o' work."

"So if you're not a Christian, what do you believe in?" asked Kate.

"Reincarnation," said Sloan.

"So you're a Buddist?" responded Kate.

"Moor o' a capitalist, tae be honest," said Sloan, matter of factly. "Referral business is great. But repeat business? E'en better."

"Wow," said Kate.

"Wow indeed," added Malcolm.

Once within Sloan's inner sanctum, the funeral director settled into the overstuffed leather seat behind his desk and directed Kate and Malcolm to occupy the pair of matching wooden chairs on the opposite side.

"First thin's first," said Sloan. "As ye've instructed, we took custody o' yer father's body an' transported it from the community hospital in Lochgilphead earlier this mornin'."

"So he's here now?" asked Kate.

"Aye," said Sloan. "Wha' happens next is entirely up tae ye. We will adhere tae yer wishes, wi'in the constraints o' Scottish law. Have ye had an opportunity tae think this through?"

"If you had asked me that question 10 hours ago, I would

have said no," replied Kate. "But some things my dad said, or at least was quoted as saying by his newspaper, have convinced me that this part of the world—not San Francisco—is his true home. As such, I believe it should be his final resting place."

"So ye wanne be transportin' the body back tae America?" asked Sloan.

"No," said Kate.

"Tha' makes a difficult task a wee bit easier then," said Sloan, as he opened a desk drawer and extracted some paperwork. "But theer are still many details tha' we'll need tae sort oot. The most important: Wha' would ye like us tae dae wi' the body?"

"What are the options?" asked Kate.

"Two basically. We can prepare it for internment. Or we can arrange for cremation."

Kate hesitated. It wasn't that she didn't know which way to turn. It's more that she wasn't fully prepared for the arrival of the moment—now spinning in front of her in sharp relief— during which she would be required to proceed.

"Kate, are ye OK?" Malcolm intervened.

"Yes," she replied. "It's just all so…final."

"Ye can have more tahm, if ye need it," said Sloan. "Ah'm currently workin' wi' another family. Multiple siblin's. The deceased dinna make his wishes known in writin'. So his kin need tae make the call. An' they canne agree. I's been 30 days noo. At 100 pounds per day."

"Huh?" said Malcolm.

"For the refrigeration."

"Oh, right," said Malcolm. "The thin's ye dinna thin' aboot."

"Well, works for me," said Sloan. "But na so good for the deceased. Or his loved ones. Thankfully Miss McAlonan, in this case, the decision is entirely yers."

"Yes. I know," she said finally. "And I know what to do. Cremation. I'm certain that's what my dad would have wanted. Don't you think, Malcolm?"

"Aye, Ah dae," he said. "Ah know 'tis hard. But Ah agree. I's the right choice for John."

"Very well, then," said Sloan. "We'll just need tae walk through this form. Answer some questions. Sign some papers. Ma sons an' Ah can take care o' everythin' else."

"When?" said Kate, corralling her emotions.

"Taemorrow would be the earliest," said Sloan. "Since ye're stayin' neerba, we can personally deliver the ashes tae ye—in yer preferred container."

"That would be OK," said Kate. "I'll be at or around the clubhouse all day."

Kate held herself together while Sloan guided her through the process, as if he were a mortgage broker and she were applying for a loan. But later, when Malcolm cleared the outskirts of Campbeltown and put his foot into the Vauxhall's accelerator, salty precipitation filled her eyes—though there still wasn't a cloud in the sky.

A Yankee Doodlin' Dandy

Kate awoke bolt upright, a particularly exuberant outburst of Angish in the dining room below serving as a thoroughly effective human alarm clock. Six hours before, her plan had been to take a brief nap up in Margaret's flat while waiting for the guys to wrap up their morning round. Then, rejuvenated, she longed to join them on the course in the afternoon. But she overslept, regaining full consciousness only after the day's golf had ended and the evening's consumption had commenced.

"Oh for fuck sake," she blurted out, giving rise to a soft chuckle. Much to her surprise, this place and—more to the point—these people had started to get to her. And, stranger still, she no longer felt compelled to resist. Margaret had warned her that Machrihanish had a way of latching onto one's soul and not letting go. Now, Kate began to accept the fact that she, too, was destined to fall under its subtle yet powerful spell. It seemed inevitable. And given that, by doing so, she would follow in her father's footsteps, it also felt right.

Kate made herself presentable and descended the stairs, following her ears until she laid eyes on the assembled crew at the main table. Angus, true to form, was holding forth center stage. Gavin, Malcolm and Ewan were to his right. Bernard, Alister, and Donald huddled to his left.

"Ah, Kate!" said Angus. "Welcome tae Quiz Night! So glad ye coold join us."

"Quiz Night?" replied Kate, quizzically.

"Aye, yet another o' oor time-honored traditions. An' one o' yer father's personal favorites, Ah might add," said the full-bodied Scot.

"I's a popular pastime in the pubs an' on the telie ower heer," said Gavin. "So we've adopted the format for oor use."

"A bit o' fun," said Ewan.

"An' a guaranteed laugh," added Malcolm.

"Why don't ye join us?" implored Angus.

"Doubt I'd contribute much," said Kate.

"Oh, ye might be surprised," said Angus. "Ah've added a new category for the big finish, in honor o' yer da'."

"Well, in that case, I'll give it a go," said Kate.

"O dear, she's startin' tae talk like us," said Gavin.

"Brilliant!" said Angus.

The big man flipped a pound coin to determine which

team would expand from three to four players. Alister, happily, pulled up an extra chair. As with the matches on the course that are decided hole by hole, the Quiz Night champion is determined question by question. Actually, more accurately, answer by answer. Angus, for reasons known only to him, chose a "Jeopardy"-like format where he reads an answer and the first team to raise a hand has a shot at pairing it with the appropriate question. Guess right and the team wins one point. Guess wrong and a point is deducted.

The two teams, though numerically unbalanced, proved to be evenly matched through the initial rounds, perhaps because topics such as Premier League football, world geography, British royalty and Scottish-English skirmishes through the ages fell well outside Kate's worldview. But when Angus announced that the fifth round would be devoted to Kintyre trivia, there was at least the possibility she could chime in. She'd learned a lot in just three days, or so it seemed.

"Ah'm callin' this category, 'Wha's in a Nemme?'" said Angus. "Each answer makes reference tae a specific feature o' oor li'l slice o' heaven. Heer we go then. First answer: 'Moby motor. Gun garrison. Ominous opener.'"

"Ye've git tae be kiddin' me," said Malcolm. "Ye're speakin' in riddles."

"Perhaps," said Angus. "But 'tis all theer for any o' ye tae figure oot."

An uneasy silence settled on the room. Then Bernard, out of character, began waving his hand excitedly.

"Ah've got this one," he said. "''Wha' is a battery?'"

"Ye are correct, sir," said Angus.

"A battery?" said Malcolm. "How dae ye figure?"

"A battery powers a mobile phone," said Bernard. "In battle, battery is another word for a stash o' arms. An' the 1st hole, the ominous opener, is called Battery."

"Ugh!" groaned Malcolm.

"Spot on, Monkey Boy," said Angus. "Let's proceed tae the next clue: 'Accommodation appendages.'"

"Wha'? Can ye say tha' again?" asked Donald.

"Aye," said Angus. "'Accommodation appendages.'"

"Oh wait, Ah've got this one!" said Gavin. "'Wha' is the Ugadale Arms?'"

"Bingo, Fauntluhroo," said Angus.

"Oh my, Ravi," said Alister. "Ah dae believe tha's yer most groan-inducin' pun yet."

"Like so many true artists, ma genius goes unappreciated among ma own clan," said Angus. "Nevertheless, Ah press on. Next answer: 'First stop north o' Northern Ireland.'"

Alister immediately raised his hand.

"Tha's an easy one: 'Wha' is South End?'" he said.

"A knock for the Doc," said Angus.

"Hey, wait a minute, are you saying we're close to Northern Ireland?" asked Kate.

"Aye, a mere 25 miles, as the oyster catcher flies," said Angus. "For us earthbound creatures, there's a ferry from Campbeltown to Ballycastle in County Antrim. Will git ye there in well under two hours."

"Amazing," said Kate. "My dad's family was originally from

County Antrim. Maybe I should drop by and say hello."

"It coold be arranged," said Angus. "At minimum, weather permittin', ye shoold catch a glimpse o' the Irish coast on Friday. We make a field trip on oor last day o' the week tae South End tae play Dunaverty, arguably the most entertainin' coorse under 5,000 yards on the planet. A true hidden gem."

"And here I thought it was all about Machrihanish," said Kate.

"I's the main coorse, make nae mistake," said Angus. "Think o' Dunaverty as the after-dinner sweet. But we must continue wi' oor wee contest. Next clue: 'The wee course an' Peters.'"

Bernard jumped in.

"Clearly, Ravi, retirement has left ye wi' way too much tahm on yer hands," he said. Ah believe the question is, 'Wha' are Pans?'"

This time everyone, save Kate, groaned.

"The Pans?" she said.

"Aye," said Alister. "The 9-holer Ah pointed oot tae ye on the drive in is officially known as the Pans Course. Ah'm sure ye can sort oot the other reference."

Now Kate groaned, causing the men—including Angus— to laugh.

"OK, one more for 'Wha's in a Nemme?'" said Angus. "Heer we go: 'I's English for Machrihanish.'"

Angus let the ensuing hush linger, but only for a few seconds.

"Stumped ye this tahm, noo dinna Ah?" he said.

Then Malcolm, defiantly, raised his hand.

"Na' so fast, Big Man," he said. "Ah believe the question ye ha'e in mind is, 'Wha' is plain o' whispers?'"

"How in heaven's nemme did ye come up wi' tha' one, X-man?" said Angus.

"The Internet strikes again!" said Malcolm.

"Talk aboot havin' too much tahm on yer hands," said Angus.

"Hold on, did you say, 'plain of whispers'?" said Kate.

"Aye," said Malcolm. "Tha's what Machrihanish means, when ye translate the gaelic intae oor mother tongue."

"Well, I can vouch for that," said Kate.

"Say wha'?" said Malcolm.

"My first morning here, thanks to jet lag, I woke up very early—while you were all still sleeping. So I decided to walk the course. Somewhere along the 3rd fairway, I heard something. Sort of human-like, as I remember it. But I was the only one out there."

"Ye heard a voice?" asked Angus.

"Maybe. Barely a whisper, really. I don't know," said Kate. "Not sure why I'm telling you guys this. Probably think I'm crazy."

"Aye, but ye've got plenty o' company," said Malcolm. "If we're honest, we've all had oor moments oot theer on the links. Experiences we canne explain."

"What are you saying, that Machrihanish is haunted?" said Kate.

"Haunted? Nae," said Angus. "But theer's definitely more tae those dunes than sand an' fescue. Ah think we can all agree on tha'."

"Indeed," said Alister. "An' Ah'm a man o' science."

"An' whate'er tha' mystical *it* is, it canne be described," said Bernard. "An' Ah'm a man o' words."

"Consider yersel' fortunate," said Gavin. "It took most o' us yeers tae see past the surface. Ye caught a glimpse o' the old gurl's true wonders yer first tahm oot. She must have taken a likin' to ye."

"The course is a woman? Not sure I'm ready to go that far," said Kate. "But if I were to get all 'X Files' on you, which really isn't my thing, I'd be more inclined to believe my dad had something to do with it."

"Noo theer's a fascinatin' theory," said Donald, in his trademark bolt-out-of-the-blue fashion. "Perhaps his bein' is in one o' the multiverses Ah've been readin' aboot an' we're in another one. An' the two intersect in some way on the links."

"Oh Gawd help me," said Angus. "Ah dae we believe we are in danger o' fallin' headlong doon the rabbit hole."

"Did ye say hole, Angus? A worm hole?" said Donald. "Tha's another possible explanation."

"Back tae yer Scotch, Don-Don," said Angus. "An' tahm for us tae git back tae oor game."

"I agree," said Kate. "Starting to wish I'd kept the whole whispers business to myself. Probably just sleep deprivation. Or dehydration. Or something."

"If ye say so," said Malcolm with a twinkle in his eye.

"Enough already," said Angus. "Final round. An' given the close scorin', it will definitely determine this year's champion. In honor o' Mac, Ah'm callin' it, 'A Yankee Doodlin' Dandy.'"

"Nicely phrased, Angus," said Kate. "Hopefully now I'll have a shot."

"Somethin' tells me ye'll git this first one," said Angus. "'His merriest month an' nom de Kate.'"

Kate's hand shot up.

"'What is May?'" she said. "Grandma Mac and I share the same middle name."

"We have a winner!" said Angus.

"Talk aboot a gimme. We ha' nae chance on tha' one," said Malcolm. "She's goin' tae run the table on us."

"We'll see aboot tha'," said Angus. "Next clue: 'His one an' only hole-in-one hole.'"

"Ah witnessed it," said Ewan without hesitation. "'Wha' is the 4th?'"

"Right ye are Roy Boy," said Angus.

"My dad had a hole-in-one?" said Kate. "He never mentioned it."

"Perhaps because o' the questionable circumstances," said Ewan. "He flat out sculled a wedge. He was so busy cursin', he almost dinna see his ball hit the bank just above the front bunker, jump aboot 10 feet intae the air an' slam dunk right intae the heart o' the hole, rattlin' the flagstick. Na' exactly picture perfect."

"Aye, but it still counts," said Angus.

"Well, I'm glad he got at least one ace," said Kate. "I mean, imagine playing golf your whole life and never experiencing a hole-in-one."

"Nae need for me tae imagine it," said Angus. "Ah'm livin'

it. Still waitin' for my moment o' glory. Back tae the game, though: 'His degree document an' Luke Donald's.'"

Kate raised her hand again.

"This one he did talk about," she said. "'What is a Northwestern diploma?'"

"Yep," said Angus. "The only thin' Mac had in common with the one-time woorld's No.1 player, Ah might add. OK, boys an' gurl, the score is noo tied an' we have just two moor clues tae go."

"Oh, the pressure!" joked Malcolm.

"Well, one o' ye jammy bastards gave this one away on Monday," said Angus. "But Ah decided tae keep it in the quiz, just tae see if any of ye eejits was payin' attention. Heer 'tis: 'His first-time tally on the 16th.'"

"Ooo, ooo!" shrieked Bernard. "14!"

"I'm sorry, Monkey Boy," said Angus. "Must be in the form of a question."

All four of the opposing players raised their hands. Angus rose to his feet and, like a conductor leading an orchestra, cued them to respond.

"What is 14?" they practically sung in unison.

"Oh the humanity!" replied Bernard.

"It all comes doon tae this, then," said Angus. "One last shot. Are ye ready?"

"Aye," pleaded Malclom. "Le's be done wi' it."

"Very well," said Angus. "For all the marbles, here ye go: 'His hometown an' wedge-maker Roger's surname.'"

All eyes turned to Kate who, calmly, stood up to deliver the deciding blow: "What is Cleveland?" she said.

"Winner an' new champion!" said Angus. "Well done ye!"

"I'd like to thank the Academy, my agent and all of the little people," joked Kate. "So what's our prize?"

"For ye, Kathleen, 'tis tha' pint o' Guinness Ah offered when we first met at the airport," said Angus.

"Man, that feels like a lifetime ago," said Kate. "I believe I am now fully ready to appreciate it. And I do believe it's time I tried my hand at links golf. Would it be OK if I joined you in the morning?"

"Nae, tha' woold na' be OK," deadpanned Angus.

"Huh?" said Kate, taken aback.

"It woold be bloody brilliant!" exclaimed the big man. "And it woold be oor honor."

"Oh Angus! Right back at you," said Kate.

"We head oot at 10," said Angus. "The Swedish dentists, Ah'm sorry tae report, beat us tae the punch for the early tee tahms."

"Sounds perfect to me," said Kate. "Will give me a chance to lay down a full Scottish beforehand. Do this thing right. Who knows? Maybe I'll even eat the blood pudding!"

"I dinna know wha' ye did wi' the old Kate, but Ah dinna care," said Angus, as he handed her a pint of the sudsy stout, freshly drawn by a beaming Margaret. "Yer transformation is noo nearly complete."

"Well then, this ought to finish me off," said Kate, lifting the glass to take a gulp, a golden brown mustache forming on her upper lip. "Yum!"

Guard Down, Truth In

Kate pulled back the blind on her room's dormered window and assessed the damage. She'd drifted in and out of a shallow sleep, in part excited to play her first round of links golf but even more so due to the fierce storms that had strafed the seaside enclave throughout the night.

"Really?" she said to herself as her eyes scanned the general dreariness. "Can't a girl catch a break?"

Shifting focus, Kate could hear Margaret puttering around in the kitchen down the hall. And she could smell the salty sweet aroma of bacon frying up in a pan. Her senses, by unanimous consent, decided to move in that direction.

"Guid mornin' love," said Margaret as Kate took a seat at

the table.

"You call this good?" said Kate. "Once again, larger forces have conspired against me. I really wanted to play golf today."

"Please dinna tell me ye've been on yer email again," said her hostess. "Another New York meltdoon?"

"Nope. I'm intentionally ignorant on that front. As far the office is concerned, I'm off the grid," said Kate. "I meant the weather. Can't imagine we'll play in this."

"Oh, 'twill take moor than a few sprinkles tae keep these lads from theer appointed roonds," said Margaret. "Unless conditions take a decided toorn for the woorse, an' tha's na' in the forecast, the gemme will still be on. Ye'd best ready yersel'."

"No kidding?" said Kate, craning her neck to reassess the view from the kitchen window. "I stand or, more accurately, sit corrected. Guess it's all part of the adventure then."

"Ah'm sure ye'll find everythin' ye need in yer father's gowf bag, includin' waterproofs an' rain gloves," said Margaret. "He seemed tae thrive on blustery conditions. The guys always said he was a guid mudder."

Fortified (including the blood pudding) and armored (in Gore-Tex, that is), Kate made the short walk from the clubhouse to the pro shop where she found the seven Scots holed up inside for warmth.

"See, Ah knew she'd make it," said Malcolm. "Ye owe me a pound, Ewan."

"Ah shooldn't ha'e doubted ye, Kate," said the big redhead. "Guid mornin'."

"Well, it's definitely morning, I'll give you that," said Kate.

"Once Margaret assured me you guys would play, I wasn't about to let you, or myself, down. Or, more to the point, I wasn't about to give Angus an opening."

"Ye're definitely gettin' the hang o' this," said Gavin. "Though Ah should warn ye, nae matter wha' ye dae or dinna dae, Angus will find a way tae insert his needle. Ye can count on tha'."

"Why Gavin, Ah dae believe tha's the nicest thin' ye've ever said aboot me," said Angus. "But na' tae worry Kate. Given tha' this is yer first tahm, Ah promise tae be a perfect gentleman— oor at least tae make every effort."

"No need to hold back on my account," said Kate. "After all I've been through this week, I'm ready for whatever Machrihanish has in store. Bring it on!"

"If ye insist," said Angus, just as a gust of wind whistled around the humble hovel.

"Oh my," said Kate.

"Indeed. Be careful wha' ye ask for, ma deer," said Angus. "OK, heer's the plan: We've got two fourba's on the docket. First off are Ewan, Donald, Gavin an' Alister. Kate, ye an' Ah, along wi' Bernard an' Malcolm, will follow. As always, everyone tosses in a quid for the best individual Stableford scoore. Gemmes wi'in yer group are up tae ye. Taeday's overridin' objective: survival."

"Come on boys," said Gavin. "Nae point in delayin' the inevitable."

The banker pushed hard against the pro shop door, then held it open as his playing partners trudged by. A haphazard metallic clanging sound—produced by the wind and the fasteners that secured the still half-mast Scottish flag to its halyard—added a percussive accompaniment to their steps. Through the window overlooking the first tee, the players still inside the pro shop watched as the wind whipped the waves into an angry froth—a stark contrast to the steaming hot cappuccinos Margaret served in the cozy clubhouse just across the B843.

As the first four combatants struggled to tee up their balls and whack them over the beach and onto the turf, Kate gathered herself—much in the same way, when seated in a client's lobby, she would prepare to make a new business pitch. It's just that in this moment and on this foreign soil, she had no past experience to fall back on.

After all, golf in Los Angeles is rarely influenced by weather, unless you count triple-digit temperatures or oppressively thick layers of smog. Rain of any amount, a rarity, shuts the whole operation down, much in the same way an inch of snow paralyzes ill-prepared southern U.S. cities such as Atlanta or Dallas. Santa Ana winds, that sweep off California's blistering inland deserts, can be troublesome. But at least the players who brave those torrid blasts can count on ample warmth to minimize their clothing and maximize their movement. In Scotland though? On a bleak day in May? Golf in wind, rain *and* cold? Try as she might, Kate failed to see the upside.

"All four are safely away noo," said Angus. "Tahm for us tae follow."

Kate gave the lid of her dad's Olympic Club cap a tug to shield her eyes and followed closely in Angus' wake, employing his generous girth as a windshield. Then she shouldered her father's already sodden golf bag and lugged it a few steps, setting it down next to the members' yellow marker. Though a woman, she never plays from the forward tees in the States. No point in starting now.

Angus, in character, went first and—perhaps slowed by the multiple layers of apparel—managed to stripe his ball down the center of the fairway. As Bernard and Malcolm followed, Kate quietly dug through the pockets of her father's golf bag in search of a few tees, a Cleveland Indians Chief Wahoo ball marker and—of course—a golf ball. To her surprise, he played Titleist Pro V1s. That was her brand of choice, too.

"On ye go then, Kate," encouraged Angus. "Since ye've walked this hole, nae need for me tae show ye show the way."

"I've hit this drive in my mind a thousand times, thanks to that photo above my dad's desk," she said. "But I never imagined it in conditions like this."

"Nothin' tae lose," said Malcolm. "Just dae yer best."

With the exception of her dad's PeeWee 3-iron, only six days had passed since she'd swung a club, at that muni with Joe on a carefree Friday afternoon in L.A. But given all that had transpired since, that round of golf felt like a lifetime ago.

"Let's see if I can remember how do this," she said, as much to herself as her playing partners.

Kate teed up a ball then attempted a few practice swings, feeling her body turn and muscles stretch underneath her father's rain suit. His rain gloves, already soaked, kept a firm hold on the rubber grip. That's helpful. But she couldn't detect much feeling between her hands and the club. That's not. Muscle memory would have to fill the gaps.

As she took her stance, a steady flow of raindrops dribbled off the lid of her cap, partially obscuring her view of the tiny dimpled orb that oscillated precariously on its wooden peg down below. Out of habit, Kate swiveled her head to the left to fix the target in her mind. But with the 1st hole swathed in fog, there really wasn't much to see.

"Hit and hope," she thought, just as she started into her motion. The rest was largely a blur. Kate recalled making contact with the ball. And she was able to track its initial flight path along her intended target line. But then a splash of wind-aided rain filled her eyes, forcing her to look away.

"Well done, Kate!" said Angus. "Our ba's are nearly side ba side."

"Really!?" said Kate. "It seemed about right. But I lost sight of it."

"Aye," said Bernard. "The University o' Machrihanish is noo officially in session."

"Ye've done yer da' proud," said Malcolm.

"Well alright then," she said. "Let's do this."

Kate lashed her dad's double loop bag to her body with an extra dose of deliberation, allowing the men to get a head start as they made their way gingerly down the rain-slicked slope from the 1st hole's tee to its fairway. Like her father's relationship with single malt, she was slowly but surely acquiring a fondness for their company. But as this inaugural round began, she longed for a bit of space—and a bit of time—to let the experience linger, free from commentary.

"So this is the game my dad loved to play?" she thought to herself as she followed in their footsteps. "Seems like such a hard way to go. Still, there's gotta be something to it. I'm willing to be wowed."

As it turned out, Kate had ample opportunity to take it all in. Malcolm had pulled his drive onto the beach and Bernard had blocked his to the right, the soggy rough grabbing hold of his ball well short of the nefarious pot bunkers. So when it came to the second shots, she was third in the batting order. Angus, his ball having rolled just a few yards ahead of hers, would hit cleanup.

Back home, Kate would have raced from the tee to her ball in a motorized cart, focused entirely on the next shot, letting everything in between zip on by. But here, the walking—especially against the wind—slowed the pace and helped her stay, well, fully grounded. So while only a few minutes had elapsed and only two hundred yards had been traversed, she was fully immersed in this fescue-and-marram-blanketed world. The fragments of reality that weren't Machrihanish had already fallen away.

As such, when it was her turn to play, Kate was calm. Restoratively so. For the past six days, she had been lashed against her will to an emotional roller coaster that tossed her to and fro, relenting just enough to tease her with a moment of respite before hurtling, once again, in an unanticipated direction.

But once she'd set foot on Old Tom's linksland, the

turbulence—suddenly yet softly—had ceased. Yeah, sure, Mother Nature still packed a punch. But those blows, even when they landed, were at most skin deep. At the level of the soul, Kate nestled into a state of serenity—somewhat akin to what she'd experienced during her walkabout on Tuesday. Just as then, she hadn't seen it coming. And she certainly hadn't done anything to bring it about. Like a mountain climber who—after a long and arduous journey—is exhausted yet also exhilarated upon attaining the summit, Kate simply leaned into Machrihanish, allowing the larger-than-life linksland to engulf her in its strong and steadfast embrace.

In that surrender, her true self—not the false self that had railed for so long against her life's injustices, both real and perceived—was set free. And, like a genie let loose from a centuries-old bottle, it was chomping at the bit to have some fun.

"Still roughly 200 yards oot from heer, plus the wind," said Angus. "Give it all ye got."

Kate struggled to spot the pin, not that it mattered. From this distance, she simply aimed for the center of the green and pulled the trigger after just a mere flicker of indecision. This time, her ball and her 3 wood's sweet spot achieved perfect alignment. An instant later, while the Titleist was still gaining altitude, she knew it would find its mark.

"Boy did that feel good!" she said.

"Ah should say so," said Angus, as Kate's ball bounced smartly through the run-up area and onto the putting surface. "Ye sure ye dinna sneak oot heer when we weren't lookin'?"

"Beginner's luck," said Kate out loud. But internally? "I am locked in today. Just put it in cruise control and enjoy the ride."

Angus, a bit flustered, botched his approach and opened with a bogey. Bernard and Malcolm bunted their balls back in play and wound up with matching 6s. But Kate? She narrowly missed her birdie putt, settling for a tap-in par.

"Gotta love this linksy golf," she said playfully.

Kate led the group to the second tee with a spring in her step. From her early morning walkabout, she remembered that a watery burn crossed the fairway about 230 yards out. She set down her bag and rested a hand on her father's 3-wood.

"Given yer distance, this woold normally be a lay-up hole," said Malcolm, offering some unsolicited advice. "But in this wind, even Ah hit driver."

"Got it," said Kate, pulling the big stick instead. Moments later her ball came to rest dead center of the fairway about 15 yards short of the hazard.

"Perfecto," said Angus. "Guid thing Ah dinna engage in a little side bet. Your da' always said ye had a guid gemme."

"Thanks Ravi," said Kate, for the first time opting for Angus' official nickname. "Truth be told, I'm as surprised as you are."

"Ye really are yer father's daughter, aren't ye?" said Bernard. "The blusterier the conditions, the better he played."

Then the scribe, perhaps overcorrecting for his blocked tee shot on the 1st, proceeded to pull hook this attempt dangerously close to the white OB markers on the left. Angus and Malcolm, perhaps influenced by Bernard's flirtation with a stroke-and-distance penalty, pushed their drives into the heavy stuff on the right.

"The fairway is all yers, m'lady," said Angus. "We'll see ye at the green, hopefully ba nightfall."

Kate strode confidently to her ball. But that self-assuredness slowly dissipated as she sized up her second shot. She knew the green rested atop the tall dune dead ahead. But neither the putting surface nor the flag were in view. An aiming post at the crest of the hill, though, did offer some guidance for line. But yardage? With her playing partners otherwise occupied along the hole's periphery, Kate would just have to figure that out for herself.

"8-iron, I guess?" she said softly. "Oh, what the heck."

Kate, luxuriating in a state of relaxed concentration, struck the ball flush and watched with fascination as it soared high and true, seeming to pierce the cloud bank directly over the red-and-white post. The shot felt right. But she'd need to scale the dune to find out if it *was* right.

"A little links drama," her internal monologue continued. "This is kinda fun."

"Ah think ye're goin' tae like tha' one," said Angus, catching up to her as they crossed the footbridge that spans the burn.

"Well, I certainly enjoyed hitting it," she said, tacking into a gust of wind.

"Ye know Kate, theer's a guid chance tha' Monkey Boy an' ye are goin' tae have the X-man an' me two-down after just two holes. And, strangely enough, Ah'm OK with tha'," said Angus. "Ah really want ye tae have a guid experience oot heer.

Ah know yer da' woold have wanted it tha' way."

"Well, so far so good," she said. "I know I've just begun. But it feels like I've been playing this golf course forever. Weird."

"Want tae know somethin' even weirder?" said Angus.

"Fire away."

"Yer father said almost exactly the same thin' durin' his first tahm aroond Machrihanish."

"Hmmm, maybe Mr. Sloan was right," said Kate.

"The funeral director? Aboot wha'?"

"He believes in reincarnation," she said with a wink.

"Guid Lord!" said Angus as he nearly crashed his trolley into one of the two put bunkers cut into the face of Machairinnean's massive dune.

Angus' prediction proved accurate: Kate's two-putt par bettered Malcolm's scrambling bogey, giving the writing partners the early lead. The laborer managed to stop the bleeding on Islay (aka the 3rd hole), securing a regulation par four to match Kate, who continued to cruise. But the newbie struck again on the short but devilish par three Jura, calmly rolling in a 20-foot putt for the deuce and a three-hole advantage.

"Ah might na' have much o' a gemme taeday," said Bernard, "but Ah surely have one heckuva partner. Kate, did ye realize ye're one-under par after four holes?"

"Really!?" she said. "I do now. To be honest, I haven't had the bandwidth to keep track of my score. I've been on sensory overload."

That changed one swing later, on Punch Bowl. As Kate prepared to attack the mischievous dogleg left with a 3-wood,

Bernard's commentary filled her head, displacing the blissful silence that had resided there since the start of the round. And the internal chatter, as is its wont, took its toll.

"Ugh!" groaned Kate as she watched her ball dive bomb hard, low and left into the cack.

"Sorry tae say, Kate, but ye might want tae reload," said Malcolm. "Na' sure we'll find tha' one."

Machrihanish giveth. But in the less than three seconds it takes to swing a golf club, it can also taketh away. Kate, though still absorbing the blow, regained enough composure to hit a serviceable back-up tee shot in the short stuff. But she had no intention of using it. The competitor within was hellbent on tracking down the first ball, blasting it out of the hay and somehow making a par to stay in red numbers.

The three gentlemen, in keeping with golf etiquette, silently joined her in the search—though, without saying a word, they all knew the effort would prove futile. A minute or two later, it dawned on Kate that Malcolm's uncertainty about her tee shot's outcome was actually his polite way of saying, "Ye can kiss tha' one guidba!" Given its wicked duck hook trajectory, Kate's ball was almost certainly buried deep in the calf-high rough. She'd probably have to step on it to find it. And even then, the lie would be unplayable.

But just as she was about to call off the bloodhounds, Kate felt a hardness through the sole of her father's waterproof Foot Joys.

"Maybe," whispered Kate, as she dug into the thicket of marram grass underfoot. Moments later, she extracted a Titleist

Pro V1 and held it up against the still roiling sky, rotating the ball to and fro between her right thumb and index finger, examining its markings. "Unbelievable!"

"Ye found yer ba'!?" asked Angus incredulously.

"Close, but not exactly," she responded. "This is a Titleist 1. I'm playing a Titleist 3. But look here."

Angus moved closer.

"That's my dad's imprint," said Kate. "See, in red: 'Wee Mac Mon.'"

"Well, if tha' dinna beat all!" said Angus. "Ah gave him tha' nickname, in honor of Ben Hogan. He's known in these parts as the Wee Ice Mon."

"Yeah, my dad told me the story. The 1953 Open at Carnoustie, right?"

"Tha's the one. Hogan's only appearance ower heer. He marched methodically tae victory, havin' already won the Masters an' U.S. Open tha' year. No one afore or since—na' Bobby, na' Jack, na' Tiger—has equaled it."

"Well, this ball might not be the Claret jug, but it means just as much to me. It's making the journey home, that's for sure," said Kate as she slipped the rare find into the left pocket of her father's rain paints.

And just like that, Kate's fierce competitive drive—unleashed when Bernard's innocent comment shifted her focus from being in the moment to posting a score—scurried back into the cage that had contained it through the first four holes.

Those of a spiritual bent would have called it an epiphany. The skeptics? Merely the recognition of a moment that, for whatever reason, had separated itself from the rest. But for Kate? In the instant she found her father's ball, she knew this round was never meant to be about a number—whether it be her medal score or even the outcome of the match. Rather, it was about following in her father's footsteps, at times quite literally. And by so doing, it was about finding her way forward—not just along this tumultuous terrain, but to whatever awaited her in the wide world beyond.

So that became Kate's mission over the remainder of this journey within the journey, this game within the game: to let her guard down and, just as crucially, to let the truth in.

Simultaneously, the match continued. Bernard's perfectly executed bump-and-run shot off the right side of the 5th hole's green set up a winning par, pushing the margin to four-up. At Balaclava, the wind relented—an early sign of a change in the weather—and Malcolm took advantage of it, nearly driving the green en route to a birdie that narrowed the divide to three. At the 7th, the ever-ominous Bruach More, Angus rose to the occasion, puring a hybrid to find the blind green 190 yards away. Two putts later and the margin was back to two. Kate, who had been floating along stress-free since the pull hook at the 5th, appeared to claim the honors at the 8th, coaxing her 9-iron approach to a stop just six feet below the hole on Gigha's fully exposed dune-top green. But before she could convert her birdie, Malcolm holed out from the front right greenside bunker—the shot of the round, it would turn out.

"The X-man striketh!" said Kate, who in her Zen-like state didn't begrudge Malcolm's good fortune. "But I do believe I'm going to strike back." And she did, draining the putt for the halve.

The quality of the play was clearly on the upswing and, as the four made the longish hike to the 9th tee, so were the conditions. The rain had subsided. The wind had downshifted to no more than a zephyr. And the sky, though still overcast, was brightening.

"Guid news, Kate," said Angus. "Ah dae believe the worst is behind us. Shoold be smooth sailin' on oor way back tae the clubhoose."

"Smooth like that ferry ride to Dunoon?" said Kate lightheartedly. "I'm not going to fall for that one again."

"Point taken," said Angus. "Bad form o' me tae even say such a thin'."

"Aye, ye've jinxed us for sure noo," said Malcolm.

Upon arrival at Ranachan's tee box, nearly the furthest point out on the course, the players parked their bags and removed their rain jackets. Bernard glanced back at the 8th green to confirm that, essentially, they had the course to themselves. Then he approached Kate.

"Theer's somethin' heer Ah think ye shoold see," he said. "It will only take a minute. Follow me."

Kate, in an agreeable mood, did as she was instructed, tracing Bernard's steps along a footpath worn into the steep dune that bracketed the back of the tee. Then they cleared the crest, revealing the view.

"Oh my!" said Kate as she took in the vast expanse of beach along Machrihanish Bay, leading all the way back to the first tee. Fortuitously, a few rays of sunshine managed to sneak through minute breaks in the dissipating clouds, illuminating the picture postcard setting.

"The other guys dinna know this, but this was yer father's favorite spot in all o' Machrihanish," said Bernard. "He told me tha' he'd come heer whene'er, as he put it, he 'needed tae thin' deep thoughts.' Seems rather certain tha' many o' those thoughts were aboot ye."

"It's breathtaking," said Kate. "Thank you for sharing this with me, Bernard. It means more than you know. Heck, more than I know."

"Ye're most welcome," said Bernard. "But we'd best git back tae our gemme before Angus an' Malcolm petition for a forfeit."

Kate remained in a blissful semi-trance the rest of the way around. Yes, she did fall even more deeply in love with the links, especially the one-of-a-kind 10th and the wildly wonderful 13th. She did hit many good shots, most notably a soft-drawing 5-wood to 12 feet on the long par three 11th. And the outcome of the match was still in the balance until Bernard chipped in for birdie at the 17th, closing out Angus and Malcolm three-and-one. But those mundane details paled in comparison to the overall transformative effect.

Simply put, the Kate who, after the final putt dropped, shook her playing partners' hands on the 18th green and began to make her way back to the clubhouse, was not the same Kate who stepped warily onto the first tee less than four hours before. The weather, in dramatic fashion, had changed. But so had Kate. Far more so.

Now, she knew why her father—once he'd stumbled upon this place and these people more than 20 years ago—was so adamant about returning each May to experience it and, more to the point, them again. In that knowing, she understood him in ways that went beyond words, beyond memories, beyond even the thin veil that separates this world and the next. And in that understanding, Kate reconnected with her core self—that happy, easygoing, fun-loving little girl who went into hiding that fateful Saturday morning so long ago, leaving a chocolate banana waffle, half eaten, on the plate in front of her.

"Enough," said Kate out loud as she spun around and took in the panorama. "Time to get on with my life. Time to simply…be."

Buon Divertimento!

Margaret, who'd spotted Kate as she crossed the B843, walked out to greet her, coincidentally meeting near "The Spot" in the car park.

"So, Ah see ye survived yer first tour o' Machrihanish," said the steward. "So glad the weather took a toorn for the better."

"Absolutely!" said a luminous Kate. "I couldn't have asked for more, especially after such a gloomy beginning. I mean, look at this, my dad's golf bag is completely dry."

"Aye, sometimes a wee wind can be a very useful thin'," said Margaret. "Feel free tae store everythin' up in yer room. Which brin's me tae the real reason Ah've abandoned ma post behind the bar: Mr. Sloan made his delivery while ye were oot wi' the boys."

"Oh, right," said Kate softly. "I'd almost forgotten about that."

"Ah took the liberty of placin' the package on yer bed. Dinna want ye tae come upon it unprepared."

"Thank you, Margaret. Always so thoughtful. But I'll be OK. I know now what needs to happen next."

Meanwhile, Angus returned his trolley to the pro shop and caught up with the two women as they conversed.

"Ah believe these belong tae ye, Kate," he said, handing her three pound coins. "Ye an' Monkey Boy swept us—the outward nine, the inward nine an' the 18. Well played, young lady."

"Ma guidness, Ah wish Ah had ma camera," said Margaret. "The big man is payin' up, an' wi'out the slightest hint o' arm twistin' nae less!"

"So we won?" said Kate. "To be perfectly honest, I kind of lost track. There was a lot going on out there."

"Aye," said Angus. "Theer's moor tae the old gurl than meets the eye, an' tha's sayin' somethin' given the views."

"What say we put these nuggets back into circulation?" said Kate. "Can I buy you a beer, Angus?"

"Ah'd love tae accept," said the Glaswegian. "But perhaps we coold put tha' on hold until we gather in the clubhoose in a wee bit. I's Music Night, dae ye know?"

"Music Night?" said Kate. "What do you have up your sleeve this time?"

"Craig McMillan, a local one-man band, is settin' up inside

as we speak. He'll git the party started wi' a few ditties on his keyboard, accordion an' whate'er instrument strikes his fancy. Then, once the bevvies have begun tae take hold, everyone steps up tae the mike for a go at karaoke."

"Oh my god!" said Kate in a panic. "Everyone?"

"Aye, well nearly. Don-Don usually begs off, when he's na' threatenin' tae lay a heapin' helpin' o' Robert Burns poetry on us. Ah sincerely hope ye'll join in, though."

"Oh, I wouldn't miss this for the world!" said Kate. "As an observer that is, not a participant."

"We'll just ha'e tae see aboot tha'," said Angus with a grin as he began to make his way in the general direction of the Ugadale.

Kate took that as her cue to return to Margaret's flat. She peeled off her father's still-damp golf shoes at the base of the stairs and hung his rain suit on the coat stand that stood guard at the top. Then she proceeded warily to her room, taking care not to bash her dad's golf bag into the walls until she'd propped it securely against the far corner. From there, she had no choice but to turn around and make eye contact with the silver metallic canister that, as Margaret had forewarned, rested unassumingly on the center of the comforter draped over the small bed. A letter-sized manila envelope—containing her father's wedding ring, Kate surmised—lay alongside it.

For the first time since Monday, Kate and her father's physical remains shared the same room. But this time, there was no audible gasp, no loss of conscious control. If pressed, Kate would admit to a slight quickening of her pulse and a barely perceptible shallowing of her breath. But this was a decidedly different encounter than that at the mortuary.

Kate knew, with a stark finality, that the ashes inside this sterile container were all that was left of her father's body. But she also knew, having just spent the past four hours on the linksland communing with his spirit, that the body was not the man. In the six days since he'd died, the two had been rent asunder. She could feel it. And just as assuredly, she knew there was only one way to repair the breach.

But that could wait until tomorrow. For now, she had more urgent tasks to attend to: the taking of a long hot shower, the changing into dry, warm clothes and—if she could muster the courage, aided by enough single malt—the singing of a song. Life, in all its transcendence and triviality, went on.

By the time Kate checked off the first two items on her to-do list and descended the stairs, the joint was already jumping. As Angus had promised, Craig was cranking up the crowd—supplemented by dozens of locals and a gaggle of dumbfounded Swedish dentists—with his accordion, powering through an up-tempo traditional Scottish jig. Many, including Donald, clapped in time and a few, most vociferously Angus, hooted and hollered. Music in these parts, Kate quickly deduced, was a full contact sport.

As Craig downshifted to a mellow pop song, Kate made her way to the bar where Margaret was doing a brisk business.

"Guid evenin', love," said the Steward. "Oh ma, ye look especially nice taenight!"

"Oh, thanks Margaret," said Kate. "This is the last of my

clean clothes. I severely under packed. Have been mixing and matching with my dad's stuff to somehow get through the week."

"Wish ye had said somethin' earlier," said Margaret. "Please help yersel' tae anythin' ye see in ma closet, but only if ye thin' ye can pull off the dowdy look!"

"I just might take you up on that, though I'm thinking tomorrow will be my last full day here," said Kate as she fidgeted with her father's ring that had taken up residence on her right index finger. "With Mr. Sloan's delivery, I've nearly fulfilled my reason for being here. As much as I'd love to stay on, I can't ask the office to cover for me forever."

"Ah understand," said Margaret. "But rest assured, we'll all be very sorry tae see ye go."

"Me, too, Margaret. Me, too."

Kate made eye contact with Angus, who'd saved a seat between him and Gavin. But before she could take a step in their direction, she felt a hand gently touch her arm.

"My excuse, Miss McAlonan," said Angelo. "I jussa wanna say *buonasera*."

"Angelo!" said Kate. "A very good evening to you, too. We missed you out there today."

"*Si,*" said the Italian. "I onna the wee course. Work onna things. Maybe we play *domani?*"

"Oh, I wish I could," said Kate. "But I promised the guys I'd join them at Dunaverty. Hoping to catch a glimpse of Ireland, my family's homeland."

"Ah, *si*, family. Buona. Your father say he go Ireland some day. But no chance."

"You seem to have known my dad well."

"We talk, *si.*"

"Just wondering what you talked about, if you don't mind my asking."

"Well, I not say before, but your father tell me about Machrihanish. Whya I move here."

"What!? You met my dad *before* Scotland?"

"*Si.* We met Bandon Dunes."

"The golf resort in Oregon?"

"*Si.* I caddy there, for your dad. He like those links. But say Machrihanish *il migliore.*"

"Huh?"

"*Numero uno.* The best."

"Oh, right. But how did you get from Italy to Oregon? I bet that's one heckuva story.

"*Si.* Your father wanne write it. But no chance that, either."

"Would you be willing to roll the highlights for me? I'm really curious."

"Roll what?"

"Tell me your story. The short version."

"Oh, *capisco.* Well, I grow up on *vigneto.* How you say? A vineyard. My papa not owner. He dig dirt, care vines. So we poor. But happy. Then papa die. So I dig dirt. But like school. Make things. Invent wine cork. It screw into bottle. Screw out. But not, what you say, screw top. Not metal. Is cork. Real cork. Company buy idea. Give me money. *Molto.*"

"*Molto?*"

"A lot."

"Oh, got it."

"*Si*, so I try buy *vigneto* in Italy. Too much. Then I hear Oregon. New *vignetos*. Not too much. I go there. No good. No sell to me. They say, 'You a furriner.' So need job. See Bandon Dunes. Try caddy. Not play golf then. So study game. Watch players. Work on things. They givva me try. I do good. Then, I meet your father. I caddy for him."

"This is unbelievable," said Kate. "I mean, what are the odds?"

"He say Machrihanish better. So I come here. Live cheap. Like people. I stay. Play golf. Now? Never leave!"

"I understand that," said Kate. "What a story. I'll bet my dad would have told it well."

"*Si*," said Angelo. "I lika your father very much."

"Me, too," said Kate. "I'm sorry Angelo, but I'm just dying to ask you one more question."

"*Si*, is OK."

"That leather satchel. You always have it with you. I'm just really curious to know what's inside."

"Oh, my man purse?" said Angelo with a smile.

"*Si*," said Kate.

"OK, I say you," whispered Angelo. "But you not say guys."

"I can keep a secret," said Kate, leaning in.

"Issa my money. From cork invention. Keep safe."

"Oh my!" said Kate, a bit too loudly. "I'm sorry," she whispered, "but you might want to try a bank."

"My *nonno*, my papa's papa, he lose everything in bank.

Was 1930s. So my papa no trust bank. And I no trust bank."

"Well, do you trust Gavin?"

"*Si*, Mr. Gavin. He's gooda man."

"Then you might want to give him a try. He'll take care of you, I'm quite sure."

"Maybe. I think about it."

"OK, good. And I'm going to think about your story. Someone, maybe Bernard, needs to write it all down and share it with the world. Turn it into a screenplay. As Angus would say, it's brilliant! In the meantime, enjoy the music, Angelo. Time we had some fun."

"*Grazie*, Miss Kate," said Angelo. "*Buon divertimento!*"

Kate procured a Guinness from Margaret and then redirected her gaze toward Angus, its intended owner. But now there were two empty seats next to the big man. Gavin, to her surprise, was making his way to the stage.

"This should be interesting," said Kate as she handed Angus the fresh pint and settled into the chair next to him.

"Aye," said Angus. "Gavin is always the first man oot o' the gate in this wee frivolity. Inexplicably, it sets his alter ego free. Right as rain."

With that, Craig fired up the karaoke machine. And Gavin ignited the room.

"You can tell the world…you never was my girl…you can burn my clothes when I'm gone," belted the banker, doing a remarkably credible Billy Ray Cyrus impersonation. "Oh, you can tell your friends…just what a fool I've been, and laugh and joke about me on the phone."

Kate looked on, speechless. Gavin continued to croon.

"You can tell my arms…go back onto the farm, you can tell my feet to hit the floor. Or you can tell my lips…to tell my fingertips, they won't be reaching out for you no more."

Then the crowd joined in on the refrain:

"But don't tell my heart…my achy breaky heart, I just don't think he'd understand. And if you tell my heart, my achy breaky heart, he might blow up and kill this man."

"Aaaaoooooooooh!" howled Gavin.

"Oh my!" said Kate. "I didn't see that coming."

"He does it e'ery year," said Angus above the din.

"Well, I'm thinking he just lost Angelo as a customer," said Kate.

"Say again?" said Angus.

"Oh, never mind," said Kate.

After unleashing his last and lustiest howl, Gavin gave a bow to acknowledge the standing ovation, then made his way back to his seat amid a flurry of high-fives and fist-bumps.

"Well done, Gavin!" said Kate. "I'd never figured you for a natural born ham."

"Like tae keep the people guessin'," he replied. "As long as none o' ma coworkers at RBS e'er see it, Ah'm fine."

"Uh oh," said Kate. "Guess I shouldn't have been so hasty to upload the video to YouTube. Free Wi-Fi is a dangerous thing."

"Oh ma gawd!" said Gavin, the blood draining from his face. "Please tell me ye dinna."

"Oh, I'm sorry Gavin," said Kate. "Just joking with you. I'd never do such a thing. But Angus? One can never be sure."

"Na' tae worry, Fauntluhroo," said the big man. "Theer are some lines tha' even Ah won't cross."

Once Gavin had blazed the trail, his compatriots dutifully followed. Bernard was next with a heartfelt, though tone deaf, version of, "When I Fall in Love." Ewan, in keeping with his relative youth not to mention his search for the perfect golf swing, offered up U2's, "I Still Haven't Found What I'm Looking For." Alister, appropriately enough, went with Jackson Browne's, "Doctor My Eyes." And Angus and Malcolm wrapped up the set with a campy rendition of the Elton John and Kiki Dee duet, "Don't Go Breaking My Heart," the perfect end bracket to Gavin's opening salvo. It was quite the display—of what, exactly, Kate could not say. But she had to admire these middle-aged men's willingness to make complete fools of themselves, a card that, until she'd arrived at this most unlikely moment in her life, she had resolutely refused to play.

Kate also couldn't silence the little voice in her head that kept repeating, "Oh, what the hay?" So after downing the last of her snifter of Springbank, the once and former control freak cast her trepidation aside and made the long and lonely walk to the front of the room.

"Tha's oor Kate!" bellowed Angus in encouragement.

"Aye, indeed, ye go gurl!" echoed Malcolm.

Gavin fired off another Billy Ray howl. Bernard whistled. Ewan hooted. Even Donald joined in, clapping exuberantly.

"Oh geez," she thought to herself. "No turning back now."

Kate whispered her selection into Craig's ear who nodded in approval as he cued up the mechanism.

"My thanks and apologies to Stevie Nicks, in advance," she joked nervously as an anxious hush fell over the room. Then softly, slowly, the song's prelude gained momentum. It only took a few notes for the Scots to identify her selection.

"I took my love and I took it down," started Kate, timidly. "I climbed a mountain and I turned around. And I saw my reflection in the snow covered hills, till the landslide brought me down."

Kate gasped for air, then continued.

"Oh mirror in the sky, what is love?" she sang, a bit more forcefully. "Can the child within my heart rise above? Can I sail through the changin' ocean tides? Can I handle the seasons of my life? Mmmm, I don't know. Mmm, I don't know.

"Well I've been afraid of changin' cause I built my life around you," she continued. "But time makes you bolder, children get older. I'm gettin' older, too. I'm gettin' older, too."

Kate started to lose her composure during the instrumental interlude and the men knew it. But they, too, were falling prey to their pent up emotions and were powerless to offer much help. Kate, somehow, managed to steady herself and sing on.

"Well I've been afraid of changin' cause I built my life around you," Kate warbled. "But time makes you bolder, children get older. I'm gettin' older, too. I'm gettin' older, too.

"So, take this love, take it down. If you climb a mountain and you turn around. If you see my reflection in the snow covered hills, well the landslide will bring you down, down."

Then, adlibbing, "And if you see my reflection in the grass-covered dunes...well maybe, the rain storm will bring you down. Well, well the rain storm will bring you down."

The music stopped. For what felt like forever but was actually a mere second, no one reacted—until everyone in the room burst forth as one. And Kate, who had lost herself in the music, finally broke. Shoulders slumped. Knees buckled. Tears streamed. In a classic life-imitates-art moment, "Landslide" had brought *her* down.

The seven Scots rushed forward to surround her. Then Angus, looking over his shoulder, gave Craig a nod—and the one-man band knew exactly what that meant: Time for the evening's grand finale. Everyone else apparently sensed it, too, rising to their feet yet yielding to Craig. So the musician took the lead on the first verse, delivering his solo with great solemnity:

"Ba yon bonnie banks an' ba yon bonnie braes, wheer the sun shines bright on Loch Lomond, wheer me an' ma true love will ne'er meet again, on the bonnie, bonnie banks o' Loch Lomond."

But the audience, even the Swedish dentists, couldn't resist joining him on the refrain, with an equal measure of gravitas:

"Oh ye take the high road an' Ah'll take the low road, an' Ah'll be in Scotland afore ye. For me an' ma true love will ne'ei meet again on the bonnie, bonnie banks o' Loch Lomond."

Craig reassumed the reins on the second verse, once again with measured intensity. But as he led the crowd back into the refrain, he picked up the pace. Big time. And Kate, who had begun to rally, could hardly believe her eyes: the people had started to dance. Every last one of them. Donald included.

"What the hay," said the voice in her head once again. So Kate, her karaoke moment having purged what little remained of her conditioned restraint, joined in.

"Oh ye take the high road an' Ah'll take the low road, an' Ah'll be in Scotland afore ye," the assembled throng practically shouted. "For me an' ma true love will ne'er meet again on the bonnie, bonnie banks o' Loch Lomond."

And so they continued, wailing and waving, some swaying to and fro in their place, others engaging in what appeared to be military issue calisthenics, and still more—a large splinter group actually—forming a conga line that wound its way serpentine throughout the room. Before long, the mass of humanity's collective body heat had steamed up the clubhouse's picture windows, obscuring the ocean view. Everyone, even Kate, was all in.

It was sheer madness!

After at least a dozen such frenzied refrains, simple exhaustion began to take hold. So Craig improvised a stirring finish on his synthesizer that the crazed choir, in sync with his last note, punctuated with a unison yawp—followed by a full minute of hearty hand clapping and back slapping.

Kate was spent.

"Good heavens," she said. "What just happened here?"

"Release," said Angus, dripping in sweat. "I's na' tha' we Scots lack emotion. I's just tha' we rarely let it oot. But when we dae, all Ah canne say is, 'Duck an' cover!'"

"Aye, indeed," said Gavin, who had flopped into a vacant chair nearby. "But like Christmas, i' only comes once a year.

Oor dispositions need 364 days tae recover."

Kate, like the locals, was physically and emotionally drained. But she wasn't quite ready to call it a night. One more task remained. So she scanned the room in search of Bernard, and—once she had him in her sights—threaded her way in his direction amid the slowly thinning crowd. Soon, the pair engaged in what appeared to be a serious discussion. But neither spoke loudly enough for anyone else to hear, until the very end.

"Sounds perfect, Kate," said Bernard. "Consider it done."

I'm in the Painting

"Here, check this one out," said Kate as she handed her iPhone to Margaret across Machrihanish's bar, bathed in the Friday afternoon sunlight that poured through the clubhouse's west-facing windows. "Something tells me it's going to wind up on my PC's desktop back at the office."

"Glorious!" said the steward. "Ye cooldn't ha'e asked for a better day. An' theer's na' better place tae be on such a day than Dunaverty."

"Angus was right: a true hidden gem," said Kate. "I took that one from 11th tee, the highest point on the course. The landmass out in the distance, across the water: That's Northern Ireland. So close to home."

"Aye," said Margaret. "Perhaps 'tis na' just happenstance tha' yer father found his way heer, an' found it all so familiar. Perhaps if Ah traced ma' genealogy, Ah'd discover some distant relatives who passed this way, too. Woold explain a lot."

"All part o' the mystery," inserted Bernard as he loaded up a tray of bevvies for delivery to his friends who had gathered at their favorite round table in the adjacent alcove. "Speakin' of mysteries, Kate, Ah've shared yer plan wi' the lads. We're all wi' ye on this. An' we're ready tae proceed, whene'er ye are."

"Thanks, Bernard," said Kate. "Let's let it go a round or two here first. Give the sun a chance to set a wee bit more before we make the trek."

"Guid call," said Bernard. "The weather gods have taken kindly tae us, tha's for sure."

"Confirmation that we're doing the right thing," said Kate.

"Aye," said Bernard. "Cooldn't agree moor."

Kate, with Guinness in hand, joined the circle of Scottish men who, in a week's time, had become something less than a staunch "He-man Women Hater's Club." Make no mistake: Her time with them had altered her view of reality, irrevocably. But the reciprocal was also true. For the first time in the more than 20 years they'd been gathering at this spot each May, they had begun to imagine including a person of the female persuasion in their midst. Gloria Steinem would have been stunned, and heartened.

That development was easily trumped, however, by a far more base emotion: sadness. In part, certainly, its source was the tragic events that led off the week. But even more, their blue mood had to do with the simple fact that their time together was rapidly coming to a close and that another 51 weeks would need to pass before they'd get to reconvene. Their first few days had been excruciating, unfolding at a glacial pace. But their last few, especially once they'd found their way back on the course, had flown by—accelerating with each passing second.

"Ah canne believe 'tis Friday already," said Malcolm. "How is tha' possible?"

"Aye, afraid so, ma guid man," said Alister. "Another Machrihanish reunion has come an' is nearly gone."

"Back tae reality?" said Ewan. "Noo theer's a depressin' thought."

"So perhaps Ah'm na' the only one who suffers from PMS," said Angus.

"Angus! Lest ye forgit, theer's a lady present," said Bernard.

"Na' *tha'* PMS," said the big man.

"That's a relief!" joked Kate. "For a moment there, I was afraid that, somewhere in your murky past, you'd had a sex change operation."

"Noo theer's a scary thought!" said Malcolm.

"An' an e'en moor frightenin' mental image," added Ewan.

"Very funny, Miss MacAlonan," said Angus. "Nae, Ah'm talkin' aboot Post Machrihanish Syndrome. Ah dinna know aboot ye, but Ah dinna have the heart tae play gowf at ma home club after Ah git back from this trip. Parkland gowf, after gorgin' yersel' on links gowf, just dinna seem worth the effort."

"Ah hear ye, Ravi," said Gavin. "Ah strooggled wi' tha' mahsel', until Ah secured ma berth at Western Gailes. A wee bit o' a commute from the house, but worth e'ery minute o' it—if ye ask me."

"Aye," chimed in Bernard. "Once ye've tasted a fine wine, 'tis hard tae go back tae the bargain bottles."

"But the guid news is tha' PMS does eventually pass," said Angus.

"Same for my PMS, thankfully," said Kate playfully.

"Well, this strain usually sorts itsel' oot wi'in a few weeks, nae moor than a month. Eventually, Ah'm achin' tae git oot an' knock it aroond again—e'en if the coorse is landlocked an' tree-lined."

"I's still gowf," said Ewan. "An', when 'tis all said an' done, 'tis this infuriatin' gemme tha' keeps us goin' an' holds us taegither."

"I think I'm starting to get that," said Kate in earnest as she set down her pint. "Before I came here, golf was a challenge for me—just like all the others I've sought to conquer in my life. But, to be honest, it was entirely interchangeable with those other pursuits. I mean, I'd just assume run a 10K as play 18 holes. But now? When I think about my dad? I can see that there really is something more to this game. It's the one thing—or at least the most tangible thing—that binds me with him. And now, all of you are a very important part of that connection, too. So is this clubhouse and those dunes out there. I don't think I've ever felt closer to him—really understood him— than I do right now, right here, with you. I'm just so—what's the word?—grateful. I'm going to miss this, just like you must miss it when you're not here and giving each other a hard time.

But I also know there's a part of all this that will stay with me—deep down inside—forever. And no matter where I am in the world and no matter who I'm with, that inner core will be there. And I can tap into it, whenever I need to remember what I've learned here. And, more importantly, whenever I need to remember what my dad truly means to me."

Silence followed Kate's soliloquy. But unlike the anxious hesitations that had filled Gavin's Jaguar her first day in Scotland, this cessation of sound was enveloped in an aura of mutual understanding. She was one of them now. And without uttering a word, they knew their paths from this point forward would be interlinked with hers.

Angus, after a bit, broke the meditative state.

"So Kate, ye claim ye've changed?" he offered. "Well Ah dare say we have, too. An' once we git past the heartache, Ah trust tha' we'll see tha' we've changed for the better. Wha' a week!"

"Ah'd like tae propose a toast," said Gavin, as ever the stickler for protocol.

"Please proceed, Fauthluhroo," said Angus.

Gavin stood and raised his glass.

"Tae gowf, tae the linksland, an' tae deer friends—old an' new: May we always be taegither, in person an' in oor thoughts, in oor minds an' in oor hearts, in this woorld an' whate'er awaits us in the next!"

"Cheers!" responded the choir, this time resonating on the high end with a lone soprano voice.

"Gentlemen," said Kate. "I do believe it's time. I'm heading out to my dad's favorite spot at Machrihanish. Would you please join me?"

"Ye woouldn't be able tae stop us," said Angus.

Kate retreated to her room to retrieve the silver canister, then joined the seven men and one woman who had gathered in the car park, reveling in the scenery. The western sky along the Argyll coast was in particularly fine form that evening, the slowly setting sun painting dramatic cloud formations in pinks and purples offset with dollop or two of green. For the only time that week, everyone was in shirtsleeves, in part due to the unseasonable warmth but even more so to the complete absence of wind. Johnny Mac himself could not have dialed up a better sendoff.

As they made the mile-and-a-half hike along the outward holes toward Ranachan's tee box, they shared stories about their old friend's exploits on that auld sod: the time he made par from the beach on the 1st; the lighting-bolt moment he holed out his blind approach for a very rare eagle on the 2nd; his lone hole-in-one on the 4th; Kate's against-all-odds discovery of his golf ball in the cack on the 5th; the pure joy on his face when he finally found the green in regulation on the 7th; and, on the 8th, the anguish when his approach bounded over the back of the dune-top green followed by an overcooked third shot that rolled down the front, right back to where he'd started.

"Ah'll ne'er forgit the look on his face when he marched back doon tha' dune an' arrived a' his ba'," said Bernard. "One second, he was so furious he wanted tae scream. But then a second later, he was overcome wi' the sheer absurdity o' it all an' began laughin', uncontrollably."

"Aye," said Angus. "He just let it all hang oot. It was a beautiful thin'."

And so John's friends continued, delivering their walking eulogy of the good, the bad and the ineffable. Kate, hungry for details, hung on every word. For her, it was simply Papa.

Once they reached the 9th tee, Bernard assumed the lead and the others followed single file along a narrow footpath worn into the side of the dune. Then, collectively, they paused at the summit to catch their breath and, even more restoratively, to take their fill of the image that appeared before them.

"Ma friends, is theer anyplace on Earth ye'd rather be?" said Bernard.

"Amazin'!" said Ewan. "All the times Ah've played this course, an' Ah'd never seen this. Thank ye for bringin' us heer, Kate."

"Thank you for joining me," she said. "When Bernard told me what it meant to my dad, I knew in an instant this is where he belonged. This is his true home. And you are his true family."

"Well, Ah hope ye know ye're noo part o' this clan, too young lady," said Angus. "Ye dae the MacAlonan nemme proud."

"I *do* know that," said Kate. "And I am so grateful. I guess that's why, strangely, I'm feeling OK about all of this. Don't get me wrong: I miss my dad, something fierce. But it's so clear to me now: his spirit lives on, at this place and in all of you. And every time I come back to Machrihanish, especially to this very spot, I know I'll find him here."

"Aye," said Bernard. "This is wheer Johnny Mac foond hi'sel'. An' heer, intae perpetuity, he shall remain."

"Speaking of remains, there's something I need to do," said Kate. "But I need to do it alone. I hope you understand."

"As ye wish," said Gavin.

"Thank you," said Kate. "I won't be long."

With that, the others held their ground on the massive dune's crest as Kate slowly worked her way to the caramel brown beach below. Then, after removing her shoes and socks, she continued along for another 50 yards or so, enough to create a generous cushion between herself and the group behind and the barely visible clubhouse ahead.

Amid the solitude, Kate could hear the soft murmur of the waves as they lapped lazily against the shore. She could see the oyster catchers patrolling majestically from above, their search for sustenance never ending. She could taste the hint of sea salt in the gentle breeze that drifted over the eerily calm surface of the North Atlantic. And she could feel the cool moisture in the coarse sand as it tickled the gaps between her bare toes.

This is the place, she thought.

Kate sat down and nestled the canister into the sand before her. Then she reached into her pocket and pulled out her phone, touching the voicemail app icon on its screen.

This is the time.

Kate, without hesitation, pressed play:

"Hi Katie! Papa here. I'm in Scotland, making my way to Machrihanish and I just had to call. Sure wish you would have picked up. But can't say I'm surprised you didn't. I know. you're busy. *Always* busy. Guess I've been guilty of that myself from time to time. Pot calling the kettle black, and all that. Anyway. I really don't want to go there. Not now. On a night like this, none of that matters. Here's what *does* matter: It's just stunningly beautiful here! The sky is, I don't know, how can I describe it? Remember after you graduated from high school and I took you to Paris? And we went to the Musee D'Orsay? And you raved about the vibrant colors of those impressionist paintings…especially the Van Goghs? Well, this is the *real* deal…and I'm *in* the painting…and, well…I guess I was just wishing you could be here, too. I know. I know we've talked about it. But I think it's time we actually *did* it. The golf courses over here *are* different. I'm not going to sugar coat it. But I really think, if you gave it a chance, you'd like it. Maybe even fall in love. But hey, that's just me talking. Anyway kid, I hope you're doing well. I sure as heck am. Can't wait to get there! Man, it feels good to be home again. I love you!"

"I love you, too, Papa!" cried out Kate, even if only an adventurous oyster catcher, who just then walked by, could hear her.

A normal human being, at such a moment, would have been overcome with emotion. And tears *did* stream down Kate's cheeks. But for John McAlonan's daughter, who is most decidedly not normal, they were tears of gratitude not grief. After all, her father was right about this place. He was right about her. And in ways that no one could have anticipated, his wish *did* come true. Kate was here. And like him, she was subsumed by this vast natural canvas. She had taken her rightful place amid the whole.

Kate slid her phone back in her pocket, grabbed hold of the canister and stood up. But before going any further, she turned around to catch a reassuring glimpse of her new Scottish family—just as they'd begun to pass around a flask of, she was quite certain, single malt. When it was Angus' turn to take a nip, he hesitated, made eye contact with Kate and raised the silvery container in her father's—or was it her?—honor. So Kate, lacking an alternative, raised her father's silvery canister in silent reply.

That was her cue: Kate pried the top loose and, for the first time, peered inside. But the ashes held no sway over her. Only a trace of her father's full being resided there. All it took was a slow, purposeful twirl—aided by the mellow sea breeze—for his lifeless remains to reunite with his vibrant spirit.

It was done.

And Kate, even more deeply than when she fell prone on Islay's dewy fairway her first morning at Machrihanish, was at peace.

Up 4 Some Golf?

The pilot touched the appropriately-named 787 Dreamliner down on the LAX runway with a skilled hand. But the gentle transition from air to land still rousted Kate from a full-on Technicolor drama, the germination of a seed planted during the first minutes she'd spent in Gavin's Jaguar. From what she could remember, her subconscious was trapped in an Oz-like world. With the help of some friendly natives, though, she was slowly making her way back home. But instead of lions, tigers and bears, the forces at work against her were bunkers, burns and bogies. Oy vey!

The apparition, though, struck Kate as more funny than fearsome as she slowly got her wits about her. After everything she'd been through, the linksland was, at minimum, a second home to her now. There certainly was no need to escape it for another realm. Yet here she was, once again in Los Angeles, her first home. In less than a week, *it* had become the foreign country.

Kate deplaned and made her way to the long-term parking shuttles. En route, she couldn't help but notice that most of her fellow passengers had someone waiting to greet them. And she suddenly couldn't help but wonder how she ever thought the lack of a welcoming party—a hired limo driver didn't count— was perfectly normal. A part of her, foolishly, even scanned the crowd in the faint hope that she'd spot Gavin and Malcolm. But that was their world. This was hers. Alone in a crowd.

Kate arrived at her Porsche, deposited her carry-on bag in the sports car's afterthought of a trunk and took a seat behind the wheel. Good thing Margaret offered to store her dad's possessions. "Theer's a reason they call it a 'clubhoose,' dinna ye know," she'd said. His kit never would have fit in the Boxster, even without a passenger to occupy the empty seat next to her.

"This is still one heckuva car," said Kate, attempting to cheer herself up. "It's good to be back."

But the words, though only in her head, rang hollow, as if they begged to be punctuated with question marks. Something was amiss. Or perhaps she was the thing that was out of place. Angus, no doubt, would have been quick with his diagnosis: "Ye've got PMS, young lady," he'd say. "An' ye've got it bad."

Kate sat motionless in the speedy car, not quite sure what to do next. After a minute or two, she retrieved her father's golf ball—the one she'd found in the rough—from its safekeeping in her pocket, gave it a long look and carefully placed it in the Porsche's center console. Then, reflexively, she pulled out her iPhone. A quick glance at its world clock told her it was late at night in Scotland. It would be impertinent, not to mention a wee bit desperate, to call there now.

But maybe, just maybe, there was an even better alternative closer to home. Joe's week-old text, sent when she'd made the flight over, was still atop her list of IMs. When she'd first read it, upon arrival in Tarbert, she'd hesitated to respond, though not entirely sure why. Now, she hesitated again, but for good reason: like a vulnerable schoolgirl, her stomach was all aflutter.

"Hey Joe! Back in LA," Kate typed at last. "Up 4 some golf?"

Appendix A:

A Scottish-to-English Dialect Translator

As you'll quickly discover, I've populated this story with several Scottish characters and have attempted to write their dialogue in the local dialect. Having done so, I fully recognize there's no such thing as one Scottish accent any more than there's a definitive British or American way to speak the English language. As such, no accent—let alone the highly complex Scottish derivation—can be fully captured on the written page, not if strict literal accuracy is your measuring stick.

So here's what I suggest: Rather than attempt to read the Scottish "words" verbatim, simply use the odd spellings as mental triggers that a local is speaking. Then trust your inner ear—the apparatus you employ when you read silently—to recreate the Scottish accent for you. If you've encountered variations on the theme in a movie, television show or—better yet—live and in person, you'll hear it. Trust me. Trust yourself. It works.

However, if for some reason this literary alchemy doesn't quite happen for you, I offer up the following wee guide to ensure nothing essential gets lost in translation.

Either way, if I've managed to convey a sense of what it's like to be an American surrounded by Scots without getting in the way of the reader's enjoyment of the story, then I will be pleased. And greatly relieved. I'm sure my friends on the other side of the pond will let me know if I have offended. So, in advance, I beg forgiveness!

A

A' = At
Aboot = About
Accordin' = According
Affeers = Affairs
Adae = Ado
Afore = Before
Ah = I
Ah'd = I'd
Ah'll = I'll
Ahea' = Ahead
Ah'm = I'm
Amazin' = Amazing
Amusin' = Amusing
An' = And
Anythin' = Anything
Appeers = Appears
A'ready = Already
Aroond = Around
Arse = Ass
Ashoor = Ashore
Askin' = Asking
Assumin' = Assuming

Auld = Old
Aulder = Older
Aye = Yes

B

Ba = By
Ba' = Ball
Bailin' = Bailing
Bankin' = Banking
Bein' = Being
Belongin's = Belongings
Bevvies = Beverages
Beyoond = Beyond
Blabbin' = Blabbing
Blendin' = Blending
Blowie = Windy
Bonnie = Beautiful
Boond = Bound
Boorden = Burden
Boot = car's trunk
Borderin' = Bordering
Bouncin' = Bouncing
Braes = Hills

Breedin' = Breeding
Broon = Brown
Buggered = Screwed

C

Cack = Deep Rough
Canne = Can't/Can I
Carryin' = Carrying
Chappies = Chaps/Friends
Clammorin' = Clammoring
Clubhoose = Clubhouse
Cogitatin' = Cogitating
Collaboratin' = Collaborating
Conductin' = Conducting
Coold = Could
Coorse = Course
Counselin' = Counseling
Crackin' = Excellent
Crawlin' = Crawling
Cursin' = Cursing
Cuttin' = Cutting

D

Da' = Dad
Dae = Do
Daein' = Doing

Dinna' = Didn't/Don't
Daftie = Imbecile
Dealin' = Dealing
Deer = Dear
Demandin' = Demanding
Dependin' = Depending
Depresssin' = Depressing
Developin' = Developing
Disappoonted =
Disappointed
Doon = Down
Drinkin' = Drinking
Drivin' = Driving
Durin' = During
Dae ye = Do you

E

Eejit = Idiot
E'en = Even
E'er = Ever
'Em = Them
Embarrissin' = Embarrassing
Endin' = Ending
Enjoyin' = Enjoying
Entertainin' = Entertaining
Expectin' = Expecting
Evenin' = Evening

Everythin' = Everything

F

Fascinatin' = Fascinating
Fauthluhroo = Fauntleroy
Feelin' = Feeling
Flashin' = Flashing
Fleein' = Flying
Foond = Found
Forgit = Forget
Frontin' = Fronting
Frustratin' = Frustrating
Fulfillin' = Fulfilling

G

Ga' = Gall
Gazin' = Gazing
Gawd = God
Gemme = Game
Gents – Men's restroom
Gettin' = Getting
Git = Get
Goin' = Going
Groon = Ground
Gowf = Golf
Gowfin' = Golfing

Guessin' = Guessing
Guid = Good
Guideness = Goodness
Gurl = Girl

H

Ha' = Had
Ha'e = Have
Hauf = Half
Healin' = Healing
Heapin' = Heaping
Heer = Hear/Here
Helpin' = Helping
Hi'sel' = Himself
Hols = Holidays
Hoors = Hours
Hi'self = Himself
Hurtin' = Hurting
Hyperventilatin' =
Hyperventilating

I

I' = It
Imitatin' = Imitating
Includin' = Including
Inflictin' = Inflicting

Intae = Into
Intimidatin' = Intimidating
Invitin' = Inviting
I's = It's
I'sel' = Itself
Isnae = Isn't

J

Joinin' = Joining
Joodgment = Judgment

K

Keepin' = Keeping
Knockdoon = Knockdown
Knockin' = Knocking

L

Leadin' = Leading
Leakin' = Leaking
Learnin' = Learning
Livin' = Living
Loo = Bathroom
Lookin' = Looking
Loomber = Lumber
Loong = Long

Loord = Lord
Lorry = Truck

M

Ma = My
Maddenin' = Maddening
Makin' = Making
Marketin' = Marketing
Masel' = Myself
Meanin' = Meaning
Meetin's = Meetings
Mobile/Moby = Cellphone
Moor = More
Moornin' = Morning
Muppets = Fools

N

Nae = No
Neerba = Nearby
Ne'er = Never
Nick = Condition
Noo = Now
Nothin' = Nothing
Numpty = Incompetent

O

O' = Of
Ontae = Onto
Oor = Our
Oorsel'es = Ourselves
Oot = Out
Ootter = Utter
Operatin' = Operating
Ootta = Out Of
Ower = Over
Owerwhelm = Overwhelm

P

Pairin's = Pairings
Partne's = Partners
Peltin' = Pelting/Hard Rain
Placin' = Placing
Playin' = Playing
Poosh = Push
Prayin' = Praying
Prevailin' = Prevailing
Proceedin's = Proceedings
Pronoonce = Pronounce
Puttin' = Putting

R

Rampin' = Ramping
Rattlin' = Rattling
Readin' = Reading
Redeemin' = Redeeming
Reel = Real
Regardin' = Regarding
Rimember = Remember
Roonds = Rounds
Ruminatin's = Ruminatings
Runnin' = Running

S

Sayin' = Saying
Scoore = Score
Scroungin' = Scrounging
Seemin'ly = Seemingly
Semme = Same
Scribblin' = Scribbling
Shapin' = Shaping
Shillin' = Shilling
Shockin' = Shocking
Shooldn't = Shouldn't
Sibblin's = Sibblings
Sippin' = Sipping
Sittin' = Sitting

Sleepin' = Sleeping
Smilin' = Smiling
Soakin' = Soaking
Soberin' = Sobering
Sometahms = Sometimes
Somethin' = Something
Soom = Some
Soonds = Sounds
Soorender = Surrender
Soorry = Sorry
Surprisin' = Surprising
Sorrowfool = Sorrowful
Speakin' = Speaking
Surroundin' = Surrounding
Strikin' = Striking
Strin' = String
Stroogle = Struggle
Swally = Beer
Swingin' = Swinging
Swoorls = Swirls

T

Tae = To
Taeday = Today
Taegither = Together
Taemorrow = Tomorrow
Tahm = Time

Tahmin' = Timing
Talkin' = Talking
Telie = Television
Tickin' = Ticking
'Tis = It Is/Is it
Tha' = That/Than
Tha's = That's
Theer = There
Theer'd = There'd
Theer's = There's
Thin' = Thing
Thin's = Things
Threatenin' = Threatening
Tipetoein' = Tiptoeing
Toold = Told
Toorn – Turn
Trackin' = Tracking
Transportin' = Transporting
Tryin' = Trying
'Twas = It Was
'Twill = It Will
Twistin' = Twisting

U

Underlyin' = Underlying
Undyin' = Undying
Usin' = Using

V

Viewin' = Viewing

W

Wakin' = Waking
Wanderin' = Wandering
Warnin' = Warning
Watchin' = Watching
Waitin' = Waiting
Wanne = Want To
Wee = Small
Wha' = What
Wha's = What's
Whe' = When
Wi' = With
Wieldin' = Wielding
Willin' = Willing
Wi'in = Within
Winnin's = Winnings
Wi'oot = Without
Whate'er = Whatever
Wheer = Where
Whene'er = Whenever
Woold = Would
Wooldn't = Wouldn't
Woondered = Wondered

Woonderin' = Wondering
Woord = Word
Woorld = World
Workin' = Working
Woulda' = Would Have
Wullny = We Won't
Wumman = Woman

Y

Yawnin' = Yawning
Ye = You
Yeers = Years
Ye'd = You'd
Ye'll = You'll
Yer = Your
Ye're = You're
Yersel' = Yourself

Appendix B:

A Glossary of Golf Terms

While I wrote this story primarily with golf aficionados in mind, I'm hopeful it will also appeal to those who've never played the game. As such, I had a choice to: 1) dumb it down for the uninitiated; or 2) let the golf jargon fly in the hopes that non-players would still get the gist of the action in context. In deference to the game, I've opted for the latter strategy.

And in a nod to curious non-golfers eager to learn more, I offer up this modest glossary of the golf terms used in the book. Maybe, just maybe, the newbies will be emboldened to take the plunge. Those of us who already have know golf is the greatest game that ever was, or ever will be.

3-wood: A club that's designed to produce long shots, second only to the driver.

7-iron: A mid-range iron, used mostly for shortish approach shots into the green.

8-iron: A bit shorter and with a more lofted face than the 7-iron when less distance and a higher arcing trajectory is required.

9-holer: Half of a regulation 18-hole golf course. In Scotland, also referred to as a wee course.

15-handicapper: A little better than average player. If par for 18 holes is 72 strokes, a 15-handicapper would typically shoot 87. Basically.

A

Ace: A hole-in-one.

A-game: A player's best stuff.

Aiming post: Indicates the ideal line of flight on blind shots. A staple of links courses, rarely seen on parkland layouts.

Approach: The shot into the green.

Arnie: As in Arnold Palmer, the charismatic go-for-broke champion who—in sync with the emergence of television in the 1960s—helped broaden golf's appeal in America beyond the upper to the middle class.

B

Backswing: The first half of the golf swing, from the club at address behind the ball to parallel at the top. See also "Downswing."

Bagger Vance: Mystical caddy at the heart of Steven Pressfield's wonderful novel, *The Legend of Bagger Vance.* Was later made into a so-so movie directed by Robert Redford and starring Will Smith, Matt Damon and Charlize Theron.

Ball marker: Coin or other small flat item used to mark the ball's position on the green.

Bandon Dunes: A multi-course golf purists' mecca along the Oregon coast. Besides its authentic linksland, perhaps its most endearing quality is that all players are required to walk the course. You can carry your bag, push/pull it along with a trolley or hire a caddy. No motorized carts/buggies are allowed. Their slogan: "Golf the way it was meant to be played." Amen to that!

Best ball: A team game, usually two-man, where the team's score is based on the player who posts the lowest score on each hole.

Big stick: Slang for driver.

Birdie: Holing out in one stroke less than par.

Bump-and-run: A shot, generally near the green, that flies a short distance before hitting the ground running. Much more common on links courses than parkland due to wind and topography.

Bobby: As in Bobby Jones, arguably the game's best amateur player of all time. In 1930, he won the U.S. Open, British Open,

U.S. Amateur and British Amateur—the original Grand Slam and a feat that's highly unlikely ever to be equaled.

Bogey: Holing out in one more stroke than par.

Bomb-and-gouge: Slang for booming a driver off the tee without regard for accuracy (the "bomb"), then digging the ball out of the rough with a wedge and onto the green (the "gouge").

Bridgestone: Popular brand of golf ball.

Buggy: Scottish term for a cart.

Burn: Scottish term for a narrow winding creek or stream.

Byron Nelson: Arguably the best player of the 1940s. Posted 52 PGA Tour wins, including a record 18 total and 11 straight in 1945.

C

Cack: An irreverent term for deep, nasty rough.

Caddy: A hired hand who carries your golf bag and, if experienced, offers guidance in how to negotiate your way around the course. An endangered species since the introduction of carts/buggies.

Carnoustie: Recognized as one of the world's best links courses. Has hosted the Open Championship seven times as of this writing.

Cart: American term for a motorized on-course vehicle to carry your clubs and, ill-advisedly, to minimize walking. See also "Buggy."

Club championship: Annual tournament that crowns each golf club's best amateur player.

Clubhouse: Back in the day, it really was the house where the players stored their clubs. Now? It's where the players gather before and after their rounds.

Cross bunker: Unlike pot bunkers, which are generally positioned along the border between the fairway and rough or around the green, cross bunkers are found in the center of the fairway.

D

Dance floor: Slang for green/putting surface.

Dogleg: A hole with a pronounced bend in it, either left or right.

Dormie: In match play, it means the trailing team can—

at best—tie the team in the lead, and must win all of the remaining holes to do so.

Downswing: The second half of the golf swing (see "Backswing"), from parallel at the top to impact.

Draw: A shot that curves gently right-to-left for right-handed players (and in the opposite direction for lefties).

Drive: The opening shot on a par 4 or par 5 hole.

Driver: The club designed to hit the ball the farthest. Generally reserved for the opening shot on a par 4 or par 5 hole with the ball perched on a tee. Using a driver without benefit of a tee is referred to as "hitting it off the deck." See also "Big stick."

Duck hook: A low, hard shot that curves violently right-to-left for right-handed players (and in the opposite direction for lefties). See also "Hook" and "Pull hook."

E

Eagle: Holing out in two strokes less than par.

Etiquette: In a golf context, it's the mostly unspoken rules that govern the way players interact with one another on the course. Example: Standing still and silent when a competitor is executing a shot.

European Tour: The top rung on the professional golf ladder on the other side of the pond.

F

Fairway: The tightly-mowed grass between the rough that stretches from tee to green.

Flagstick: A metal post with a flag on it that's placed in the hole so you can spot the target from long distance. See also "Pin."

Flat stick: Slang for putter.

Flip wedge: Something less than a full swing with the shortest club in the bag, generally producing a shot in the 30-to-70 yard range.

Foot Joys: Popular brand of golf shoes.

Four ball: Four players in a group formed by two opposing two-man teams. See also "Best ball."

Forward tees: Most courses have more than one teeing area to accommodate players of different abilities. Skilled players usually use the back tee box. Beginners or short hitters tend to start each hole from the front position. At one time, the latter was called the "ladies tee."

Freddie Couples: A 15-time winner on the PGA Tour, including the 1992 Masters. Does not wear a golf glove on his left hand, unlike most right-handed players.

G

Green: The putting surface, where you can mark your ball and pick it up between putts.

Golf Pride: Popular brand of golf club grips.

Gore-Tex: Popular brand of waterproofing material used in golf outerwear.

H

Halve: In match play, a tied hole.

Ham and Egg: In best-ball match play, refers to a two-man team that works well together. When one player struggles on a hole, his or her partner steps up and posts a low score. Then the roles reverse on the next hole. Common phrase: "We won our match because we ham 'n' egged it pretty well."

Hazard: Where you don't want to hit your golf ball. Includes such stressful locations as bunkers and burns.

Hogan's secret: Perhaps golf's longest-running rumor that

Ben Hogan, through countless hours pounding practice balls on the range, discovered some "secret" move that made him one of the game's all-time greatest ball strikers. If so, he never revealed it.

Hole-in-one: Knocking the ball in the hole with just one swing of the club. Generally reserved only for par 3s, in which the green can be reached with one shot. See also "Ace."

Hollow: A deep depression in the linksland. Basically, the corollary to a dune.

Hook: A sweeping shot that starts to the right of the intended target line and then moves dramatically to the left for right-handed players (the opposite direction for lefties). The bane of the good player's existence.

Hybrid: A fairly recent invention in golf clubs that's part fairway wood and part long iron. Excellent for hitting longish shots from iffy lies.

I

Impact: The moment of truth, when the club face collides with the ball.

Iron Byron: A robotic machine designed to emulate a perfectly repeatable golf swing. Allegedly modeled on Byron Nelson. See also "Byron Nelson."

J

Jack: As in Jack Nicklaus, arguably the game's greatest champion of all time. His 73 PGA Tour wins include 18 major titles, the most ever.

K

Knockdown: A low trajectory shot executed mostly by making an abbreviated follow through. A links staple, especially when playing directly into a strong wind.

L

Layout: Another word for golf course. See also "Routing."

Laser range finder: A modern handheld contraption that, with the touch of a button, quickly measures distance by bouncing a laser beam off an opaque surface, such as a flagstick. Traditionalists contend it undercuts the importance of feel in the game.

Lob: A short, very high shot meant to hit the green softly and stop quickly near the hole. Played with a wedge with a high-lofted club face, typically 60 degrees or more.

Linksland: The grass-covered sandy soil between the beach and the arable farmland. Shaped into dunes, hollows and natural bunkers by wind, rain and sheep over the centuries.

M

Match play: A golf competition decided by who wins the most holes among all played.

Medal play: A golf competition decided by who records the fewest strokes to complete all holes played.

Middle iron: Typically a 5-, 6- or 7-iron for shots in the 130-170-yard range for average amateur players.

Mudder: Someone who plays well in inclement weather, in particular heavy rain.

Myrtle Beach: Resort town in South Carolina famous for its many golf courses.

Muni: Short for municipal, refers literally to golf courses owned by cities. But is also commonly used generally to refer to all public-access (aka no private membership) facilities.

O

Old Tom Morris: Icon of 19th century Scottish golf. Four-time winner of the Open Championship, but his lasting legacy was golf course design, including Machrihanish. After touring the linksland he was entrusted to shape into a full 18-hole layout, he reportedly said it was "specifically designed ba The Ahmighty for playin' gowf." You'll get no argument from me.

Olympic Club: A top-rated club in San Francisco. Has hosted five U.S. Opens, including the 1955 edition, when journeyman pro Jack Fleck upset heavy favorite Ben Hogan.

One-shotter: A hole in which the green can be reached with one swing of the club. More commonly known as a par 3.

Out-of-bounds: A golf course's outer border, usually marked with white stakes and/or white lines. Shots that are hit out of bounds (or, simply, OB) must be replayed from where the previous shot was struck, with a one-shot penalty.

P

Par/regulation par: The number of strokes a good player would require to get the ball in the hole. Assumes two putts per green. So a regulation par is the two putts, plus however many are needed to get to the green (one on a par 3, two on a par 4 and three on a par 5).

Past parallel: Refers to the position of the club at the top of the swing. Textbook form calls for the shaft to be parallel to the ground at the top. Rotating past that point is doable but fraught with danger. Can be a cause for inconsistent ball striking.

Pin: Another term for flagstick.

Pot bunker: After wind, a links course's primary line of defense. Compared with American-style parkland bunkers (sometimes referred to as sand traps), pot bunkers are generally smaller and deeper with flatter sides that can make it difficult to make a stance, let alone extract the ball.

Power fade: A shot, usually with a driver, that moves gently from left to right for right-handed players (the opposite direction for lefties). Easier to control than a draw, though perhaps offset by some loss of distance.

Pro shop: Where the golf club's resident professional sells equipment and apparel, books lessons and manages the flow of tee times. At some clubs, the latter takes place at a starter's shack.

Pull hook: A shot that flies straight left of its intended target line for right-handed players (to the right for lefties). Less severe than a curving, diving duck hook but still highly problematic.

Putter: A club specifically designed to roll a ball on a green. With the wedge, considered one of the critical scoring clubs.

R

Rain gloves: Made of a special fabric that gets tackier as it gets wetter. A must-have for the links golfer.

Range: Also referred to as a driving range or practice area. It's a patch of land set aside from the course specifically for the purpose of working on your game.

Red numbers: Slang for a score that's under par. Unlike an accountant's balance sheet, being in the red in golf is a very good thing.

Roger Cleveland: Founder of Cleveland Golf, a popular club maker. Particularly revered for their wedges.

Rough: Opposite of the fairway. Shaggy grass that can make it more difficult to hit the intended shot.

Routing: The overall flow of a course's holes, one to the next.

S

Sergio Garcia: Standout Spanish tour professional who went through a phase of, at address, gripping and then regripping his club a dozen times or more before starting his swing.

Scratch: Term for a very good player with a zero handicap.

Typically plays at par.

Scottish Golf Union: Organization that governs player handicaps and sanctions amateur golf tournaments in Scotland.

Shank: Technically speaking, what happens when you strike the ball on the clubhead's hosel (the part that fits into the bottom of the shaft) rather than its face. Superstitious players fear that merely uttering the word can bring on a case of the sh?nks. So have a heart and keep it to yourself, please!

Shinnecock: Short for Shinneock Hills Golf Club on New York's Long Island. Founded in 1891, the links-like layout—host to four U.S. Opens—is considered to be the oldest formally organized golf course in America.

Shivas Irons: Mythical Scottish golf pro at the center of Michael Murphy's seminal book, *Golf in the Kingdom.*

Short game: Basically, any shot within close proximity of the green. Includes chips, lobs, bump-and-runs, greenside bunker blasts and putts.

Short iron: Generally speaking, any club from the 8-iron through the wedges. When playing a shot with one of these sticks, the anticipation is that you'll knock the ball relatively close to the pin.

Slice: A sweeping shot that starts to the left of the intended target line and then moves dramatically to the right for right-handed players (the opposite direction for lefties). The bane of the hacker's existence.

Srixon: A popular brand of golf ball.

Stableford: Individual scoring system that tracks points per hole rather than strokes. So, for example, a bogey might be worth one point, a par two, a birdie three and an eagle four. In some variations, points are deducted for holes played over par. Compared with medal play, can minimize the negative impact of a disaster hole, which is always lurking on a links course.

Sticks: Slang for golf clubs.

Stroke and distance: The penalty for a lost ball as well as hitting out of bounds. You add one stroke to your score and you must replay your next shot from where you last made a swing (thus also loss of distance).

T

Target line: An imaginary line connecting the point where your ball is currently at rest to the point where you want it to end up. So, for an approach shot, that second point would most often be the hole.

Tee: The teeing ground or tee box designated as the starting point for a hole. Also refers to the small peg (made of wood or plastic) that you place into the teeing ground and upon which you place your ball. After the tee shot, the ball must be played as it lies, though you can mark, lift and replace it on the green.

Tee sheet: Order of the groups scheduled to play the course that day, generally maintained by the pro shop staff.

Three-shotter: A par 5 hole. Three shots to the green and then two putts.

Tiger: As in Tiger Woods, arguably the game's most talented player of all time. As of this writing, has won 79 PGA Tour events, including 14 major championships.

Tiger line: Slang for the most aggressive path along which to play a hole. High risk but also high reward.

Titanium: Space age material of choice for today's oversized driver heads. Compared with wood or steel, it allows club designers to make the head (and thus the effective hitting area) bigger without making it heavier.

Titleist: Popular brand of golf equipment, especially balls.

Trolley: Scottish term for a two-wheeled cart that carries a golf bag and is pulled (or more commonly now pushed) by the player.

Two-shotter: A par 4 hole. Two shots to the green and then two putts into the hole.

U

Unplayable: A lie so bad that the ball cannot be moved, at least not in a reasonably predictable manner. The player has different options for picking up the ball and dropping it in a playable lie, but all incur a one-stroke penalty.

Up and down: Slang for hitting a short shot (such as a chip or bunker blast) onto the green—the "up"—and then sinking the putt—the "down."

Urethane: Cover material of choice for today's premium golf balls. Replaced balata, whose softness delivered the desire feel but, alas, was also highly susceptible to cuts and abrasions.

W

Waterproofs: Scottish term for rain suit.

Wedge: A club designed to hit short, high shots, generally within 100 yards of the green.

Western Gailes: A classic Ayrshire links course founded in

1897 that, today, often serves as a qualifying site for the Open Championship.

Y

Yellow marker: The members' tee box on a links course. The white markers are generally reserved for medal competitions. American translation: yellow = white tees and white = blue tees.

Acknowledgements

Writing this book was largely a solitary journey. But that's not to say the end product exists in a vacuum. Far from it. If you're reading these words, there are many to thank (besides your grade school teachers), most notably:

- **Anna Anderson**—The club secretary at Machrihanish who graciously negotiated permission for me to refer to their incomparable club by name. Settling for a pseudonym simply wouldn't have done the place justice.

- **Brad Nelson**—My writing partner on "Ham 'n' Egg on Golf" and the one brave soul among our inner circle who made that first epic journey to Machrihanish, then insisted we join him a year later. As he would put it, we've "eaten our peas" and returned dutifully every year since. Great call, Bud. Next round (golf and Guinness) is on me!

- **Craig Eisentrout and Dave Tyson**—With Brad and me, the other half of the ironically-named "Dream Foursome." I grew up and learned the game with Craig and Dave. All four of us went to Northwestern University. And now we meet annually at Mach. I would have considered myself blessed to have one lifelong friend. But to have three? It's like winning the relationship lottery.

- **The Parsons Family**—They literally dug Bath Golf Course out of northeast Ohio dirt with their bare hands. OK, I exaggerate. Slightly. Back in the day, the green fee was just $3.50 for 18 holes, most of which were easily reachable in regulation—even for a short hitter like me. It was the perfect Petri dish, allowing my fledgling game to take hold. Lamentably, my old playground no longer exists, having since been subdivided into home lots. Oh the humanity!

- **Dwight Greer**—The coach of my high school golf team, who had virtually no faith in my playing ability. If not for all that teenage angst he *unwittingly* (emphasis mine) unleashed, would I have written this book? I think not.

- **Lisa Yamada**—Best editor with whom I've ever had the good fortune to collaborate. Writing a book is like stepping out on a high wire. Doubt I would have made it very far without a net of fresh eyes and a non-golfer's perspective.

- **Jack Jones**—The first actual golfer and non-family member who read the work in progress. His enthusiastic support kept me going. I'll let you decide if that was a good thing.

- **Liz MacLarty Jones**—The lovely and multi-talented artist and friend who very generously offered to create the illustrated map at the front of this book. If that doesn't inspire you to make your own journey to Machrihanish, perhaps a physician should check you for a pulse.

- **Billy Dixon and Duncan Sloan**—Two members of my adoptive Scottish clan who offered their counsel on the dialect, not that I always followed it. See Appendix A for my full mea culpa.

- **Paul Galuppo**—My Italian language tutor. Thanks, even more so, for including me in your regular weekly game and for booking those crack o' dawn tee times. *Grazie mille!*

- **Phil Alden Robinson and Bill Forsyth**—The directors of "Field of Dreams" and "Local Hero," respectively, two of my all-time favorite films and, I'll confess, creative inspirations for this tale.

- **Grace, Claire and Emily**—Three compelling reasons why this story centers on a father-daughter relationship. Their presence can be felt throughout these pages, each in their own wonderfully unique way. As with my tutelage in golf, their lessons for me in what it means to be a good dad are ongoing.

- **Vivi**—Last and by no means least, my adorable and inexplicably adoring wife. She is my emotional support system, the love of my life and—it kills me to admit it—a highly constructive critic. If not for her unwavering belief in me, none of this would have happened. "Always!"

Credits

Achy Breaky Heart (Don't Tell My Heart)
Words and Music by Don Von Tress
Copyright (c) 1991 UNIVERSAL - MILLHOUSE MUSIC
All Rights Reserved Used by Permission
Reprinted by Permission of Hal Leonard Corporation

"Landslide," written by Stevie Nicks. Copyright © 1975 by
Fleetwood Mac.

About the Author

Dan Miller's parents met because their parents were friends and members of the same golf club. So it's not an exaggeration to say that, if not for the game, he probably would not exist. Perhaps that's why he's been in love with golf almost as long as he's been in love with writing and that the two have been, and likely forever will be, intertwined.

Professionally speaking, he got his start in newspapers, transitioned to magazines as a freelancer (including *Travel & Leisure Golf*, *Inside Golf* and *Golf Illustrated*—though only one of those publications still exists) and established a foothold in the online world (on *golf.com* and, most notably, the late great *Ham 'n' Egg on Golf*). These days, he feeds his need through *weeeggmon.com* and—against all odds—this debut novel. Along the way, he's had the opportunity to experience many of the world's best links courses in Ireland and Scotland. With great joy and humble gratitude, he is proud to say that the latter is now his second home.

Given the choice, his first option is to play the game. But when the evils of darkness, atrocious weather and/or the day job intervene, he'll happily settle for Plan B: bantering about golf with his fellow adherents/victims. As such, comments, questions and condolences—sent to dan.miller@weeeggmon. com—are always warmly welcomed.

Fore!

www.ingramcontent.com/pod-product-compliance
Lightning Source LLC
Chambersburg PA
CBHW050527110726
47899CB00005B/1626